CRESTMORE

THE LOST ELMKEY

SEAN CLARKE

ISBN: 978-1-5272-7578-2

First Released, 2021
www.seanclarkeauthor.com

ABOUT THE AUTHOR

Sean Clarke is an author, blogger and freelance writer who lives in Saltcoats, Ayrshire. He writes fantasy and supernatural horror fiction. When he's not writing, Sean enjoys gaming, swimming, and spending time with his family and friends.

To learn more about Sean, check out his website:
www.seanclarkeauthor.com

Table of Contents

Acknowledgments

A big thanks to Marc Nimmo, whose typically Scottish, depreciative humour kept me going when I wanted to quit. To Stephanie Clarke, for believing in me. Thanks, Gary Young for all your help. Sometimes we need the benefit of experience to give us a guiding hand. A collaboration is hopefully not too far off.

Last but certainly not least, special thanks to my fiancée, Samantha for her help and patience during the six long years it took to complete the novel. Without you, none of this would have been possible.

I love you all.
Sean

Chapter 1

A decade had passed since Jacob swapped the small town of Oakhedge for the Capital of Uthovaya, but life in the big city had proved to be anything but the paradise he believed it would be. Everyone was less friendly, for a start; too busy rushing from place to place to offer so much as a friendly hello. The roads were busier, too. If you didn't hurry across, you risked not making it to the other side.

Oakhedge was a close-knit community by comparison. A place where everybody knew each other's business. There was also no chance of being knocked down by careless drivers or mugged while out for a leisurely stroll. In fact, Jacob reckoned Oakhedge was superior in every way, except for one small detail: his foster parents, Pirlie and Raszlo lived there.

The two oddities had raised him in a small house on the edge of town, only a stone's throw away from the Polan Burn. All the local kids played on the banks of that burn, but Jacob rarely got to join them. He spent most of his time cooped up in the house, hidden away like a monster too hideous for the world to see.

Jacob escaped to the Capital on his tenth birthday, and for years after, he wondered why his foster parents had treated him so horribly. It was only when he got older that he began to suspect their behaviour stemmed from the fact he wasn't Human, like them.

Jacob was a Mixling, and like all Mixlings, he was born to a Dakew and a Human. Some people struggled to tell the difference between the Dakew and Mixlings, but Jacob was usually ready with an explanation. The Dakew were similar to Humans but had hairless skin, a flatter nose, and more rounded eyes. Mixlings predominantly inherited the physical traits of the Human parent, with the only exception being a flatter nose that came from the Dakew side.

Jacob had no memory of his birth parents, but often wondered why they gave him up. Would life have been different if they had stuck around? Jacob had no idea, but he was sure there would have been no Pirlie and Raszlo.

His past still scarred him, and he always vowed never to return to Oakhedge without good reason. Right now, as he struggled through the Capital's busy streets, trying to avoid the stares from passers-by who studied the contents of his trolley, he could not think of a single one.

Although he was tired, footsore, and hungry, Jacob knew he had to keep going. Dragging the trolley made things more difficult, especially with the dead creature on top, lying underneath a white sheet. He dabbed his forehead with a grey cloth and then looked across the busy street at the Hunters Depot sandwiched between two run-down office buildings.

Just a few more tugs.

Visiting the Hunters Depot could be a long and tedious experience, but Jacob had gotten used to the process since becoming a fully-fledged hunter almost two years ago. He knew it was a means to an end, the struggle before the big payday. Once he reached the counter, he would collect his reward for a hard-earned kill. Payment could be anything from food parcels to money, and although Jacob had never received the latter, he felt quietly confident his latest kill was worth at least fifty nova.

Such a large sum of money would enable him to buy edible food. No more of those out-of-date parcels from the depot. Maybe, the money would even stretch to some new clothes. His tatty grey t-shirt was full of holes and two sizes too small, and his brown jacket was faded and dirty.

Still dreaming of a substantial payday, Jacob joined the queue of battle-scarred hunters, each one spending what probably seemed like an eternity shuffling towards their payment. One hour later, Jacob reached the counter, and was greeted by an overweight, middle-aged Human attendant he had never seen before. She tapped on the bullet-proof glass and ordered him to come closer.

"Name?" she barked through the speaker.

"Jacob."

"Your full name," she said, sounding exasperated with his response.

"I don't have a surname."

"Everyone has a surname."

"Not me. I haven't used mine since I came to the Capital."

The attendant stared blankly. "Why not?"

It was a good question. The thought of using Pirlie and Raszlo's surname made Jacob feel physically sick, but he had no intention of admitting that fact to a total stranger. He shuffled from side-to-side, hoping the attendant would get the hint.

"Never mind," the attendant finally said. "What have you brought us today?

Jacob could hardly contain his excitement as he pulled the white sheet away and let the lady's gaze settle on his kill – a terrifying beast with six-legs, three arms, and two red eyes. Capable of camouflage, even in death, it had turned dark blue to match the colour of the trolley.

"H-how did you catch one of those?" the attendant stammered, forcing glasses onto her plump face.

The other hunters broke from the queue, chatting excitedly about the youngster who had single-handedly slain a Villfaar Dragon. The attendant signalled a colleague over, and a short man in a crumpled suit made his way around the depot counter to inspect the haul.

"Impressive, huh?" Jacob grinned, enjoying the positive attention from his fellow hunters. Praise was a rare commodity for him, so he intended to make the most of the adulation. He took a deep breath and then puffed his chest out.

"Where are the others?" the man in the suit asked.

"Others?"

"Come on, kid. There's no way you caught this by yourself. You obviously worked with a hunting party and then plundered their haul."

"No, I ha –"

"Or you've swiped it from a hunter's camp."

Jacob could not believe the gall of the man. Capturing the Villfaar Dragon was his crowning achievement as a hunter to date. Yet this perfect stranger wanted to take the credit away from him. How dare he?

"I nearly died three times trying to capture this creature," Jacob said in a tone that was a mixture of anger and hurt.

"Maybe if you had been killed, I might have believed you."

It was a ridiculous statement, but the man in the suit seemed completely oblivious to his own stupidity. He clicked his fingers, and two staff members carrying shotguns burst from the depot. Without saying a word, they began to drag the trolley away.

"Leave it!" Jacob cried.

"I'm afraid not." Said the man in the suit. "We're keeping your haul. You're lucky I'm not revoking your licence as well."

Jacob dashed forward to block the trolley's removal, but a third armed guard exploded from the depot to keep him at bay. Exasperated, he turned back to the man in the suit.

"I can't face going home hungry. Is there any way we can resolve this?"

But the cold-hearted man barely mustered a change in expression. "On your way, thief."

Jacob looked on helplessly as his trolley disappeared into the depot. Too tired and hungry to continue his protests, he started the long walk back to the place he called home, a derelict army recruitment centre in the backstreets of Capital-West. He was overcome by dizziness on the way, and the environment around him adopted a dreamlike quality, as hunger began to affect his mind, leaving him weary and disorientated.

By the time he arrived at his bomb-damaged home, Jacob was exhausted. He collapsed on the cold hard ground but managed to pull a threadbare grey blanket over himself. He looked up at the stars through the broken roof, counting them one by one, and hoping they would take his mind off the hunger pains stabbing into his belly like a thousand knives. Perhaps, tomorrow would bring some luck.

***

The next morning, Jacob threw the blanket away and peeled himself off the ground, just as the bell from the nearby Church of the Dakew began to chime. Although he didn't believe in a higher power, Jacob never complained about the bell. Its familiar ring meant he had made it through another cold winter's night.

After a long stretch, he trudged to the closest water fountain for a wash and then made his way to Main Street, hoping to find a familiar face amongst the claustrophobic mess of bodies and traffic. Eventually, he found one in the form of the local tailor, a jolly Dakew by the name of Mr. Janmano, who was seated inside a vehicle that stood out from the everyday cars, trucks, and motorbikes whizzing past.

"You don't see many Fast-Wheels around here," Jacob said, as Janmano brought the single wheeler with a seat at either side to a halt.

"What can I say? Business is booming," Janmano replied, twirling his long, pencil-thin moustache. "Where are you going today, ma'boy?"

Jacob tore himself away from the smooth surface of the impressive vehicle.

"I'm going to meet Orla."

Orla Paton was eighteen years old; two years younger than Jacob and had been his best friend since he arrived in the Capital. Three days ago, she had gone for an interview at North-West University, hoping to gain a place in next term's Political Science course. Jacob had agreed to meet her at the train station when she returned.

"Need a ride?" Janmano asked, pointing to a passenger seat on the left side of the wheel.

Jacob nodded. "Train Station West, please."

"Yes, sir," Janmano replied, starting up the engine.

Jacob hoped his friend could not hear his stomach screaming for attention as the disc rolled through the congested streets. There was a sandwich wrapped up in a see-through bag beside him on the passenger seat but looking at it only made his hunger worse.

Finally, the Fast-Wheel came to a stop outside the dilapidated station, and Jacob jumped onto the pavement. "Thanks for the lift."

"No problem, ma'boy."

Janmano pulled out three nova from his pocket and thrust them into Jacob's hand.

"What's this?"

"Get yourself some breakfast."

"Are you sure?" Jacob replied, secretly hoping Janmano wouldn't change his mind.

"Of course." He beamed. "I'm off to work now. Say hello to Orla for me."

Jacob waved goodbye and then studied the money in the palm of his hand. Was there time for a quick bite to eat? No, he concluded, Orla's train was due to arrive any minute. His rumbling stomach would have to wait.

He scaled the dirty marble steps at the station entrance and made his way towards a grim-faced Human employee sitting inside a worn-out booth. There was a sign situated above the employee's head, instructing all Dakew and Mixlings to check-in. Jacob took a deep breath and prepared to do what he always did whenever he entered a public place–swap his dignity for a permission slip.

"Sign this form," the man at the booth ordered, pushing the piece of paper through a gap underneath the glass.

"Does your job not embarrass you?" Jacob replied as he signed the form and passed it back.

The man behind the booth ignored the question and handed over a blue permission slip.

"That'll be a no, then?" Jacob added, shoving the slip into his pocket.

"Look, I'm not happy about this either, but I've got a wife and two kids to support. If you've got a problem with how things are done, take it up with the Antantan government. They're the ones who make the rules; I only enforce them."

Jacob knew he had a point. It was hardly the man's fault that Uthovaya was under the control of another nation. The Antantans were Humans who hailed from the country of Antantis, possibly the strongest superpower in the world of Lozaro. Antantis was ruled by a maniacal president who hated the Dakew and Mixlings in equal measure. It was the president who had ordered his troops to storm the Capital, murder the royal family, and take control of the country, twenty years ago.

Jacob reached the timetable screen and scanned the jumbled-up words and numbers, but his lack of schooling meant understanding them was difficult. A kindly old lady came to the rescue, explaining the train would arrive on time at platform fourteen. He thanked her and then sprinted to the platform in question, feeling dizzy and weak again by the time he got there.

"Can I help ya?" a rough voice asked as he leaned against the nearest bannister.

Jacob spun around and came face to face with a muscle-bound military man decked out in the silver full-face helmet and matching uniform of the Antantan army.

"I said, can I help ya?" the soldier barked.

"No thanks," Jacob replied, turning away.

The soldier wasted no time in swinging him back around by the shoulder.

"Don't even think about it, boy."

Jacob wriggled away, but the soldier appeared to sense his discomfort and stepped further into his personal space, leaving him almost frozen with fear. Jacob took a backwards step, but the soldier came forward again, making him feel even more uneasy.

"Leave me alone. I'm waiting for someone."

"Not in this spot, you're not."

Jacob held up his permission slip. "I have as much right to be here as you do,"

"Your kind will never have as much rights as me," the soldier spat. "Anyway, this area is being kept clear for the Antantan army recruitment drive. Be on your way."

Scared he would be ejected from the station, Jacob hurried to another spot and waited for the train. It arrived minutes later, stopping with a hiss and the release of thick white smoke. The doors opened and passengers spilled onto the platform. Orla was among them, sporting a smile and clasping a light green duffel bag. She looked smart in a grey trouser suit and crisp, buttoned-up cream shirt. Her strawberry blonde hair was clipped to the top of her head, making her look older than her years.

"Hey, you," she greeted him.

"Hey, yourself." Jacob grinned in response. "Well, don't keep me in suspense. How did you get on at the interview?"

"Brilliant." She squealed. "I start the Political Science course next week."

"That's the best news ever," Jacob replied, doing his best to look happy.

Although he supported Orla's dream of becoming a politician, he did not share her view that she could make a difference for the people of Uthovaya. The Antantans had installed their own government and would never allow a Uthovayan to call the shots. Not to mention the course would require her to relocate to Capital North-West. Jacob would be lucky to see her once a week, and that wasn't enough as far as he was concerned. He wanted Orla to succeed in her goals, but the prospect of life without her came with almost painful loneliness. Not that he would ever voice his feelings on the matter. Orla would probably feel betrayed if she knew the truth.

"Let's get going," Jacob said.

He reached out to take her bag, but she playfully snatched it away and burst out laughing.

"Fine." He said, pulling a funny face and then wandering away.

"Oh, you're terrible," she quipped, slinging the bag straps over her shoulder, and then jogging to catch up with him.

"And don't I know it." He grinned.

They chatted back and forth as they walked through the station, mainly about what Orla could expect when she started her course. Before they reached the exit, two Antantan soldiers stopped them in their tracks, demanding a closer inspection of Jacob's permission slip.

"What's the problem?" Orla asked.

"Stay out of this." one of the soldiers replied.

Jacob did not resist as the soldiers dragged him away from Orla and bundled him into a squared room. There was an examination table inside with a tray of medical instruments on top.

"Make it quick." Jacob snapped, glaring at the two soldiers.

There was no response, but he felt anger and shame burn inside him as they conducted a full-body search.

"Are you two finished?"

"Keep it zipped," one of the soldiers snarled. "Ah, what do we have here?" The soldier removed Jacob's hunting pistol from his cocoa-coloured trousers. "Care to explain why you have a firearm in a public place?"

"I'm a hunter; I use it for hunting."

"A likely story," the other soldier remarked as he slipped the gun into a small grey pouch with tie strings. "We have a bit of a problem here."

"What problem?"

"How you intend to pay your fine, for a start."

"Licensed hunters can carry their registered weapon at all times. Page two, paragraph seven of the Hunter's Law. You guys should have done your homework."

"This will have to do," the first soldier crowed, as he held up the money Mr. Janmano had given Jacob.

"That's mine," Jacob countered, his voice shaking from a combination of anger and fear.

"It *was* yours," The soldier laughed, putting the money into his breast pocket. "Put your clothes back on and get out."

Jacob dressed quickly and then headed back outside to Orla. She put a hand on his shoulder and gave him a sympathetic look. It was a look he had seen many times before. A look he hated.

"They didn't even check the slip." He whispered.

"Those soldiers are beneath contempt," Orla spat. "Are you OK?"

"I'll just have to be."

Despite the bravado, Jacob was more than fed-up with the constant mistreatment, tired of being a second-class citizen. Even after a decade in the Capital he had not gotten used to Antantan persecution.

As they left the station, Jacob felt a deep rumbling coming from down the street, shaking the ground. A group of protesters had gathered across the road, screaming obscenities at passing Antantan soldiers. Suddenly, two monstrous tanks rolled past them in single file., leaving the trail of raging protesters in their wake.

"Another day, another round of intimidation," Orla said quietly.

Jacob nodded. "C'mon, I'll walk you home."

Chapter 11

By the time he walked Orla back to number 14 Gonga Grove, Jacob could barely muster the energy to open the freshly painted front gate. His weak attempt drew a suspicious glance, and she demanded to know if he had eaten anything.

"I had breakfast this morning," he lied.

"Where?"

"Bins behind Roscoe's Eatery."

Another lie, but anything was better than seeing her look of pity again.

"Sorry. You just seemed a bit…"

"Tired."

She nodded. "That must be it."

As Jacob held the gate open, he saw the nosey old woman from next door gawping in his direction and got the all-too-familiar sense of not belonging in such a prestigious neighbourhood. There was no overgrown grass here, no garden ornaments out of place, or weeds struggling to escape cracks in the pavement. The residents, usually dressed in expensive clothes, turned their noses up at anyone not from the area.

As far as Jacob was concerned, Orla and her mother, Kaira, were the only exceptions to this rule of snobbery. Her father, Dinah, was an Antantan who had moved to Uthovaya before the takeover. He hated the Dakew and Mixlings with a passion, refusing to even acknowledge Jacob when he came to visit. Dinah had ordered Orla to stay away from Jacob many times, but it was an order she always ignored.

"Want to come in?" Orla asked when they reached the front door.

"I'd better not. Your dad said he'll kill me if he catches me hanging around with you again."

"Don't worry," she chuckled. "He's been away on a business trip since last week."

"When's he due back?"

"Tomorrow morning."

Jacob mulled it over for a few moments.

"Are you coming in or not?" Orla asked.

"Sure."

He followed Orla into the quaint hall, removed his shoes, and left them by the front door. Kaira was in the living room, sponging down paint-covered overalls she had obviously worn to the paint the front gate. Kaira was around fifty-three years old with blonde hair and a fringe that hung to the left-hand side of her soft, pale face.

"I'm home, Mum," Orla announced, as she led Jacob into the living room.

"It's about time," Kaira replied, pulling her daughter in for a hug.

Jacob stepped back to admire the visible bond between mother and child. It was a bond he had never experienced; Pirlie and Raszlo's idea of a family moment was letting him out of the house for a few hours. He had never spoken about their behaviour to anyone. Not even his best friend.

"How did the interview go?" Kaira asked, her voice dripping with anticipation.

"I got in." Orla screamed.

"Splendid," Kaira cooed, clapping her hands with obvious excitement. "You're going places, girl. Nothing can stop you now."

Feeling a little out of place, Jacob cleared his throat to let Kaira know he was there. She greeted him with a smile.

"Nice to see you, Jacob,"

He waved. "You too, Mrs. Paton."

"Care to stay for dinner tonight? We're having poached Yelfish."

"That would be lovely," he replied, feeling a twinge of excitement at the thought of food in his belly.

"Make yourself comfortable until dinner-time." She turned back to Orla. "And as soon as I've washed these overalls, you can tell me more about university."

Jacob spent the rest of the day in Orla's living room, counting down the hours until it was time for dinner.

He felt a little stronger, as though the promise of food had re-energised his entire body. Although he struggled to think about anything other than his stomach, he couldn't help but be impressed at Orla's passion for her course. She talked about it all afternoon. Kaira got in on the act, too, mapping her daughter's future out in fine detail.

The proceedings were interrupted by a knock at the door, and a tall, slender man in a grey suit and black tie came into the living room. He introduced himself as Mr. Slade, an organiser of the upcoming Dance for Liberty – otherwise known as the biggest social event on the Uthovayan calendar. The dance had begun as a small protest against Antantan oppression but had grown to a nationwide event in the fifteen years since its inception.

"What can I do for you?" Kaira asked.

"Actually, I am here to speak with your daughter," Slade replied, grinning in Orla's direction.

They retreated to the hall for privacy, leaving Jacob and Kaira to speculate about the reasons for his visit. When Orla returned, she had an envelope in her hand and a smile stretching from ear to ear.

"Mum! Mum!" she cried excitedly.

"What's all the commotion."

"Mr. Slade wants me to give a speech at the Dance for Liberty tomorrow."

"You're kidding?" Kaira said with a visible tear in her eye.

"I applied last year but got a rejection letter. They're looking for younger speakers this time, and they'd kept my name on file."

Kaira pulled Orla in for a hug. "I'm so proud of you."

"Let's hope Dad feels the same way."

Kaira's visible excitement evaporated. "I'll go check on dinner."

Jacob watched her leave and then gave Orla a thumbs up. He was delighted his best friend would finally get the chance to speak her mind, even if he did not believe the speech would make a difference in the grand scheme of things. At the very least, it would be good public speaking practice – a required skill for anyone hoping to go into politics.

"What's in the envelope?" Jacob asked.

"Mr. Slade has given me an extra ticket for the dance."

"That was nice of him."

"It sure was," she replied, ripping the ticket from the envelope, and handing it to Jacob. "Please, say you'll come."

"Me?"

"You're my best friend. Who else would I invite?"

"Your mum for a start?"

"Mum already has a ticket. I want you to have the extra one."

Jacob was speechless. He had gotten used to Orla's acts of kindness over the years, but even now, she still had the ability to surprise him. He had never been to the dance due to the expensive ticket price but was curious to experience the magic for himself.

"Will it be OK to wear these clothes?" he asked, feeling less than hopeful about a positive response.

"I…I don't think so," Orla replied awkwardly.

Kaira came back into the living room and must have caught the looks on their faces. "What's all this?"

"I want Jacob to come to the dance, but he has nothing to wear."

"That's not a problem," Kaira replied, going into the kitchen, and returning with a tape measure. "I'll call Mr. Janmano and hire you a suit. My treat."

Jacob felt a little awkward about accepting more charity. A meal was one thing, but hiring a suit would cost a lot of money. He was about to protest, but Orla clasped her hands together and squealed with delight before he could offer an objection.

"Oh, Mum, do you mean it?"

"Of course, I mean it." Kaira took down Jacob's measurements. "He can't miss your big day. It wouldn't be right."

Realising it was pointless to argue, Jacob decided to remain quiet and simply thank Kaira for the kind offer.

"Think nothing of it. Now, both of you into the kitchen. Dinner's ready."

Finally, Jacob thought.

He accepted Orla's invitation to sit beside her at the kitchen table and looked on with glee as Kaira served the tasty-looking Yelfish. It took all his powers of restraint not to wolf the meal down like a savage. After a lifetime seemed to pass, Kaira joined them at the table and gave the go-ahead to eat. Jacob shovelled the first piece into his mouth, savouring the flavour as it exploded onto his taste buds.

"Are you still hunting?" Kaira asked between mouthfuls.

"Still hanging in there." he admitted. "Been a few years now."

Jacob thought back to how it all started. He had found his way into the business by accident when a city official had trouble with Rinkals on his estate. The omnivorous creatures had eaten his exotic birds and caused massive damage to his plants. Jacob overheard the official complaining in the street and offered his services free of charge. The official was so pleased with Jacob's work, he bought him a five-year hunting licence to say thank-you.

Hunting made Jacob small sums of money, but it rarely excited him. He longed to experience something different in life. Perhaps, he mused, losing his pistol was a blessing in disguise? It would force him to think outside the box; find a new way to make money.

A purpose. That is what he lacked most of all. There had to be more to life than sleeping outside and rummaging through bins for scraps. He had to get away from the Capital before it dragged him down even further than it already had.

"I hate when you go on those hunts," Orla said, as she twisted succulent meat around her plate. "They're so dangerous."

Kaira frowned at her and noted, "He has to earn a living, dear."

"I know, but the risks far outweigh the benefits."

"I don't think that's going to be much of a problem anymore," Jacob said, quietly. "The soldiers at the station confiscated my gun."

"They can't do that," Orla protested. "You've got a licence."

"Yeah, that didn't stop them."

"So, what will you do now?"

"If I continue hunting then I'll go for something different. I never liked guns much, anyway. Too clunky."

"What do you mean *if* you continue hunting?" Orla asked, sprinkling yellow spices on the remains of her Yelfish.

"I've been thinking about a change of career."

"Be careful what you wish for," Kaira interjected. "There isn't an abundance of jobs out there, thanks to the Antantan government selling off our industries."

Orla tutted. "Those Antantans make me sick."

"We shouldn't generalise, dear," Kaira insisted. "I'm sure there are lots of good Antantans living in Antantis and all over the world. Your father is one of them."

Jacob almost choked on his food.

"Dad still hates the Dakew and Mixlings though. He said teachers back home, actively encouraged the hatred in school, and I bet things haven't changed since then."

Mother and daughter continued to converse between mouthfuls, covering a range of topics Jacob knew nothing about. After eating the last piece of Yelfish, he licked the plate clean but was suddenly aware of Kaira and Orla staring at him.

"Sorry."

"Don't apologise," Kaira soothed. "I hope you've still got room for pudding?"

"Oh, I'm sure I'll manage."

Pudding consisted of vanilla ice-cream smothered in a chocolate sauce. Orla and Kaira couldn't finish theirs, so Jacob helped them out. Afterwards, he washed the dishes as a way of saying thanks. Then he bid them goodbye.

"I would let you stay if I could," Kaira assured him, "but my husband…"

"Hey, it's fine," Jacob replied, saving her the embarrassment of an explanation.

He hugged Orla in the hallway, put his shoes on, and then thanked them both again before heading out into the night. He had almost reached the gate when it swung open in front of him. Dinah Paton was standing in his way, looking less than impressed at his presence.

"What are you doing here?" Dinah barked.

Kaira rushed between the pair before things could escalate. "You're home early."

"Never mind that. Why is this thing standing in my garden?"

"I invited him to dinner. But it doesn't matter because he's leaving now."

Orla backed Kaira up by telling her father to keep calm, but Dinah ignored them both and grabbed Jacob by the neck with both hands.

"Leave him alone!" Jacob heard Orla scream.

Dinah was not listening. "I tell you to stay away from my daughter, and you invite yourself in for tea with her. Who do you think you are?"

Jacob was too busy fighting for breath to reply. He could feel Dinah's cold hands gripping tighter and tighter around his throat and saw the blank expression on his attacker's face. Kaira attempted to pull her husband's hands apart, but it was no use.

"Let him go!" Kaira screamed. "I told you it was me who invited him."

The irate father pulled Jacob onto the street and then released his grip. Jacob sank to the ground, coughing and spluttering on the way down. He rolled onto his back and saw Dinah standing over him.

"Don't let me see you around here again," he snarled before turning back to Orla and Kaira. "Get in the house."

They did not need to be told twice. Dinah spat at Jacob's feet and then followed them inside, slamming the door behind him. Raindrops landed on Jacob's nose, so he got back to his feet and saw Orla pressed against the upstairs window.

She mouthed, "I'm sorry," and then closed the curtains.

Jacob was unable to stop tears of anger from coming and would have continued to let them cascade down his face, were it not for the nosey neighbour's friendly hello giving him a brief respite from his despair.

"Are you OK?" the lady asked.

Embarrassed, Jacob covered his face with his hands to wipe the teary evidence away.

"I'm fine."

Her expression morphed into a frown. It was clear she did not believe him.

"Really, I'm fine," he said in an unconvincing manner.

"OK, if you're sure," she said, trundling back into her garden.

By himself again and shaking from the cold, Jacob took quivering breaths as anger raged inside him. How dare Dinah throw him on the street like a bag of trash? He was nothing more than a bully; no better than Pirlie and Raszlo. It was then Jacob felt the first drops of rain wash his anger away, leaving nothing but loneliness that choked him far worse than Dinah did.

Cold and wet, he took one last look at number 14 Gonga Grove and wandered away into the night.

Chapter III

Alone in the darkness of her room, Orla lay on her bed and tried to process the awful things her father said after Jacob left.

"*Those Mixlings and Dakew are disgusting.*"

"*They should all be drowned at birth.*"

It hurt Orla to see him so full of hate.

A light knock on the door got her attention, but she stayed motionless on the bed, staring through the window at the cloudy sky. There was a second, louder knock quickly followed by a third and then a fourth.

"Open the door," she heard her father say.

"Go away."

"Open this door, or I'll break it down."

Orla knew it was not an empty threat, so she leapt from the bed and turned the key, allowing her father to burst in with a face like fizz.

"I don't want you in here," Orla snapped, as she turned on the light.

"Don't speak to me like that," he roared, marching past her into the centre of the room. "I'm going to say my piece, whether you like it or not."

Orla spun around to face him. "I'm not interested, Dad. Jacob's my friend, and you treat him like something that's stuck to the bottom of your shoe."

"And why do I do that?"

Orla opened her mouth to call him a bigot, but he cut her off.

"He's a complete waster of a boy, that's why. Hanging around with younger girls. No job, no family, and no prospects. Why would you even entertain someone like that? Honestly, I thought we raised you better."

"He's a hunter," Orla shot back. "And he's only two years older than me in case you haven't noticed. The only reason you don't want him hanging around is because he's a Mixling."

"Mixlings are vile. They were created by something…" He paused as if searching for the right word to describe a Dakew and Human relationship. "Unnatural."

Orla rushed forward to point an angry finger in her father's face. "You're the vile one. Get out of my room, I'm too angry to speak with you right now."

"Fine. Keep away from that freak, and we won't have an issue."

Orla nearly jumped out of her skin when he slammed the door on the way out. Hurt swelled from deep inside her, and she battered both pillows with her fists. How dare he dictate her choice in friends? Poor Jacob was out in the rain right now, probably needing comfort.

She tried to open the window, but it would not budge. Feeling even more smothered, she trudged to the wooden cabinet in the corner of the room and pulled out a small penknife. After prising the window open, she climbed down the drainpipe and went to find Jacob.

By the time she arrived in Main Street, darkness had shrouded the city, choking the light, and exposing the murky underbelly of the once innocent Capital. Her search lasted two hours, but she found only horrible sights–burnt-out vehicles smouldering by the roadside, and homeless souls, most of them children, huddled together in sleeping bags to keep the cold at bay, their young lives in the ruthless hands of mother nature. Even the drug dealers were out in force, selling to addicts willing to trade anything for a fix.

The abandoned building where she knew Jacob usually slept was deserted, except for an empty food parcel, and an old blanket weighed down by a boulder. Shivering, Orla breathed warmth into her ice-cold hands and exited the building. She then crossed the road and sat on a vandalised bench to take the weight off her aching feet.

Where could he be?

A familiar figure called out her name. It was Mr. Janmano with a concerned look on his face. He wore a thick grey duffel coat with a matching hat, scarf, and gloves. After checking both ways for traffic, he waddled across the road and sat down beside her.

"What are you doing here?" he asked. "Don't you know how dangerous these streets are?"

"I can't find Jacob. He was at my house for dinner, there was a big fight and…" She stopped, too embarrassed to go into detail.

Janmano removed his scarf, hat, and gloves and handed them to Orla. "Put these on."

"Thanks."

"Where have you looked for him?"

"Everywhere. I even checked the back streets."

"You shouldn't be anywhere near the back streets. My Fast-Wheel is just over there. Let me take you home?"

"Not until I've found him."

"OK, let's think this through logically. Where else could he be?"

Orla tried to think, but Jacob had never ventured further than Main Street. Not unless he was hunting.

"He could be at the hunter's depot," she said excitedly.

"No, the depot closed hours ago."

"That's right. I forgot it closed early today. Sometimes we sit at the harbour. Maybe, he's gone there?"

"Well, what are we waiting for?"

Twenty minutes later, the Fast-Wheel came to a stop, and Orla felt her routine sadness at the state of the harbour. She had read many books in history class and seen lots of photos of the harbour in its heyday. Back then, it provided jobs for workers up and down the country. Now, due to a lack of funding, the harbour had fallen into a state of disrepair. All that remained from its industrial peak was a few damaged shipping containers and a crane rusting in the elements.

"Back in a moment," she said, stepping onto the pavement.

"I'll come with you," Janmano replied, removing his ample frame from the Fast-Wheel.

"It's best I go alone."

He sighed and then nodded. "If you're not back in twenty minutes, I come and get you. Deal?"

Orla chuckled. "Deal."

She found Jacob straight away. He was right where they always hung out, dangling his feet over the harbour's edge with a pile of pebbles beside him. Bracing herself, she rolled underneath a decaying barrier and sat by his side.

"I've been looking everywhere for you."

No reply.

"Have you been here all night?"

Still no reply.

His silence left her deeply worried. Jacob had never refused to speak with her before. It was clear he was still angry and hurt about what her father did. She hated seeing him in such obvious pain, but it was impossible to turn back the clock. Maybe a sincere apology on behalf of her cowardly father would do the trick?

"Look, my father's behaviour was unforgivable. I can't tell you how sorry I am."

Jacob turned to face her. "You shouldn't be out this late. It's dangerous."

"Oh, don't you start." She laughed. "I've already had a lecture from Mr. Janmano."

"Janmano?"

"He's waiting to take us hom..." She stopped herself from finishing the sentence. "He's waiting to take us wherever we want to go."

Jacob sighed. "It'll take more than a Fast-Wheel to get me where I want to go."

"What do you mean?"

"I'm leaving," he said, throwing a pebble into the murky water.

"Leaving?" Orla parroted. "Where will you go?"

"To join the Revolutionaries. Get a sense of purpose, something to fight for"

The Revolutionaries started out as a group of free-dom-fighters but had become a powerful force. Most of their soldiers came from the now disbanded Uthovayan army and would do anything to liberate their country from the Antantans. Orla believed in their goal but not their violent methods.

"It's impossible to find them," she said gently.

"They've got hidden bases all over the country."

"Yeah, the operative word being hidden. I've never seen any of them. Have you?"

He shook his head.

"So how do you plan on joining them? It's not like they take out adverts in the local paper."

"At least it's a plan," he snapped, twisting to meet her gaze. "You're not the only one who can dream of a brighter future."

His response irked her, but there was no point in a petty squabble, so she kept her cool, lowering her voice to a whisper as she spoke. "That's not fair. I'll support you in anything you do, but why let life drive you out of the Capital? Don't run away like you did in Oak-hedge."

"What do you mean, run away?"

"You had a loving family there, Jacob, and you swapped it all for a life on the streets."

Jacob jumped to his feet. "Loving family? You know nothing about my foster parents."

"That's because you never talk about them. I just assumed –"

"Well, you assumed wrongly then, didn't you? Let me tell you something about my loving family. On my ninth birthday, Raszlo came home from work the happiest I'd ever seen him. He and Pirlie were dancing around the house. I joined in, even though I had no idea why they were dancing. For once, they didn't clip me round the ear or send me to my room. They danced along with me. It's probably the happiest time I can recall as a kid."

Orla said nothing, but as he continued, she had a horrible feeling of where the story was going.

"I soon learned Raszlo had won a luxury cruise around the Eastern Islands," Jacob explained. "We couldn't afford holidays, so I understood their excitement. It was wonderful to see them so happy, but it didn't last long. Not when they realised, I could scupper their plans."

"What happened?" Orla heard her own voice crack when she spoke.

"They left a week later. Without me. I was chained down in the cellar with just enough wiggle room to reach a bowl of water and a loaf of stale bread."

Orla's mouth fell open, and her blood ran cold at the thought of her best friend's suffering. What kind of monsters left a child locked in a basement? The knot in her stomach tightened as she fought back tears. Jacob looked in her direction, but then quickly looked away again as he continued the story in a flat tone.

"For six days, the cellar was home. Six days in complete darkness with nothing but the squeaks of a Weavel Rat for company. That little guy got me through that ordeal. We shared the bread equally. When my foster parents finally returned, they were horrified to discover my little friend in the cellar...and they killed him."

Orla could not halt the quiet sobs as she stared at her best friend, broken by the memory of his horrific childhood. He was pale, and he had a look of terror on his face that suggested he was reliving the terrible ordeal right in front of her.

"I remember Pirlie shouting, 'Get that vermin.' He threw another pebble into the water, aggressively this time. "The only vermin in that house was those two."

Orla threw her arms around him, desperately hoping to take his pain away, if only for a second. Neither of them said a word, until Mr. Janmano appeared behind them, his flat nose red from the cold.

"Come on, kids, time to go."

"I can't leave him here," Orla whispered, still with her arms around Jacob.

"Don't worry," the tailor replied. "I'll take him back to the shop. He can sleep there tonight and change for the dance in the morning."

Chapter IV

Jacob was still tired when he woke up the next morning on Mr. Janmano's stockroom floor. He could have gone back to sleep, but his sudden regret about telling Orla his childhood secret prevented him from switching off.

Had he done the right thing in letting his feelings out? He certainly never intended to tell his best friend about life in Oakhedge. In fact, he never intended to tell anyone. The pain was still too raw, too close to the surface for any positive discussions. Yet, the more he lay and contemplated his actions, the more it felt like a weight had been lifted from his shoulders.

Ping.

The noise of the counter bell made Jacob venture through to the shop-floor, where he found Mr. Janmano clutching a white bag.

"You're awake." Janmano said.

"Sure am. Thanks for letting me spend the night."

"No worries, ma'boy."

"What you got in there?" Jacob asked, gesturing towards the bag.

"Breakfast," Janmano said, emptying assorted fruit and nuts onto the counter. "Tuck in."

Janmano went about his usual morning routine, preparing the shop for opening time, while Jacob ate breakfast and thought about the previous night's events. His desire to leave the Capital had not subsided. He was even more determined to find the Revolutionaries and join their fight to free Uthovaya. Not because he believed they would succeed, but because it would be a one-way ticket out of his pathetic excuse for a life.

There was a knock at the door. It was Orla, staring through the window and gesturing for someone to let her in. Jacob always got nervous when Orla became animated. Usually, it was a sign she had something up her sleeve.

"Morning," she said in a serious tone, bursting into the shop the second Jacob opened the door.

"What's going on?" he replied, dispensing with the small talk.

Orla looked disappointed. "What makes you think something is going on?"

"Because it's you. There's always something going on, especially when you get all bouncy like you are now."

"OK, you got me. I have a plan."

"Why don't I like the sound of this?" Jacob sighed.

"Hey!" she protested grumpily.

"Sorry."

"Just listen for a moment. What if we go to Oak-hedge to visit your foster parents?"

Despite the seriousness of the conversation, Jacob hoped she was joking.

"Why would we want to do that?" he asked. "Why would *I* want to do that?"

"Hear me out," she replied quickly. "Your childhood was horrific, but what if there was a way to make you feel better and stop you from wanting to leave the Capital?"

Jacob sighed again. "I'm listening."

"OK, here goes," Orla said, before taking a deep breath. "I was heartbroken for you last night. Carrying that pain around with you can't be healthy so I figured you should face your foster parents. It might give you closure."

Jacob jumped backward to sit on the counter as he gave Orla's suggestion serious consideration. On the one hand, taking such a drastic course of action seemed reckless, but on the other, he could see how facing his foster parents might help him come to terms with his troubled childhood. He was a big boy now–no longer a frightened tyke, unable to defend himself.

"What do you think?" Jacob asked Janmano, who had been pottering about the entire time.

"Up to you, ma'boy. If you feel it could help, then I don't see why not. Just don't expect your foster parents to show any remorse. That way you won't be disappointed."

Jacob nodded and then turned back to Orla. "Let's go for it. We'll be back in time for the dance, right?"

"I guarantee it."

At the train station, Jacob went through the usual rigmarole of signing in at the entrance and collecting his permission slip, while Orla bought two return tickets for Oakhedge. As they made their way to platform 7, Jacob did his best to avoid the guards from before. The last thing he needed was more hassle – not today.

The train was three minutes late, but Jacob barely spoke a word to Orla as they waited. It was the prospect of facing Pirlie and Raszlo that made him stand in silence. Truth be told, he still feared them.

"Here comes the train," Orla announced.

The train was empty, save for a few young undesirables running through the carriages. They continued clowning around until the ticket inspector came and told them off. Jacob found somewhere for him and Orla to sit. It was a small-boxed cabin with a curtain for privacy and two seats on either side of a wooden table attached to the side of the carriage.

"Hope you're not travel sick," Orla said as Jacob felt the train slowly pulling away from the station.

"It usually only happens on twisty roads."

"Well, if you do feel ill, make sure you run to the bathroom. It's about four carriages away."

"Should be a life or sick dash then," Jacob joked.

Orla's chuckle in response sounded forced, almost like it was designed to bridge the gap between a humorous comment and a more serious discussion.

"Try not to worry about seeing your foster parents again." Orla blurted out, almost as if she were privy to his innermost thoughts and fears.

"Can we leave it for now?" Jacob snapped. "I don't want to talk about them all the way to Oakhedge."

"What will we talk about then?"

"Let me hear your speech for this afternoon."

"You really want to hear it?" Orla cried, excitedly pulling a crumpled sheet of paper from her bag, and ironing it out on the table with her palm.

Jacob grinned. "I really want to hear it."

Orla cleared her throat and then read from the paper. Jacob had to admit she delivered her message beautifully. So beautifully, the ticket inspector stayed for the duration of the speech. Orla spoke of equality, a better future away from the Antantans, and the importance of helping those less fortunate. After the speech was over, she folded the piece of paper and put it away again.

"That was marvellous!" the ticket inspector remarked, clapping his hands enthusiastically.

Jacob shot him a look to remind him of the cabin's intended privacy.

"Er, I'll be on my way," he stammered.

Orla smiled at Jacob. "Well, what do you think?"

"Boring," he replied sarcastically.

She chuckled nervously at his comment. "You don't really think it's boring, do you?"

"Of course not. You're onto a winner there. I never knew you could write and speak such poignant words."

"I'm a girl of many talents."

"Clearly," Jacob replied, playfully hitting her arm with the back of his hand.

They joked around throughout the journey, their laughter taking Jacob's mind off the impending reunion with his foster parents. It was only when Orla revealed they were coming up on Oakhedge station that Jacob's worries resurfaced, and he began to feel apprehensive again – apprehension that built as he followed Orla off the train and into the station.

Oakhedge was exactly how Jacob remembered it; wide-cobbled streets with carts everywhere, wooden houses with kids running wild in gardens, and the smell of freshly cut grass temporarily transporting him to a childhood that should have been full of laughter and fun, but instead brought pain and suffering. Only the Polan burn seemed different because the trees and bushes had grown so large the water was no longer visible.

Orla said, "I can't believe the horror behind such a beautiful place. Which house did you live?"

Jacob pointed to a house sitting near the burn. It was the largest by far, a fact his foster parents bragged about to anyone who would listen. Just seeing the front door to the house where his unhappy childhood took place was enough to make him want to turn on his heels and get the train back to the Capital, but he stood his ground like a warrior facing the fight of his life.

"Are you ready for this?"

"Ready as I'll ever be," Jacob replied, taking a deep breath.

He took a few steps forward and pushed open the rusty gate into the garden but hesitated to knock on the wooden door. Orla took the lead and did it for him. There was no answer, so she knocked again. This time, a stocky Human lady with short auburn hair answered the door. She wore a flowery dress and had a wart on the side of her lip that Jacob tried not to stare at.

"Yes, may I help you?" she asked in a posh manner.

Jacob opened his mouth to speak, but nothing came out. He felt Orla's comforting hand on his shoulder almost immediately.

"Leave it to me," she whispered, turning back to the irritated woman whom Jacob did not recognise.

"Are you Pirlie?" Orla asked.

The woman's expression instantly changed from one of irritation to a more sorrowful look. "Oh, you must not have heard," she said, shaking her head in pity. "Pirlie and Raszlo are dead."

Jacob felt a sudden dizziness, this time not from hunger.

"D...dead?" he echoed.

"I'm afraid so," the woman replied softly. "Are you two relatives?"

"They are..." Jacob corrected himself. "They *were* my foster parents."

"Oh, you poor thing. Both of you come in, and I'll explain everything."

Jacob entered last, trailing both ladies through the kitchen. The pink tiles were different from the black-papered theme he remembered from his childhood. Pots and pans hung on the wall by the window, and there was a scratched table with two chairs in the centre of the room. It was strange being back in his childhood home. There seemed an aura about the place, a dark energy that hinted at the horrific goings-on from the past. Entering the living room did nothing to ease the uncomfortable sensation he felt. The furniture was different, but everything else remained the same, right down to the musty brown carpet and damp walls.

The woman who invited them in took a seat on a single chair and then gestured towards a black two-seater directly across from it.

"Have a seat."

"Do you live here now?" Jacob asked, planting himself beside Orla.

"I only moved in last week."

"How did Pirlie and Raszlo die?" Jacob asked, bracing himself for the news.

"Raszlo was first to go. A brain aneurysm about six years ago. A neighbour told me Pirlie was never the same after his death. There's no easy way of saying this, but she took her own life a few weeks ago."

Jacob went numb. "Took her own life, how?"

"I'm afraid she hung herself."

The woman continued talking, but Jacob had zoned out of the conversation completely. He should have been happy his foster-parents were dead, but he felt sorry for them instead. Disgusted with the unexpected emotion, he excused himself from the room, ran back outside, and threw up by the side of the rusty gate. Orla was behind him in a matter of seconds, gently rubbing his back to provide comfort and support.

"Are you OK?"

"Not really," he replied, forcing himself back up.

"It was a mistake to come here," she said quickly. "I'm sorr –"

Jacob stopped her before she could finish the sentence.

"No. You were right to make me come here. Even if my mixed emotions have come as a surprise. At least now I can try to put my foster parents behind me. They can't hurt me anymore. Or anyone else for that matter."

Orla smiled and placed a hand on his shoulder. It was the same beautiful smile Jacob had seen many times before. She was trying to keep his spirits up. Maybe even let him know there was no shame in feeling mixed emotions. In that moment, he was once again reminded how positive an influence Orla was on his life, and how much he needed her around.

"The lady has a box of Pirlie and Raszlo's valuables." Orla explained. "Want to go look?"

Jacob nodded and then trudged back inside the house where the lady was waiting by the door that led into the hall.

"The box is in the cellar," she explained, turning to Jacob. "Can you give me a hand?"

"Me?" Jacob stammered, feeling nervous about descending to the scene of his very own private hell.

"Yes, please. If you don't mind."

Orla offered to help instead, but Jacob shook his head. "I'll go."

The lady unlocked the door leading down to the cellar and started down the stairs ahead of him. Jacob steeled himself and put one foot onto the top step. As soon as he breathed the stale and musty cellar air, he was instantly reminded of the time Pirlie and Raszlo had chained him there so they could go on holiday. By the time he eased off the bottom step, he could feel the familiar sense of panic from all those years ago, the genuine fear the walls would cave in and crush him.

It was then that he saw it…the chain wrapped around a support beam in the middle of the cellar. The chain was so close he could almost feel the cold metal against his skin again. Jacob took deep breaths to control his panic, which was now in danger of spiralling out of control.

"Everything all right?" the lady asked.

"Fine," Jacob found himself saying as he glanced quickly at the chain.

"I don't know why that's there," the lady said, pushing it away with her foot. "They must have kept a pet down here. Very cruel if you ask me."

Jacob said nothing.

"Can you give me a hand with this?"

The large box was heavy, but they managed to drag it towards the stairs and pull it up into the living room. It was filled with old clothes, shoes, and bags. Nothing of any value from what Jacob could tell.

"Anything you want to keep?" the lady asked softly.

"I don't think so," Jacob replied as he rummaged deep inside. He pulled out a small blue book with yellow writing on the front that read: Fiona's Journal.

Jacob had no idea who Fiona could be, but the journal seemed to be written in a strange language. Thinking it useless, he almost tossed it back in the box, but a strange feeling stopped him. Something that told him he would regret throwing it away.

"Do you mind if I keep this journal?" he asked the owner of the house.

"Be my guest. It's rightfully yours, after all."

"Thanks," he said, turning on his heels and heading back into the kitchen towards the front door.

"What will I do with the rest?" the lady cried after him.

"Dump it," he replied without looking back.

Back outside, he passed the journal to Orla for a look.

"Who is Fiona?" she asked upon seeing the front cover.

"No idea. It's written in a different language. Do you recognise it?"

"I don't," she admitted. "We studied Pavellian at school, but that's all."

"Typical," Jacob remarked, walking through the gate, and waiting for Orla to join him.

"There are various names mentioned in here," she told him. "One of them is of particular interest: Lady Kadesha."

"What's interesting about that name?"

"I've heard it before," Orla replied, as she came out the garden with her eyes still buried in the journal. "Mr. Janmano knows someone named Kadesha."

Jacob narrowed his eyes. "Could be a different person."

"Could be, but it's not likely. Kadesha is an unusual name. It's very old-fashioned."

"Let's ask him."

"Good idea," Orla replied as she handed the journal back. "We need to get back for the dance, anyway."

Chapter V

"Can't you two see I'm busy?" Janmano moaned as he folded a customer's tuxedo.

"It won't take a minute," Jacob promised, flashing the customer a rueful smile. "It's about something we found in Oakhedge."

Janmano bid goodbye to the customer and then took possession of the journal, slowly reading the words from the front cover.

"Fiona's journal?"

Orla explained, "It belonged to someone named Fiona."

"Well, colour me shocked," Janmano replied, sarcastically. "I would never have guessed."

"Very funny." Orla scowled.

Jacob stepped forward. "Do you recognise the language?"

"I'm not sure," Janmano admitted. "Why do you ask?"

"The journal mentions someone named Lady Kadesha. Orla thinks you might know her."

"The Kadesha I know was a follower…no, surely, it can't be?"

Jacob gave Orla a suspicious glance. "What can't be?"

"Never mind," Janmano said quickly. "It's probably nothing. Would you like me to contact Kadesha and ask if she knows anything about the journal?"

"Yes, please," Jacob and Orla said unison.

"Watch the shop for me. If anyone comes in, tell them I won't be a moment."

Jacob watched him grab his communicator from under the counter and then head through the back. He was only away a short while before he returned.

"Well?" Jacob asked.

"She'll be here soon for a look at the diary. Maybe, you should wait in the shop until she arrives."

"I don't mind if you have to stay here," Orla offered.

Jacob was horrified at the suggestion. "And miss your big speech? Not a chance. Kadesha can come and meet me at the ballroom."

Janmano let out an exasperated sigh, pulled out his communicator, and disappeared through the back to relay the message. Jacob said goodbye to Orla, who was heading home to get ready for the dance. When Janmano came back, he seemed more content, informing Jacob that Kadesha had reluctantly agreed to meet him at the ballroom.

"Honestly, you'd think it was you doing her the favour," Janmano commented.

"I can be a tad selfish," Jacob admitted, as he searched through the nearest rack of suits. "Which one's mine?"

"None of them. Yours is the burgundy one over here."

"Very nice. Must have cost Mrs. Paton a lot of money to hire."

Janmano shook his head. "I gave her a discount."

After throwing on his suit, Jacob stepped out of the tailor shop into a scene full of chaos. Revellers clogged the streets, some huddled around open fires, others singing songs of freedom. Flustered drivers struggled to get through the mass of abandoned vehicles, and drunken locals taunted the Antantan soldiers trying to stop the festivities.

"Are you coming?" Jacob cried to Mr. Janmano, who was standing in the doorway with his arms folded.

"I have a few more customers coming in. Once they've gone, I'll lock the shop up and head on over."

"Fair enough."

Jacob walked briskly to Penfold Tunnel, where he had agreed to meet Orla. On the way, he passed through Stardent Park and found it overrun by a gang of alcohol-swigging youths, one of whom was burning a tatty Antantan flag at the top of the climbing frame. Thumping dance tunes blared from a nearby music box. By the time Jacob reached the tunnel, the noise was nothing more than an irritating hum in the distance.

Free from the stressful goings-on, he took a deep breath and smelled the crisp, fresh air. A small bird hopping around the tunnel caught his attention, and he watched its carefree movements for a while, wishing he could forget his troubles in a similar fashion, if only for a few hours.

"Sorry I'm late," came Orla's voice from behind him.

"Don't w…" He trailed off mid-sentence, stunned at the figure of immense beauty smiling in front of him.

She wore a long white gown that showcased her slender, toned frame. One side stopped at the thigh, exposing a long, tanned leg to the world. Her hair was not imprisoned by its usual clip, but instead, flowed freely past her shoulders like a golden waterfall.

"What's wrong?" she asked, twisting for a peek at herself. "Do I not look nice?"

"Y-you…you look…" He cleared his throat in a feeble attempt to regain his composure. "You look absolutely incredible."

"Stop exaggerating." She giggled, playfully punching his arm. "Let's check you out."

She put a hand on her chin as if sizing him up. Jacob puffed his chest out and stood to attention.

"You look hot," she said in an over-exaggerated flirty tone that somehow remained friendly.

"Thanks." He chuckled. Then he realised Kaira was nowhere to be seen. "Where's your mum?"

"She can't make it," Orla replied with a mix of what sounded like sadness and anger. "My dad found out you were going and made a big fuss about it. Mum agreed not to go for a quiet life. He tried the same thing with me, but I told him about the speech, and he backed down. I was surprised he did, actually."

"You OK?"

"I'll get over it. Anyway, I should be asking how you are."

Jacob held his hand up to indicate a halt to the conversation. Now was not the time to go on about himself. This was Orla's special day. He had no intention of ruining it by moaning about his own problems.

"Let's talk about things after the dance." He suggested.

Jacob had heard many stories of the glittering ballroom where the dance was held. It was once frequented by the biggest stars in the world, and he could see why when he walked through the doors and gazed upon the blend of classic and contemporary décor. Several chandeliers hung from above, and in the right-hand corner were steps decorated with sapphire gems, leading to the stage where a band wearing gold jackets played swing music with dizzying aplomb. Glass tables and varnished chairs had been arranged on either side of the dancefloor, where dancers strutted their stuff in time with the music. A thick red fog rose from nowhere, and for a moment, Jacob thought the dancers resembled phantoms gyrating against a backdrop of dazzling lights from the stage.

"Wow," Jacob murmured, his eyes wide with wonder.

Orla nodded and squeezed his arm tightly. "This is the fifth year in a row I've come here. I don't think it will ever lose its magic."

"I can see why."

She passed him ten nova and pointed to the bar. "You get us a drink. I'll find us a table."

He awkwardly accepted the money and watched her head off. While sauntering to the bar, he was surprised to find guests from all ages and races chatting with each other. There were, of course, Humans, Dakew and Mixlings, but also, Remmans – a race of bald, white-skinned Humanoids who hailed from the country of Remmania. Many Gogglos has shown up as well, and although they communicated by means of telepathy, Jacob gave them friendly nods as they passed, trying not to stare at their black pupils swimming from side to side in their oval-shaped eyes.

"What can I get you?" the Human bartender asked after Jacob finally manage to secure a space at the crowded bar.

"One Crimson Ale and a Crimson Nectar," Jacob shouted over the music.

He paid for the drinks, and then carried them into the middle of the dancefloor, trying desperately to avoid enthusiastic dancers. He could see Orla halfway up the right-hand of the ballroom, looking rather embarrassed at being the only person seated at the table.

"I'm so glad you're here," she admitted as he sat down. "Some of the guests were giving me funny looks."

Jacob burst out laughing, handed Orla her change, and then passed the Nectar across.

"You did look a bit lonesome."

"Don't you start." She giggled, taking a sip of the alcoholic drink. "Look, there's Mr. Janmano."

Sure enough, Janmano was making his way across the dancefloor towards their table. He took one look at Orla's Crimson Nectar and shook his head.

"Make sure you're not drunk for this speech, lady," he said, adopting a hilariously over the top stern tone.

"I'll be fine," Orla laughed.

Jacob said. "Any sign of Kadesha?"

"Not yet." Janmano replied as he sat down beside them and turned to Orla. "You nervous?"

"I didn't get much of a chance to rehearse, but I think I'll be fine."

"It will be excellent practice for you," Janmano insisted. "Politicians have to address the public all the time."

"As long as I keep back from Mr. Slade, I won't be tempted to cancel."

"Speak of the devil," Jacob replied, as he saw Mr. Slade come through an emergency exit not far from their table.

The man who had visited the Paton residence the previous day approached them with a toothy smile and a clammy handshake for all. He borrowed a chair from another table and planked it next to Orla, practically pushing Mr. Janmano out of the way in the process.

"Ready for your big speech?" He grinned.

Orla looked lost for words, so Jacob spoke on her behalf, assuring the chairman she was looking forward to it.

"Excellent. There are a few acts on before you so try to relax until it's your turn." He placed a hand on her shoulder. "Don't look so nervous. You'll be fine."

"I hope so," Orla replied.

The heavy clang of a bell signalled the start of the festivities, and a hush fell over the ballroom as the dancers returned to their tables. A jester was the first act on stage. He specialised in juggling any item that came to hand. Jacob thought his act was naff, but the crowd disagreed, and the jester departed the stage to widespread laughter and a round of applause.

Next up was a singer, but his gravelly-voiced efforts did not go down well with the crowd who barely clapped after his performance. The so-called vocalist was followed by an eccentric fire-eater who timed a throw poorly and almost burnt herself to a crisp. Six acts later, Jacob was ready to throw himself off the nearest building. Finally, the chairman took to the stage and signalled the end of the entertainment section.

"I must be up next," Orla whispered with a shaky tone.

"You'll do great," Jacob assured, giving her a cheeky wink for good measure.

Janmano offered his own words of encouragement as the chairman called Orla's name. Thunderous applause echoed around the ballroom when she ascended each step to the stage. The chairman re-tested the microphone, introduced her again, and then dashed down to the dancefloor, leaving Orla standing alone under the spotlight.

"G…" She cleared her throat. "Good evening, everyone."

And then she froze.

Jacob saw Orla fall apart as clear as day: the laboured foot shuffle, the continuous clearing of her throat, the endless staring straight ahead like she had become a statue. An eternity of silent agony passed, and complaints from the crowd became more and more audible.

"Come on, Orla," said Jacob under his breath. "Say something, say anything."

Orla inexplicably snapped back to life, and Jacob breathed a sigh of relief as she started the speech. Her words were forthright but lacking the same clarity and passion she showed in the train cabin. When it was over, she sat back down to a tepid reception.

"I blew it," she cried, downing the rest of her Crimson Nectar in one go.

"It can't have been easy standing up there," Jacob told her.

"Exactly," Janmano piped up. "I would love to see this lot do any better."

An idea formed in Jacob's mind as he watched Orla stir her drink with a straw. He got to his feet and held out a hand in her direction.

"May I have this dance?" He grinned.

"I'm not in the mood for dancing."

"Oh, come on. My dancing could cheer anyone up."

Orla sipped from her straw and then leaned back in her chair. "One dance?"

Jacob nodded. "One dance. If you're not laughing in ten seconds, I'll let you go and sit back down again."

Without saying another word, Orla got up and yanked Jacob over to the dancefloor by the collar.

"Careful. I have to return this tux to the shop."

Jacob swayed from side to side in a futile attempt at copying his friend's more difficult dance moves. He imagined everyone in the ballroom was laughing at his lack of rhythm, but Orla needed cheering up, so he soldiered on.

"You're not such a bad dancer." Orla smiled.

"That's debatable," he replied as the music shifted from a funky, upbeat dance track to a slower, more romantic piece.

Orla moved in closer and pulled his hand onto her hips. "I'll do my best."

They continued moving to the music, Jacob like a drunken sailor and Orla like a pro.

As the song played out, the primary doors suddenly swung open, and Jacob watched a tall stranger with dark hair march into the party. He was escorted by six Antantan soldiers, each carrying an incinerator-rifle. The stranger in charge signalled with his right hand, and the soldiers fired in unison towards the unsuspecting crowd. Bullets sheared through guests as though they were paper, and terrified screams echoed around the ballroom.

Chapter VI

"Watch out!" Jacob yelled.

He broke away from Orla, half-a-second before a bullet whistled between them. Guests ran in every direction, screaming while diving for cover behind tables and chairs. The unlucky ones lay still on the dance-floor, their lifeless eyes staring into the abyss.

With his adrenaline pumping, and fearing for Orla's safety more than his own, Jacob scanned the ballroom for an escape route. It was then he saw the emergency exit that Mr. Slade had emerged from earlier. Without a second thought, Jacob dragged Orla towards it.

"What are you doing?" she cried.

"Getting you out of here."

A bullet narrowly missed Jacob's head. It was so close; he could feel the air on his left ear as it passed. Others had pushed towards the exit now, creating a tidal wave of panic that met Jacob full force, knocking him to the floor and leaving him struggling to breathe underneath a pile of bodies. Orla screamed as he tried to shift the enormous weight pinning him down. Finally, he slithered out like a snake but saw an Antantan soldier hurrying towards them.

"You need to go," Jacob said to Orla.

"I'm not leaving you here."

"Never mind me. You've got too much to live for. Get out of here before it's too late."

The soldier was almost upon them, but Jacob anticipated his attack and sent a surprise elbow back into the attacker's nose. He recoiled in agony and lifted his weapon to fire, but another group of escapees knocked the soldier down before he could pull the trigger. Jacob moved for the loose rifle, but more bullets whistled past his head, and he scrambled back to Orla.

"Move," he ordered.

Orla refused to budge, so he threw her over his shoulder and moved swiftly through the emergency exit and out into an alley, all the while taking blows to the back from her fists.

"Let me go," she ordered.

"I'll put you down here," he replied, dumping her in the alleyway.

As he twisted back to the door, he caught sight of what looked like several dead bodies littering the street. Confused, he crept to the end of the alley and saw strategically placed snipers on the rooftops across the road, their sights set on unsuspecting innocents who crossed their path. Suddenly, a panicked Mixling rushed past Jacob, and a sniper picked him off with deadly precision, making his head explode in a messy concoction of blood, brain, and tissue.

"Oh my God," Orla screamed, backing against a large waste container.

Jacob stared at the gruesome sight for a few seconds, his fists clenched in violent anticipation. Another rush of adrenaline came as he swung back to face Orla.

"Promise you won't follow me," He begged.

"Follow you where?"

"Just promise."

She nodded and then lunged forward to grip his arm with sharp nails. "Please, don't go back in there."

"I can't stand by and do nothing," he whispered, freeing himself and rushing back inside.

He took a deep breath and tried to ignore the little voice inside, telling him not to be so reckless. It was good advice because he had no weapon and no clear plan on what to do next, but he felt a sense of responsibility to the innocents trapped inside. He had to do something, anything to help them.

Arriving back inside the ballroom, Jacob noticed the madness had been silenced, replaced by the sound of whimpering guests.

"Get your hands up."

A soldier to the left of the door had his incinerator rifle pointed at Jacob's head. Cursing himself for getting caught so easily, Jacob raised his hands and felt the adrenaline drain from his body as the soldier escorted him over to the remaining guests.

For the first time, Jacob got a good view of the vicious murderers who had stormed the party. The Human leader was around fifty with chiselled features and a sharp chin, half concealed by the high collar of a four-button blue tunic. Strangely, there was a mass of translucent red and blue wires running from his left shoulder to a metallic backpack.

What is that?

The stranger strode forward and called the guests to attention.

"My name is Gunnar Veto, and I carry a message from the President of Antantis."

Gunnar Veto?

The name had no meaning to Jacob, but he noticed other guests cowering in terror – even more so than they already had been. Veto continued to address them while the soldiers looked on.

"Terrorist gatherings will no longer be tolerated. From this day forward, the Dance for Liberty is illegal."

Jacob baulked at that choice of words. *Terrorist gatherings?* It was quite the statement coming from a man who had just ordered his troops to kill innocents in cold blood.

Mr. Janmano, who Jacob noticed had been standing beside a stricken woman lying in a pool of blood, suddenly stormed between the guests and marched straight up to Veto. Gasps filled the air as the soldiers raised their incinerator rifles, only to lower them again at Veto's request.

Veto tilted his head like an inquisitive animal. "Do you have something you wish to say?"

"Yes, we've got someone still alive over there,"

Jacob looked back across and saw a bare-chested Remman pressing his scrunched-up shirt into a gaping wound in the woman's stomach.

"Let me take her to the emergency room," Janmano continued. "She might survive if given proper medical attention."

Veto did not even glance in her direction. "I'm afraid I can't do that. Now, step back."

"Not until you help that poor woman."

Jacob shook his head in disbelief, wishing he could turn back time to stop Janmano from venturing forward. Other guests whimpered and begged the brave but foolish tailor to get back, but he stood his ground. At the same moment, the injured woman on the dancefloor drew her last breath, and quiet sobs rose from those around her.

Veto pointed his wired left arm towards Janmano. "I asked you to step back. How dare you disobey your masters."

"Masters?" Janmano snorted. "You won't be for much longer. One day we'll drive you and your government officials out of our great nation. Uthovaya will be free again."

Another hush fell over the remaining guests, and Jacob sensed a change in the atmosphere. Every part of him screamed to attack, but with what? There was nothing to fight with. Only a few upturned chairs and empty glasses lay scattered around him. Oh, how he wished he still had his gun.

"Anything else you want to get off your chest." Veto whispered through gritted teeth.

Janmano spat in his face, drawing gasps from Jacob and everyone else in attendance.

"Big mistake." Veto said, shaking with rage. "Anyone who stands against me will be put to death."

Veto clutched the tailors' forehead with his gloved palm, and his left arm shook violently. The ballroom lights flickered as Janmano's muscles spasmed, and the sickening sound of bones snapping made the guests shriek in horror. Jacob was paralysed with fear, but unable to take his eyes off the horrifying sight of the executioner staring into the tailor's eyes until the burned body collapsed to the floor. When it was over, a perverse smile crept across Veto's face.

"No," Jacob cried, propelling himself forward.

He had a soldier in his sights but before reaching his target, he felt a blinding flash of pain shoot through his head. A soldier had caught him from behind with the butt of a rifle. Jacob hit the floor with a thud. Warm blood trickled down his scalp, and dizziness made him want to throw up. He desperately wanted to jump to his feet and run, escape the flames somehow, but he

SEAN CLARKE

could not find the strength, almost like his own mind had given up and spread its message of doom to his legs. Helpless, tired, and defeated, he lay still and waited for the inevitable.

"Burn this place to the ground!" Veto screamed, before marching out the main entrance.

The soldiers did not need a second invitation. They flicked a switch on their rifles and flames spouted from the barrels, igniting the tables, chairs, and curtains. Fire danced up the walls, and thick black smoke choked the air.

The last thing Jacob saw before he passed out were two shadowy figures, rushing through the flames towards him.

Chapter VII

When Jacob opened his eyes, he was lying on his back in a soft bed, staring up at a swirl-patterned ceiling he had never seen before. Turning his head to the left brought a twinge of pain, so he turned the other way and found Orla sitting on a chair beside the bed, a look of relief written all over her face.

"Thank goodness you're awake." She whispered.

"How long was I out?"

"Almost four hours."

Jacob wanted to ask what happened in those missing hours, but the dull ache in his head gradually worsened, forcing him to grit his teeth and close his eyes until the pain lessened, and he could concentrate again.

"My head hurts."

"You've got a nasty cut. I had to change your pillow a few times because of the blood."

Jacob could not remember where the cut came from.

"Where am I?"

"A safehouse belonging to Lady Kadesha."

"Kadesha?"

The dam that blocked his short-term memory burst open, allowing the full horrors of the ballroom incident to flood back. He remembered it all now; the man with the electric arm, the snipers on the rooftops, Janmano's death, even the heat of the flames climbing the walls. He sat bolt upright, suddenly aware of his own heart as it beat in his chest.

"A soldier pistol-whipped me. There was fire everywhere. I can still smell the smoke."

Orla began to cry. "I stood outside and watched that building burn. I never thought I would see you again."

Jacob reached forward and tenderly stroked her face. "Please, don't cry."

As the tears trickled down Orla's cheek onto his hand, he stared into those familiar eyes, and suddenly noticed something different, like a world he had yet to explore.

"I'm being silly," Orla said, looking slightly embarrassed as she pulled away.

Jacob thought it best to change the subject, so he lay back on the bed and stared up at the ceiling again. "How did I get here?"

"Lady Kadesha and her bodyguard turned up just after you left me outside. They risked their lives to save you."

"I saw them coming through the smoke." He coughed several times and then exhaled breath. "That man…Veto. There was something wrong with his arm.

He could conduct electricity through it. He's the one who executed Mr. Janmano."

Orla stood up and walked towards the window. "Apparently, he's a special agent working at the highest levels of power within the Antantan government."

"Who told you that?"

"Lady Kadesha," Orla replied, still staring out the window. "She has the journal we found. Apparently, it was written in ancient Dakew. There are only a handful of people worldwide who can decipher it."

"Did she say anything else?"

Orla turned back to face him. "She said a lot more, but it's not my place to tell you."

Jacob was intrigued, but before he could press her for more information, a crash shook the room, and the door nearly came off its hinges as a colossal figure with glowing orange eyes charged into the room. He had grey, vein-scribbled skin with a tusk on either side of his lipless mouth, and long dark hair sprouting from the back of his head. Jacob found himself shrinking into the bed. What could the dangerous-looking new arrival possibly want? He urged Orla to run, but his apprehension at the monstrous sight lessened when he noticed Orla's calm demeanour.

"About time you woke up." the newcomer grunted.

"Are you a Krokiran?" Jacob asked.

"Hell yeah, I'm a Krokiran." he replied in a gruff tone. "You never seen one before?"

Jacob shook his head. The Krokirans had yet to spread their numbers across Lozaro, but hunters who spoke of them told stories of battle-hardened warriors with tremendous speed and power on the battlefield. Jacob stared at the small satchel attached to the newcomer's right hip, and the slick, silver assault rifle strapped to his bare chest.

"It's a KSF-16." He told Jacob. "All Krokiran Special Forces operatives are issued with them."

"You're in the KSF?" Jacob responded, failing to contain the admiration in his tone.

The legendary unit was known and feared throughout the world, but Jacob never dreamed he would meet one of them in the flesh.

"I used to be," the Krokiran corrected. "The name's Boocka. I'm the one who carried you out of that burning ballroom."

"Thanks for saving my life." Said Jacob.

"I won't be making a habit of it. You'll need to toughen up if you're coming with us."

Jacob looked at Orla for clarification, but she remained silent.

Boocka said. "Lady Kadesha will be along in a moment to explain everything."

As if arriving on cue, Kadesha entered the room. She was an older, elegant Dakew with flowing silver hair, and wore a yellow sleeveless dress with white sandals. Jacob could feel her powerful aura from the other side of the room.

Kadesha moved across and then touched his face, the tears rolling down her cheeks.

"I haven't seen you in such a long time."

"OK, this is getting a little weird," he grunted, swinging his legs out of bed, and getting unsteadily to his feet.

"Forgive me." Kadesha said, softly, "But I never dared dream you were still alive."

"Excuse me?" He turned to Orla, but she didn't even look shocked as Kadesha continued.

"Please allow me to explain. Years ago, I served the royal family of Uthovaya."

"Aren't they all dead now?"

"Let Lady Kadesha speak," Boocka snapped.

"Please, go on m'lady."

"I and two others were Queen Fiona's followers. It was tradition for an Elementalist to always have three followers, no more no less."

"Elementalist?" Jacob repeated.

Boocka shook his grey fist. "What did I just tell you?"

Kadesha continued, "Her majesty broke the rule when she added a fourth follower, a man named Gosford Veto, or Gunnar Veto as you know him. They were close, but he used his influence to deceive us all. He was an Antantan spy who had been sent to infiltrate the royal family, and gather information for the President of Antantis, who was preparing to invade Uthovaya. By the time we learned the truth, it was too late, and the

Antantans knew when and where to hit us. The king, queen, and the baby prince never stood a chance."

"Or so we thought," Boocka added. "Mr. Janmano's call came like a bolt from the blue."

The mention of Janmano's name transported Jacob back to the horrific events in the ballroom. The screams of everyone inside, the lifeless bodies littering the floor, and poor Mr. Janmano. The selfless Dakew was a pillar of the community and worked hard to keep his business ticking over. Jacob was sickened by his death and hated the Antantans even more for what they had done.

"He didn't deserve to die," Jacob whispered.

Kadesha bowed her head for a few seconds and then looked up again. "There's more. You must hear the full story."

Jacob took a deep breath and then nodded.

"Before Gunnar Veto appeared on the scene, the Dakew queen fell in love with a Human named Seth. They got married and had a Mixling son by the name of Jacob."

Jacob let the words sink in for a moment, but his legs suddenly gave way, and he fell backwards into a sitting position on the bed, staring blankly at the floor, but fully aware the others in the room were waiting for his reaction.

It must be a lie.

If he was a prince, he would have known about it… *right*? Then again, he had no idea who his real mum and dad were. Pirlie and Raszlo had always been cagey when he asked about them.

"There must be some mistake."

"I assure you there isn't," Kadesha said softly. "We tested your blood while you were unconscious. You are Prince Jacob Crestmore, heir to the Uthovayan throne. The journal we have in our possession was written by your mother, Queen Fiona."

Shaking his head furiously, he turned to Orla. "Are you buying this story?"

"Why would they lie?" Orla asked. "We were never allowed to talk about the royals at school, but one of my history teachers defied Antantan law and told us stories about them. The baby prince was indeed named Jacob. He'd be exactly your age right now as well."

"So, I'm a Crestmore?"

"Looks that way. Although I can hardly believe it myself."

Kadesha smiled and then retrieved a silver plate from the landing. It was loaded with delicately cut slices of bread and butter. She sat it on a table across from the bed. "You must be hungry?"

Jacob looked at the plate, and then back to Kadesha again, trying to decide whether to push for more information or wolf down the buttered bread. In the end, his stomach got the better of him, and he dragged a wooden chair across to the table and tucked into the food, hardly pausing for breath as he shovelled each slice into his mouth.

"Have some water." Kadesha insisted, pouring it from a jug into a container.

His eyes lit up, and he swallowed the liquid in one go.

"I am afraid we haven't finished yet," Kadesha added.

"I want to know everything," he replied, struggling to speak with his mouth full.

"Not here," Boocka interrupted. "We're gonna take a trip, but your friend needs to stay in this room. We can't risk this secret getting out. It's on a need to know basis."

"Fine by me," Orla replied, sitting back on the chair.

"Whose secrets are you trying to protect?" Jacob asked.

"The Revolutionaries, of course."

"The Revolutionaries?"

Kadesha walked out to the landing and beckoned him to come along.

"Will you be OK here?" Jacob asked Orla, who was sitting with her arms folded, clearly in a huff.

"I'll just need to be, won't I?"

"Hopefully, I won't be long," he replied, before following Boocka out to where Kadesha was waiting.

They led him down a spiral staircase and then outside to a cluster of trees at the back of the garden. There was a trapdoor hidden amongst the undergrowth, and a ladder descending into the darkness. Jacob went down last and found himself in an underground tunnel lit by lamps that hung from wooden support beams. There was a large object covered by a thick black dustsheet directly in front of them. It was almost as wide as the tunnel itself. Boocka pulled the sheet away to reveal a dirty white buggy with four muddy wheels and enough seating space for four passengers.

"Get in," Boocka ordered as he climbed into the driver's seat.

Kadesha had taken the passenger seat beside him, so Jacob sat behind them, and the buggy roared into life.

"Better hold on," Boocka cried as the buggy surged forward.

As the buggy tore through the network of tunnels, spraying mud everywhere, Jacob noticed unmarked buildings built into off sections that shot away from the main route, and two enormous machines that looked like tanks being serviced by engineers.

"What is this place?" Jacob asked, leaning forward until he was cheek to cheek with Kadesha.

"This is the reason your friend had to stay back at the house. Everything you see is part of a covert plan by the Revolutionaries to seize control of Uthovaya from the Antantans. They call it Operation Creeper. There are hundreds of these tunnels linked throughout the Capital. Thousands of troops will mobilise from them when the time comes."

Jacob had always known the Revolutionaries were engaged in a battle against the Antantans, but until now, he assumed it was only on a small scale. It was heartening to know they were a much bigger force than he previously thought.

The buggy swerved, and Boocka hit the brake, caus-ing it to skid across the uneven ground and come to a stop beside a makeshift staircase that led to a thick wooden door. Head still spinning from all the revela-tions, not to mention the rocky ride, Jacob was led into a circular room with strange markings on the floor and a circular slot against the faraway wall. A single chest was situated to the right of the slot.

"Where are we now?" he asked.

"Welcome to the Chamber of the Elements," Kade-sha answered, sweeping her arm forward. "We are di-rectly under Crestmore Castle, your former home."

"The chamber of what?"

"The Chamber of the Elements is where Elemental magic is made possible. This is a special place, with a dimensional gateway that links to another universe. According to ancient Dakew legend, the original crea-tors of this planet were higher beings, capable of tap-ping into the power of elemental spirits. Not only did they build our entire world and everything in it, but they gifted the power of fire, wind, water, and terra to a select few inhabitants. The lucky few were part of the magic bloodline and went on to rule Uthovaya. They were your ancestors."

Jacob screwed up his face. "Magic spells? Dimen-sional Gateways? Elemental spirits? Am I expected to believe all of this?"

"Quiet," Boocka ordered.

"Your mother was the last of these powerful Elementalists who were able to cast spells. You inherited the power and should have been next in line to the throne, but the Antantans destroyed everything when they stormed the castle. They wiped the Elementalists from history after that, altering textbooks and deleting references. Even speaking the word was punishable by death in the early years of Antantan rule. Most people around the world believe they are no more than a myth."

There was a great sadness in her tone, but Jacob still wondered if the story was genuine.

"If this is true, I'll be able to do some magic for us right now? After all, I'm the next in line."

Kadesha's heavy sigh gave him the answer he expected.

"You cannot perform magic because the ElmKey no longer exists."

"What's an ElmKey?"

"An otherworldly artefact capable of powering the dimensional gateway. A few years after your mother died, it lost power and then turned to dust. The ancient Dakew believed the ElmKey was made by the Creators. They also believed there were two made, but one was lost to the sands of time. Your mother knew the importance of a backup, and spent years searching for the Lost ElmKey, detailing every clue in her journal. The same journal you found in Oakhedge."

"Did she ever find it?"

"No, but she was convinced it was kept in a special tower."

Kadesha reached into Boocka's satchel and removed the journal. She opened it to a specific page, and Jacob gazed upon a sketch of a golden tower that seemed to be rising out of sand. There was a map next to the sketch, and some other details written in ancient Dakew.

"So, where is this tower?" Jacob replied, humouring her for a moment.

"Somewhere in the Tavara desert, according to the journal."

Jacob raised a hand to his chin, pondering the information for a moment. "Well, what's to stop us – and I'm not saying I believe all of this – from going to the tower and getting the Lost ElmKey? We can power up the dimensional gateway and bring back elemental magic."

"If only it was that simple," Kadesha replied. "The coordinates were never recorded in the journal, but there's a note from someone, possibly Seth, claiming the coordinates can be found stored inside a cage in the Crestmore Family Vault."

"Where is this vault?"

"The journal doesn't say, probably to prevent the coordinates from falling into the wrong hands. Luckily, I know someone we can ask. A friend of Seth's who lives on the Isle of Charn."

Boocka added, "You will need to come with us to speak with him."

Kadesha put a hand on Jacob's shoulder. "If we can get the Lost ElmKey to the chamber, we can open the dimensional gateway. Your body will then absorb the elemental spirits, and you will become a powerful Elementalist."

"Then what happens?"

"You will take your rightful place on the Uthovayan throne, just like your mother. Assuming the Revolutionaries can gain control of the Capital, of course."

If Jacob had been struggling to take everything in before, he was now at the stage of feeling like his head would explode. All he could think about was crowns, jewels, and wizard hats. He had gone from being a homeless hunter, hated and persecuted by just about everyone, to discovering he was the offspring of royalty and potentially capable of magic all in one day. It was a lot of information to process, and even harder to believe.

"There must be someone else who can go in my place."

"No," Kadesha insisted. "The Revolutionaries have always dreaded the day they have to choose a new leader for Uthovaya but putting you on the throne will end the potential for civil war. You are the last survivor of the magic bloodline and the rightful king. Your ability to use magic will end any doubt about your royal heritage."

Jacob nodded, but it was still too much to process. "I want to get back to my friend now," he said, turning back towards the buggy.

"Wait," Kadesha cried. "Will you at least look in the chest?"

"Unless you can show me some proof of magic, there's no point," said Jacob without turning back.

"Wait," Kadesha ordered in a tone that made him freeze. "I can show you something else, something that might change your mind."

Curiosity got the better of him, so he spun back around, nodded reluctantly, and then made his way over to the chest. The lid creaked as he pulled it off, and dust flew everywhere, making him sneeze. As the dust subsided, he could see a bronze staff with a small white globe fixed to the top.

"The Dynasty Staff," he heard Kadesha say from behind. "It was your mother's weapon."

"My mother's?"

Jacob kneeled and blew dust from the staff's surface. For the first time, he felt like the weapon in his hand was an extension of himself. It fit him far better than any gun ever had. He felt an instant closeness to the mother he had never met, but the emotional moment was all too fleeting, ruined by his own resentment towards the man with the electric arm. Not only had Veto robbed Jacob of his mum and dad, but he was also indirectly responsible for the horrible events in Oakhedge that came after.

"Please, help us," Kadesha said softly as she walked behind him.

"What happens if I decide to walk away?" Jacob asked without standing up to face her.

"This is your decision. We cannot force you to come with us."

The buggy-ride back through the tunnel was mostly spent in silence, as Jacob contemplated Kadesha's assertion he must make his own mind up. Such a luxury was unfamiliar territory for him. Life on the streets rarely presented much scope for opportunity. Maybe, he did not believe in magic, but at least if he went with Kadesha and Boocka, he could escape the Capital for a while, clear his head and see a bit of the world. He would probably learn more about his parents, too. It was a win-win situation as far as Jacob was concerned.

But what about Orla? Would she be allowed to come as well? Would she even want to?

Chapter VIII

In the poorly lit cargo area of an armoured truck as it raced through the Capital, Orla listened in disbelief as Jacob explained his situation, wondering if her best friend had lost his marbles. It was bad enough he had convinced her to leave the safehouse with him, but now she was expected to believe the most far-fetched story she had ever heard.

"Run that past me again," she said quickly. "You want me to come with you to find a tower that contains the means to power a dimensional gateway…a gateway that will allow elemental spirits to infuse you with magic?"

"I didn't say I believed it," Jacob replied, emphatically. "I said it's what I've been told."

It was pointless trying to control herself. She burst into fits of nervous laughter and then tried to prise open the locked cargo area door.

"Let me out," she yelled, running back to bang on the back of the cabin where Boocka and Kadesha sat alongside a Human driver.

"Enough," she heard Boocka cry. "We'll drop you off at Main Street on the way to our destination like we agreed."

She banged a few more times, but there was no response.

"Will you calm down?" Jacob whispered. "I'm not supposed to be telling you any of this. They won't let you out of this truck if they find out I've told you."

"This is crazy," Orla replied, feeling her chest become tight with the stress of being trapped, and the burden of knowledge she should not possess.

Jacob frantically waved his arms about, in what seemed to Orla like an over-the-top attempt at getting her attention.

"Imagine for a second it was true?" he said intensely. "It wouldn't just be the key to elemental magic we'd be after, it would be the key to everything you ever wanted. The Revolutionaries have promised to launch Operation Creeper and retake the Capital, but they stand a better chance of avoiding civil war if they can put me on the throne. Uthovaya would be free again. Surely this has to be worth the risk?"

"Not if innocent lives are lost in the process. You know my feelings on the Revolutionaries' violent methods."

"You don't need to agree with their methods, but you might have to accept them. The Antantans will never let our country go. Force is the only way."

Orla shook her head. "But I'm starting university in a week. I can still make a difference if I work hard and become a politician. All we need is more Uthovayans in parliament. Then we can force change."

"We'll be back by the time university starts. You won't even miss a class."

"I said no."

Jacob jumped back, almost cowering like a frightened animal. He seemed genuinely shocked at her refusal to budge, but Orla did not blame herself. His pushiness had caused her to lash out.

"I wouldn't hesitate if it was the other way around." he told her; the disappointment clear in his tone. "I even went back to Oakhedge on your say so, a place I vowed never to set foot in again."

"It's a good thing you did." Orla shot back. "Otherwise you would never have discovered that journal."

Jacob softened immediately. "Fair point, but you always say university is a means to an end, and the only thing that matters is Uthovaya being free. It's time to prove you really mean it."

Orla felt trapped again, and this time it wasn't because of her location. She was unsure how to answer due to her conflicted feelings about the events happening around her. Of course, she wanted Uthovaya to be free. She had dreamed of nothing else since first becoming aware of Antantan oppression. But in those dreams, she had been the one to make a difference, not

Jacob or the Revolutionaries. Now, she felt guilty for being selfish and wanting all the glory.

The truck came to a standstill, and Orla heard footsteps coming around the back of the truck. It was Boocka. He opened the cargo area doors and then folded his grey, musclebound arms.

"That's us at Main Street."

Jacob urged Boocka to wait a moment and then turned back to Orla with his hand out. "I can't do this alone. I need you with me. Just like you've always been since the day we first met."

Orla struggled to imagine life without Jacob. She always expected they would go their separate ways, but now that the time had arrived, she suddenly felt terrified at the prospect. Jacob would be leaving on a dangerous mission, but how could she let him face those dangers alone? Taking his hand became an easy decision.

"I would need a good excuse for my parents," she admitted. "I can't just disappear for a week. They would worry themselves sick."

A smile spread across Jacob's face. He had obviously realised she would be coming along, after all.

"We'll think of something. You could say you're staying up North-West for a few days to check out that part of the city and the nightlife."

"Sounds a bit far-fetched, but maybe."

Jacob beamed at her response. "It's settled then," he said, excitedly.

Orla forced a smile but wondered if Jacob had fully grasped the danger they would find themselves in. The Antantans would not take kindly to an uprising. They had always shown no-mercy to those who opposed them.

"What if the Antantans get wind of this?" she asked. "We could be in danger."

Jacob shook his head. "By the time they figure out what's happening, we'll be back in the Capital with the Lost ElmKey, if it even exists."

"And then, Operation Creeper begins?" Orla asked, making sure she had all the facts.

"That's the plan."

Boocka banged on the back doors and urged her to get a move on.

"There's been a change of plan," Jacob announced, not taking his eyes off Orla. "My best friend is coming with us."

"That's not happening," Boocka replied, jumping onto the cargo bed, and trying to grab Orla's arm to pull her from the truck.

"Let go of me," she blazed, pulling away from the Krokiran.

"If Orla can't go, then neither will I," Jacob warned.

Boocka released her and stormed from the cargo area, muttering angry but unintelligible sounds as he locked the doors again.

Orla turned back to Jacob. "You still haven't told me where we're going."

"To meet Ambassador Bellis of the Revolutionaries. Looks like you and me will see a hidden base after all." He chuckled.

Less than an hour later, Orla and the others emerged into the middle of a busy facility packed with aircraft and armoured trucks. Mechanics wearing overalls rushed from one side of the facility to the other, tending to anything broken they could find.

A tall and robust Human with messy dark hair approached them. He looked in his mid-thirties and wore the green uniform of the old Uthovayan army. Lady Kadesha introduced him as Commander Jackson.

"It's a pleasure to see you again, m'lady." he said, bowing in front of her.

"You too, Commander. I have brought his royal highness, the Prince of Uthovaya along with me."

Jacob stepped forward, and Jackson eyed him with a mixture of surprise and intrigue. "It's an honour to meet you, your majesty."

Orla giggled at Jacob's cheeks turning scarlet.

"Ambassador Bellis is waiting for us," Kadesha explained to Jackson.

"Right this way, m'lady."

The no-nonsense Commander led them through a long winding corridor, continuing until they reached a steel door with a strange locking mechanism. He approached the lock and placed his right hand over a sensor, allowing the scanner to examine the lines on his palm.

"Palm-Print technology," he pointed out. "Seems over the top, but the Ambassador insists it's for the best."

There were around forty workstations inside, all manned by technicians and connected to a giant supercomputer in the centre of the room. Orla noticed one individual stood out from the others: a Bondurian wearing a skin-tight gold outfit and hooped gold earrings. Her silky-smooth emerald skin and lips shimmered in the light.

"Who is she?" Jacob whispered, his tongue practically hanging out his mouth.

"Ambassador Bellis," Boocka replied.

"She's beautiful."

Orla felt an unexpected pang of jealousy. "If you like that sort of thing."

"Actually, I've heard all Bondurian women are beautiful."

"Your Majesty," Bellis said, approaching Jacob with her hand outstretched. "I have no idea how you survived the Antantan invasion, but let me tell you it warms my heart to find you alive and well."

"Um, call me Jacob," he mumbled. "I've never met a Bondurian before. How did you come to be leading the revolution, Ambassador?"

"I worked for the Bondurian government a few years ago. In fact, I played a large part in negotiating successful trade deals for them. Our nation has thrived ever since."

"How exciting," Orla said, in a cheekier manner than she intended.

Bellis looked unimpressed with the interruption. "Who is this?"

"This is Orla Paton." Jacob explained. "She's my best friend."

Bellis did not even glance at Orla before urging them into a side room with shutters on the window. There was a large oval-shaped table inside, covered in notes and folders, and a seat for everyone except Orla. Kadesha insisted someone bring her one from elsewhere.

As Orla sat down, an older gentleman entered the proceedings. He was likely around fifty with slick, combed back hair, and carried a black briefcase that matched the colour of his crisp suit. Orla detected an immediate change in the atmosphere when he entered.

"Forgive my lateness," he began, taking a seat beside the Ambassador. "Our board meeting lasted longer than I'd hoped."

Kadesha turned angrily towards Bellis. "What is he doing here?"

"Meet Director Ottis Ryker," Bellis explained to the room. "He owns Cyclops, a weapons and technology company whose generous prices have allowed us to take our army to the next level. Thanks to him, our dream of defeating the Antantans has never been closer."

"I know who he is," Kadesha snapped. "His company is responsible for Gunnar Veto's weaponised arm, not to mention the rumours of experimentation with cloning techniques. Who knows what other unimaginable horrors they cook up in their labs?"

Orla noticed Jacob shifting uneasily in his seat, probably because Kadesha had mentioned Veto's name. His eyes darted around the room, hands violently shaking as though he feared the Antantan would burst into the meeting any minute. The last thing Jacob needed was further mental anguish, especially now, with the hopes of a nation resting on his shoulders. Orla took his hand to calm him down and then flashed a comforting smile. He seemed to relax immediately.

Ryker continued. "We do sometimes work with the Antantans, but it's just business, m'lady. I assure you I have Uthovaya's best interests at heart."

"Money is the only business you are interested in, Mr. Ryker."

Bellis tried to respond once again, but Orla saw Ryker wave a dismissive hand in her direction. She promptly sat back in her seat without saying another word. The weird exchange made Orla wonder who was really in charge.

"Things have changed since the beginnings of the Revolution." Ryker explained. "The days of businessmen throwing piles of money at personal projects are over. Nobody wants a return to the early days when the only tactic was a bomb and a prayer you didn't endanger innocent lives. We are close to launching Operation Creeper, a costly endeavour that will decide the nation's future. Cyclops is happy to continue providing cut-price merchandise, as long as we can monitor how that merchandise performs on the battlefield, but understand we have measures in place to protect our investment should you break the terms of our agreement. We can lock the technology at any time. The lock also prevents our merchandise from falling into the wrong hands."

"It's a standard clause, apparently." Bellis added. "Part of my job as Ambassador is to form beneficial relationships, and Cyclops is one I am extremely proud of. The Pulse-Fighters and Sky-Darters you saw in the hangar are evidence our mutual arrangement works."

Boocka grunted, the sound impressed. "I saw another type of aircraft back there, too. Pulse-Bombers, I think?"

"Indeed." Bellis smiled. "They will come in handy for dealing with Antantan tanks."

Orla listened intently, trying not to voice her own displeasure at the prospect of a battle in the streets. If what Jacob had told her about the barracks and underground operation was true, the Revolutionaries had a good chance at taking the Capital back. However, she did wonder how they planned on keeping a hold of it without more bloodshed. The Antantans would not take defeat lying down and would probably launch another invasion, leading to a vicious cycle of war. She could only hope such a dire situation never came to pass.

SEAN CLARKE

Boocka said, "Let's get down to the reason we came. How do you plan on getting us to Charn?"

Bellis went to speak, but Ryker cut her off again. "We have the perfect man for the job. His freighter is anchored at the harbour."

"Did you say harbour?" Boocka asked.

"I'm afraid so. There is no runway on the Isle of Charn, so travelling by Sky-Darter is out of the question."

"Pulse-Fighters have VTOL capabilities," Boocka replied. "Why can't we go in one of them?"

"It's not an option, I'm afraid. All Pulse-Fighters are being prepared for the launch of Operation Creeper. We simply cannot spare one."

Bellis nodded. "Director Ryker spoke with the Dakew you are going to see. He's a minister named Father Gambin; I believe."

"Yes," Kadesha confirmed. "He was King Seth's best friend. He moved to Charn and established a Dakew colony shortly before the takeover."

Orla wanted to ask a range of questions, but her head was spinning from all the details. Before she knew what was happening, Boocka was standing up and insisting they leave immediately. Ryker and Bellis agreed and ushered the group out the door with nothing but a message of good luck as their parting gift.

Back in the armoured truck, everyone sat in silence, perhaps, Orla thought, bracing themselves for what lay ahead. She had her own thoughts to process, specifically her own future, and how different it could be. With another avenue to explore, she was ready to leave her university dream behind, even if that other avenue led to someone else taking the starring role.

Ready to tie up the final loose end, she asked the driver to stop at Gonga Grove, so she could say goodbye to her parents. The thought of facing her father made Orla nervous, but she braved it out, telling him she was old enough to make her own decisions. Her mother understood, but her father made every effort to stop her while she packed a suitcase. She returned to the truck's cargo area in tears, ignoring Jacob's attempts to cheer her up.

Chapter IX

As he marched through the Capital airport, Gunnar
Veto felt a sea of satisfaction wash over his tired mind
and body. He was happy with his work at the Dance
for Liberty, and although an angry mob had gathered to
protest his presence in the Capital, their jeers and taunts
did not affect his contentment one bit. How could they
cause him to question himself?

He was used to playing the bad guy; in fact, he rev-
elled in causing misery for those who stood against
him. Veto was proud of his meteoric rise; nine years
of service in the Antantan military, starting as an infan-
tryman and earning the nickname Gunnar, as he rose
through the ranks to become a secret-service agent. No
one could stand in his way.

Negotiating the last of the corridors at the airport,
he surfaced on the third runway where the President's
airship lay in wait. It was a wonder of aviation, able to
house a small army and armed with enough firepower
to sink a Pavellian battlecruiser. Veto saw the airship
as the jewel in the Antantan crown. Some disbelievers
still denied its existence, believing it was nothing more

than a legend, a symbol of the President's power. Veto smirked at the thought. Like all the other doubters, they would soon learn the Shadow-Flare was no work of fiction.

Veto was met by the communications officer as soon as he entered the airship, a man named Briggs, who seemed even more agitated than usual. He was shaking, sweating, and struggling to speak in coherent sentences.

"Spit it out, Officer Briggs. I haven't got all day."

"Y…Yes, sir." Briggs saluted Veto with an unsteady hand. "Vice-President Gex commands you to speak with him at once."

Veto shuddered at the mention of his superior's name. Gex was the President's right-hand man, but the decision to keep him around had contributed to Veto's growing disillusionment with the President's leadership.

"Did Gex say what he wanted?" Veto asked sharply.

"N…No, sir."

He nodded and then began the long and laborious process of removing the power pack connected to his artificial limb. It was important not to break the wires when disconnecting them; one wrong move could be fatal. Once satisfied the backpack was safely off, he ordered a nearby guard to take it away for recharge, and immediately felt the familiar emptiness that came with missing an arm.

A second officer approached from the east side of the corridor. He handed Veto a communicator and stepped back. A scientist named Dr. Diala was visible on the screen. He had grey hair and heavy bags underneath his eyes.

"We'd appreciate a moment of your time, sir." the scientist said. "I think it would be in your best interests to come down to the lab."

There was no hesitation. Anything was better than having to speak with Gex. Veto thrust the communicator back into the second officer's hand and then started walking in the direction of the Teleport Booths.

"Sir," Briggs called out. "What will I tell the Vice-President?"

"Tell him to wait." Veto replied, without glancing back or breaking his stride.

The labs were located on the bottom floor, but Veto despised the method of travel between levels on the Shadow-Flare. Stairs and elevators had been decommissioned a long time ago and replaced by Teleport Booths, a series of futuristic contraptions built into every corridor wall. For teleportation to work, there needed to be a booth at both the starting point and destination. Veto appreciated the quick results but hated that each booth could only support one traveller at a time. He took a few deep breaths as he stepped inside and waited for the blue-force field to lock him in place. There was a whirring noise, and a strange floating sensation overtook him as he dematerialised and then re-materialized on the bottom floor.

The lab was eerily quiet, save for the barely audible hum of scientific equipment. The men and women in the white coats seemed oblivious to Veto's presence. All except Dr. Diala, who rushed across the moment he saw the new arrival.

"It's good to see you again, sir," Diala greeted him, shaking Veto firmly by the hand.

"You too, Doc. What have you to show me?"

"Come this way." Diala motioned, leading him to a pile of junk on a nearby workstation.

Veto studied the smashed silver object in greater detail but felt a bit embarrassed at not knowing what it was. Although he had great respect for the men and women in the white coats, science and technology were alien concepts to him.

"What am I looking at?"

Diala grinned as he ran his hands over the coarse surface of what Veto guessed was once a much larger piece.

"It's an SS-1. We recently replaced them with the SS-2 due to the vulnerability of the outer shell."

Veto looked up at Diala. "You haven't called me down here to explain the history of Seeker-Spheres. Get to the point."

Diala took a deep breath and looked around the lab, as though checking no one else could hear the conversation.

"This one was tracking Lady Kadesha as she moved through the Capital, but as you know, Seeker-Spheres can also scan a person's DNA and tell us their identity based on what we already have on file. Its last scan was of a Mixling being helped outside the burning ball-room."

"Who was it?" Veto asked, genuinely intrigued by Diala's words.

"A Crestmore. Specifically, Prince Jacob Crest-more."

Veto felt like someone had taken a sledgehammer to his stomach. Not because he was shocked the young prince was still alive, but because he never expected the kid to show up again. His mind wandered back to the day Antantan soldiers stormed Crestmore Castle. The President wanted the royals captured alive and taken to him immediately. Veto had secretly defied the direct order by arranging for the baby prince to be smuggled to safety and handed over to a couple named Pirlie and Raszlo. It was a secret Veto had carried with him since that fateful day. Now, he had a problem that required urgent attention. A problem with the potential to put him on a charge of treason.

"Good work, Dr. Diala." Veto replied tightly, trying to remain calm in the face of adversity.

"Thank you, sir. Do you want me to inform Vice President Gex of the development?"

"No, leave it with me."

"As you wish."

Back upstairs, Veto left the teleport booth and steeled himself for what was coming. A meeting with Gex usually went one of two ways: either Gex came out on top, or Veto did. Victory usually hinged on who won a battle of wills. This time, Veto had no intention of coming second best to the man he despised.

He thumped the door with his fist and waited for the Vice-President to open it. There was no answer, so he pushed the door open and cautiously entered the plush quarters. Gex had furnished the room with soft chairs and full-length mirrors. There was even a fully stocked mini-bar containing a selection of alcoholic beverages from around the world. The benefits of brown-nosing your way to the top, Veto mused.

"Are you in here?"

"I am busy right now." came the shrill response from the other room.

Veto hated being kept waiting. Especially when he suspected his rival was doing it on purpose. Before he could stop himself, he had picked up an empty drink container and hurled it against the wall. It smashed into a thousand pieces on the floor.

Gex appeared promptly from the back room, clad in a black and gold waistcoat. His straight black hair had been slicked back.

"What do you think you are doing?" Gex growled, upon seeing the shards of glass on the shaggy red carpet.

"My time is precious, Mr. Vice President; I don't wish to hang around here all day."

Veto sensed anger at the remark and grinned like a Krokiran Wild-Cat. They were now equal for Gex keeping him waiting.

"Having fun, are we?" Gex sneered, rubbing the side of his hooked nose. "Clearly, your good mood stems from the fact you have managed to apprehend the last of Queen Fiona's followers. Or did I get that wrong?"

"We have much bigger problems to worry about than Kadesha now."

"Really? Enlighten me."

Veto explained that Prince Jacob Crestmore had been found, alive. Gex seemed displeased with the news.

"So, the prince has turned up after all these years?" Gex said. "I always suspected he was still alive. We never did find his body. The only question is how a baby evaded capture."

Veto knew the answer, but he had no intention of admitting responsibility. It was far better to tell Gex a palace aide had likely smuggled the kid to safety and kept him hidden all these years, even if he wasn't sure his direct superior bought the story.

"Jacob being alive causes a major problem," Veto admitted.

"I fail to see how. The ElmKey apparently lost power years ago. The means to access elemental magic have been taken away from them. Without magic, the boy is just another imposter claiming to be the lost prince."

"Queen Fiona once confided in me that there was a second one, a Lost ElmKey she was working tirelessly to find."

"Why did you not mention this before?" Gex said, eyeing Veto with suspicion.

"Never mind that now," Veto objected. "Kadesha might have been privy to the same information. What if she leads Jacob to the Lost ElmKey? A return of the rightful king with the power of the elements could cause an uprising. The Uthovayans are already at breaking point with how we rule them."

Gex nodded. "Go and retrieve this Lost ElmKey at once."

"Fiona never revealed its location."

"And yet, you two were so close. Is this just another failure we can add to your list?" Gex sighed loudly. "You never found the Chamber of the Elements either."

"Now, hold on –"

Gex surged forward until Veto could almost feel the tip of the Vice-President's nose touching his own.

"No, *you* hold on. I am the President's eyes and ears. I have a duty to ensure things go smoothly and problems are taken care of in a timely and efficient manner, and you continue to make my job even harder. We cannot afford to lose Uthovaya. The money generated from their water, timber, and alcohol industry greatly benefit our economy. Do you want to tell the President all of that could be in jeopardy?"

SEAN CLARKE

"Is the president here?" Veto asked, his body tensing as he wiped the sweat from his forehead.

"What's wrong?" Gex sneered. "Afraid he will shine a spotlight on your list of failures? Maybe, he will start with your pathetic begging to spare Queen Fiona's life all those years ago?"

Veto had no comeback. It was a dereliction of duty as far as the President was concerned. Only Veto's stellar army record saved him from suffering a traitor's death at the President's hands. He had lived on a knife-edge ever since, with fleeting moments of glory, but never quite regaining the trust of the most powerful man in Antantis.

"I will explain myself to the President," Veto said, trying to remain calm at the thought of facing the ruthless leader.

"Save your excuses for another time. Lucky for you, the President is still in Antantis."

Veto relaxed as Gex continued.

"Find the Lost ElmKey before Kadesha and the boy do, or find yourself in a mess even you won't be able to clear up."

"But where do I start?"

"Start with anyone who was close to the royals back then?"

"Most of their acquaintances went into hiding after we took over."

"Then go back to Crestmore Castle. Keep looking until you find a lead. There has to be something."

Veto started for the door, but Gex said something that made him stop in his tracks and turn back to face his rival. It was a comment about Fiona's death, and one that had Veto squaring up to Gex.

"Fancy your chances against me?" Gex growled. "It would be another battle you can't win. Remember King Seth sliced off your arm when he found out about you and his loyal wife? Mess with me, and you'll lose more than your remaining arm."

Veto stared at the empty space where his arm should be and thought back to the battle in question – a battle that ended with King Seth sparing his life. It was a deadly mistake for the Uthovayan royal, who was killed shortly after by the President. Veto hated thinking back to that fateful day, and as he left the quarters, fiery rage engulfed him so completely that he lost control and fired four punches into the corridor wall. Blood seeped from the wounds on his knuckles and dripped onto the metallic floor.

Gex had won the battle of wills…this time.

Chapter X

As soon as Jacob and the others arrived at the harbour, most of the chat revolved around the beaten-up ship they would be sailing to Charn on. The Rad Veteran had more visible rust than lifeboats and a crew who looked more than a little rough around the edges.

"We aren't really sailing in that thing, are we?" Orla asked as Kadesha led everyone up the gangplank.

Jacob said, "Trust you to say what everyone else is probably thinking."

A tall, middle-aged black man with a cigar sticking out the side of his mouth approached them when they arrived on deck. He had short dark hair, a scar above his left eye and wore a black trench-coat with a high collar. Jacob looked closer and noticed a holster on each hip, both with a handgun inside. The man coughed and then adjusted a navy scarf tied around his neck.

"The name's Zach Hudson. I'm the captain of this vessel."

Jacob found the captain most impressive. There was an aura of danger surrounding him, a hint that suggested he had fought many battles on the high seas. His soft brown eyes seemed worldly, as if showcasing the many weird and wonderful places the Rad Veteran had taken him.

Boocka said, "You're strangely dressed for a member of the Revolutionaries."

"I'm not with the Revolutionaries," Hudson replied, the cigar in his mouth looking like it might fall out at any minute. "I was brought in by Ryker."

"Ryker?" Boocka repeated.

Hudson nodded and then took a draw of his cigar. "I'm what's left of Viper's Fist."

Jacob knew the name well. Viper's Fist was a notorious mercenary group who were only too happy to kill for cash. They had built a fearsome reputation over the years and were famous for freeing a prisoner who had been sentenced to death for breaking into a secure Antantan military base and then selling its secrets. Ryker's decision to hire this man greatly puzzled Jacob.

"Where are the others?" he heard Orla ask.

"Others?" Hudson replied.

"You said you were the last of the Fists. Where are the rest?"

"Dead," the captain replied matter-of-factly. Then he looked at Boocka, who could barely hide his contempt for the man standing in front of him. "Problem?"

"I hate mercs," Boocka said, bearing his sharp teeth. "If you so much as look the wrong way at Lady Kadesha, I'll make sure you join your dead comrades. Do I make myself clear?"

Jacob could feel the tension in the air and waited with bated breath for the captain's inevitable climb-down, but he seemed unfazed as he removed the cigar from his mouth and dropped it onto the wet deck before stubbing it out with his black boot.

"Let's get one thing clear," he said with a steely gaze in Boocka's direction. "Ryker has paid me and my crew half our fee to keep the boy, Jacob, safe and make sure he completes his mission. If we do our job, then we get paid. I couldn't care less about the rest of ye."

It was a heartless response. Jacob imagined most people would be scared to death if a Krokiran threatened them, but Hudson had not even flinched. If first impressions were anything to go by, the captain was not-to-be messed with.

"Show them to their quarters," Hudson ordered a toothless member of his crew.

"Yes, Captain."

Down below, the crewmember explained it was one cabin for the men and one for the women. Surprising Jacob, Orla expressed her delight at the cleanliness of the cabins. Both were furnished with a grey sofa, a small dining table, and two-fold-down beds with freshly washed linen. The bottle green carpets were spotless, and even the door looked recently painted.

"I think ye'll be comfortable," the crewmember said.

As soon as the crewmember departed for the top deck, Boocka thumped the table.

"What's Ryker playing at?" he blasted, thumping the table again with his massive right hand.

Kadesha said, "I must admit his choice has baffled me. There must be others who could do the job. Someone without a history of bloodshed."

Jacob was about to join the conversation, but Orla beat him to it with an answer of her own. "Perhaps, Hudson *is* the best man for the job?"

"Maybe," Kadesha replied.

The tannoy sparked into life, and the captain's voice came through loud and clear. He cracked a few jokes and then announced their departure. Jacob noticed Orla sitting at the dining table with a sad expression.

"Are you OK?" he asked.

"I can't help thinking about my parents."

"No turning back now," Jacob replied with a soft but firm tone.

"I guess not." she sighed, sprawling out on the bed just as the engines on the Veteran sparked to life.

***

Although the Rad Veteran took two days and nights to reach its current position in the Gongeti Ocean, twenty miles off the Isle of Charn coast, Jacob hardly noticed it had left his homeland. He had spent most of the journey lazing around the cabin, sprawled out on the comfortable bed, and eating delicious fruit from a wooden bowl. It was a far cry from a typical day on the streets of the Capital, where food and relaxation were precious commodities. What seemed a simple standard of living to everyone else on board was like a life of luxury to him, and he intended to make the most of it.

His relaxation was interrupted by a knock at the door from Kadesha, who wanted to check he was coping with his newfound sense of purpose.

"Trust me, I'm fine," Jacob insisted. "Well, there is one question I have."

"Ask me anything."

"It's about the magic you assure me exists. What if I can't use it?"

Kadesha smiled and sat down on the bottom bunk. "Your mother once had the exact same fears. When the time comes, you will have nothing to worry about. Just like she didn't."

"But I know next to nothing about using it. Is there training involved? Does it automatically come to me?"

"Well, I only know bits and pieces about it, but the ability to cast spells come from inside the Elementalist. It involves a specific thought process."

Jacob was confused and more than a little sceptical. "I thought you said the power comes from elemental spirits."

"The spirits are required for an Elementalist to possess the power, but the spells themselves work independently from them."

"So, an Elementalist casts the spells themselves?"

"Yes. There are many spells for each element, but only the truly special can master them all. Your mother certainly did."

Although wanting to know more about the use of magic, Jacob found it impossible not to think of his mother whenever Kadesha mentioned her. He had often wondered what she was like, and even made up little scenarios in his head where he finally got the chance to speak with her. Sometimes, he was angry in those imaginary reunions, questioning why she gave him up, but other times he would chat away about anything from his latest hunt to the weather. Not once did he imagine she would have been so powerful and respected. It made him feel proud to be her son.

"You are probably wondering what she looked like," Kadesha said, out of the blue.

Jacob took a deep, calming breath and then nodded slowly. "I would love to know," he admitted.

"She had hazel eyes and skin like a porcelain doll," Kadesha said, looking lost in another world. "A true picture of beauty."

"What about my father?"

Kadesha offered a slight chuckle. "Tall, dark, and handsome. Exactly like you would expect a king to be."

The silence that followed only ended when Kadesha suggested he go up top for some fresh air and clear his head.

"Good idea."

An icy blast of wind almost knocked him over when he arrived on the top deck, but he steadied himself against a nearby barrel and then inhaled the salty sea air for all its worth.

"Smells so fresh," he said to himself.

Captain Hudson was at the bow, staring through a pair of V5 binoculars. The sight of the Isle of Charn looming in the distance suddenly made Jacob focus on the mission.

"Hey."

He whirled to find Orla shivering in the biting cold. She was wearing a faded green dressing gown and white fluffy slippers. Her usually perfect hair was un-brushed, and the bags under her eyes indicated she had not slept well.

"I thought you were bringing your best clothes?" Jacob joked as he eyed up the dressing gown and slippers.

Orla narrowed her eyes. "I'm really not in the mood. What are you doing up here, anyway?"

"Just taking in the sea air and thinking about stuff?"

"I'd be doing the same if I was in your shoes."

Jacob was confused. "Why is that?"

"Are you kidding me? There's a chance you could be ruling an entire nation soon. If that's not something to think about, then what is?"

A fair point, but if truth be told, Jacob did not be-lieve the Revolutionaries would crown him king. He had no idea how to run a country, nor did he want the responsibility. The whole idea verged on the absurd.

Someone else could rule after they got the Antantans out, he figured.

Jacob put his right arm around Orla to shield her from the cold, and together they walked across to the bow where the captain had finished looking through the binoculars. He greeted them both with an impish grin and then threw the binoculars down on a metal drum.

"Morning, folks."

"Good morning," Jacob and Orla replied in unison.

"I'm surprised to see you two up here alone."

"Why do you say that?" Orla asked.

"I dunno. That Krokiran probably thinks I'll rob ye and then throw ye overboard."

"You wouldn't dare," Orla replied.

Hudson paused. "Yer right, I wouldn't. Well, not the boy anyway."

Jacob felt a little uncomfortable with the captain's comment. Orla was staring at Hudson with a look that indicated a deep dislike.

"Only because you need Jacob alive to collect your fee from Ryker. Well, understand we don't trust you or him."

"Glad to hear it," Hudson chuckled. "I wouldn't trust us either."

Jacob watched Hudson pull a cigar from the breast pocket of his leather jacket, put it to his lips, and then light the end with a silver lighter engraved with the symbol of a clenched fist superimposed over a snake's head. It was obvious Ryker had kept details of their trip secret. Jacob was convinced Hudson would be a problem if he knew the rightful prince of Uthovaya was on board. He might even be tempted to sell the information or turn Jacob over to the Antantans. Secrecy was essential for success.

"You wanna go tell the others we'll be docking soon, Jay?"

Jay?

"I'll go with him," Orla piped up.

"Aw, and there was me thinking ye would stay, and we could get to know each other." Hudson roared with laughter at his own comment.

"I really hate that guy," Jacob whispered as he and Orla headed below deck.

Boocka gave them both barrels the minute they got there, ranting and raving about the importance of keeping safe while aboard the ship. Orla gave as good as she got, but Jacob drowned out the noise as best he could. There was little point in getting into a slanging match with someone he needed to get along with. The lecture went on and on; even when Orla was getting ready in the next cabin, Boocka was still ranting through the wall. He only stopped when they arrived back on the top deck, and Kadesha demanded everyone in the group gather round.

"Father Gambin's colony is on the other side of the island," Kadesha explained. "Our target is to negotiate the Charn jungle before nightfall."

"Jungle?" Orla repeated in an uneasy tone.

Boocka nodded. "Yes, the jungle. Don't start getting cold feet now. We all knew the potential dangers. Just keep your wits about you, and you'll be fine."

"Easy for you to say. You've got a weapon."

The Krokiran huffed and puffed as he turned his full attention to Orla. "I can give you a gun if it makes you feel better. I keep a small pistol in my satchel."

Jacob waited for Orla's reaction, and she did not disappoint by refusing Boocka's offer.

"Fine. You and Prince Jacob stay close to me, and you'll be safe."

Orla pressed, "Can we trust this Gambin not to tell anyone we're here?"

Jacob knew the question needed to be asked. The last thing they needed was someone tipping off the Antantans.

"Of course, we can," Kadesha replied. "Father Gambin can be controversial, but he was a vocal opponent of the Antantans long before they overthrew the royals. He claimed their president was the devil himself and warned of impending doom if no one stopped him."

"Why would that be controversial?" Orla asked. "It's not as if the President has proved him wrong."

Boocka chimed in, "There were other controversies as well; alleged misappropriation of church funds, affairs with members of his parish, and even rumours he paid one woman to disappear with his love child."

Kadesha shook her head. "None were ever proven. I always believed the Antantans planted the stories to discredit him. Even if those stories were true, it does not change the fact he can help us right now."

"Do we have everything we need?" Orla asked.

Boocka patted his satchel. "Torches, canteens, and some fruit."

"Perfect."

After the briefing, Hudson and his crew got busy with the preparations for lowering the boat into the water. Jacob watched the youngest man on the crew clear the davit tracks of debris while the others carried out safety checks. Once completed, they removed the gripes and ordered the group to get into the boat, stressing the importance of keeping the weight evenly distributed while it hung in the air. Then, they dropped the boat onto the crest of a wave.

"Is she looking good?" Jacob called up.

"You'd be sinking if she wasn't." a crewman shouted back.

Jacob and Boocka took the oars and rowed until they hit shallow water. From there, all four members of the group dragged the boat onto the sand before stopping to allow the two rowers to catch their breath.

It was the first time Jacob had ever seen a beach. The golden sand blending into the turquoise water made it seem like paradise. Further up the beach, Jacob noticed the edge of a sandy path leading into the darkness of Charn jungle.

"I'll go first," Boocka announced, readying his KSF-16.

After trekking under the canopy for what seemed like an eternity, Jacob was thankful to stop for a rest and get some water into his tired body. He was used to long periods of walking when he went on hunts, but the humidity on Charn was completely different from anything he had experienced back home. As he lay back on the ground, a snake dropped out of nowhere and hung in front of his face, its thin, forked tongue inches away. Boocka caught the creature in mid-air, tossed it aside, and then walked away as though nothing had happened.

"Damn snakes." he moaned.

Next up, they reached a creaky wooden bridge swinging about fifty feet above a fast-flowing river. Jacob crossed behind Boocka and Kadesha with relative ease, but as he arrived on the opposite side, he realised Orla was still in the middle of the bridge. She had closed her eyes and was gripping the ropes for dear life.

"I forgot about your fear of heights," said Jacob, slowly making his way back across to take her hand.

"Don't. I can do it if I don't look down."

"Hurry up, you two," Boocka called from the other side.

"Don't rush me," Orla shouted back, her voice echoing in the chasm below.

Minutes later, she was still in the same position on the bridge. It was as though her feet were planted to the spot. Boocka's constant jeers were obviously not helping, so Jacob told him to show a bit of compassion.

"Thanks," Orla said, still looking terrified.

Jacob could understand her nervousness. A collapsed bridge would see them crash onto the jagged rocks in the river below. He took a deep breath and then reached out to put his hands on her shoulders, but his touch made her hyperventilate.

"What are you doing?" she wheezed.

"Look at me."

"But I –"

"I said, look at me."

He watched Orla open her eyes and then manoeuvred himself behind her, trying not to shake the bridge and panic his friend further.

"We'll do it one step at a time." he soothed.

Orla responded positively to his gentle approach, and for the first time since freezing, she put one foot in front of the other. Jacob repeated his calming words, and whispered praise whenever she took another step. After a tense few minutes, Orla put her first foot on the opposite side and then moved away from the bridge.

"I did it," she cried, rushing towards Jacob, and throwing her arms around him.

"You sure did."

Their embrace only lasted a few seconds, before Boocka demanded they get a move on.

"The settlement's not far away now. We'll be there before you know it."

But, a few hours later, they were nowhere closer to finding Gambin or the Dakew colonists.

"I don't understand it," Boocka said. "It should be easy to find."

"Didn't anybody think to bring a map?" Orla asked.

Boocka's grey face turned to fizz, and he clapped his hands sarcastically.

"It was just a suggestion."

"Well, we don't need any more suggestions from you. In fact, you shouldn't even be here, so zip it from now on."

"Don't speak to me like that," Orla snapped, bravely standing up to the Krokiran.

Kadesha interrupted them. "Stop this at once. We cannot allow ourselves to be pulled in different directions. I suggest we find a clearing, build shelter, and have something to eat. Father Gambin knows we are coming, and when he realises, we have not turned up, he will send someone out to find us."

Afternoon turned to dusk, and then dusk melted into night as Jacob and the others sat beneath a makeshift shelter built by Boocka. It was nothing more than one long branch propped up against a tree with shorter branches running from the ground to support it. Leaves were used as a cover. Not perfect, but it did the job.

The Charn jungle was a scary place at night. The unsettling mishmash of howls and chirps that worked in tandem with deafening hoots from what may or may not have been a friendly animal proved difficult for Jacob to ignore. The sounds blended to forge a haunting, alien atmosphere where the jungle itself seemed to whisper a name.

Jacob… Jacob…

"Anyone…hear …. that?" he whispered.

No one answered, so Jacob concluded the creepy voice was all in his head.

Pull yourself together. You have been in situations like this before.

And he had. Jacob was no stranger to the horrors of being in dark and dangerous places. His foster parent's basement, night hunts on the moors outside the Capital, even the city itself could be scary at night with the screams of hungry children by far the worst sound Jacob had ever heard.

A rustling noise came from somewhere close; it was louder than the ones before and seemed to be coming from behind the shelter. This time, the others took notice. Boocka grabbed his weapon, and Kadesha looked panic-stricken.

"Something's out there," Jacob said to Boocka, trying to control the obvious fear in his tone.

"Of course, there's something out there. We're in the jungle."

The light from Orla's torch caught a shadow passing the shelter, and Boocka exploded from his sitting position with his weapon in hand. Jacob could hear a scuffle outside. There was no gunshot, and nothing to indicate what was happening until Boocka peered back into the shelter.

"I think you all better come out here."

Jacob grabbed Orla's torch and got out of the shelter first. He shone the light on Boocka and found him standing in front of three strangers dressed in brown robes and sandals. Each carried a small black lantern, and their faces were hidden by a hood.

Chapter XI

Jacob had no idea how to respond to the three hooded figures staring at them in the middle of Charn jungle, and no one else in the group did either judging by their facial expressions. Even Orla seemed lost for words – a phenomenon Jacob always believed impossible.

"Are you looking for the Gambin colony?" said one of the robed figures.

Kadesha was the first to reply. "Indeed, we are."

"Father Gambin believed you had gotten lost. It is a good thing he sent us out to find you. Please, follow us."

Jacob was last to follow the strange figures who led them through the cold, dark jungle to the compound entrance – two sheets of metal banded together with rope. Two guards stood at attention on either side, wearing olive t-shirts and khaki trousers joined at the waist by a belt with a buckle at the front. Glancing up, Jacob noticed vertical and horizontal spikes running the length of the compound walls.

"Place is well protected," Boocka commented.

"Sure is," Jacob replied, eyeing the guards tenderly stroking their shotguns.

The guard on the right stepped forward and beckoned the previously vocal robed figure towards him.

"Ah, you found them." He exclaimed.

"Lost in the jungle. Just like Father Gambin predicted."

"The visitors always think the jungle can be negotiated with ease."

Kadesha said. "Forgive our ignorance, but we must speak with Father Gambin immediately."

The guards appeared to be mulling it over while glancing back and forth towards the main robed figure at various intervals. It was obvious to Jacob he was the man in charge of them all. Probably, second only to Gambin himself.

"You are late," said the robed figure. "It's not good manners to keep Father Gambin waiting."

"Not good manners at all," the rest said in unison.

"That's a bit creepy," Boocka said loudly.

"Ssshhh," Kadesha scolded, before turning back to the head robed figure. "I apologise for our tardiness, but we must speak with him urgently."

The robed figure eyed the two guards and nodded his head in the direction of the entrance. Immediately, the guard on the right disappeared into the compound and returned five minutes later to whisper something unintelligible into the robed figure's ear. They conversed for a few moments before the robed figure turned to the group.

"You may enter."

Jacob hung back at the end again, but as soon as the group had passed into the compound, the guards turned their shotguns on them.

"What the hell is this?" Boocka growled, attempting to position himself in front of both shotguns.

"Do not move," ordered the head robe figure.

He clicked his fingers, and two others rushed into a nearby bush, returning with a small white box.

"Please, leave any weapons you may have in here," said the head figure.

Although Jacob dropped the Dynasty Staff into the box without complaint, he guessed the robed figure's request would cause trouble. The chances of Boocka, a no-nonsense ex-Krokiran Special Forces soldier, surrendering his weapon were somewhere between slim and nil. Sure enough, Boocka looked at the others in disbelief, and point-blank refused to comply with the request.

"Your weapons are not permitted in the compound," said the guard. "Father Gambin would insist you hand them over."

"I don't care what Father Gambin would insist," Boocka grunted. "The gun stays with me."

Jacob held his breath as the standoff threatened to turn ugly. The robed figures were huddled together now, conversing in a quiet but angry manner. They pointed to Boocka several times before restating their point that no one would pass while still possessing a weapon.

"Then we have a problem, don't we?" Boocka growled.

Quick as a flash, he released his KSF-16 and pointed it at the armed guards, who had shuffled backwards in panic, probably at the sight of a powerful Krokiran ready to take them head on. Orla rushed in front of him, frantically waving her hands to get his attention while urging him to calm down. Boocka was oblivious to her pleas and continued arguing with the locals, his gun still trained on them. Jacob tried to pull Boocka away, but he was impossible to budge, and the situation threatened to turn nasty.

"ENOUGH!" Kadesha shouted. "Put your weapon down."

"But m'lady…"

"That is an order," she replied, in a forceful tone Jacob had never heard her use before.

Boocka reluctantly lowered his KSF-16 and then dropped it into the white box.

"I'm doing this under protest," He muttered.

"Thanks," said the head robed figure. "I will take you in now."

They walked the length of a cobbled road that veered off in two separate directions. One side led to a darkened path, while the other took the group to a square filled with quaint wooden huts. The entire area was illuminated by floodlights on all four sides. Jacob tried to say hello to the other robed residents, but none looked remotely interested in making conversation, avoiding eye contact as they rushed to a large building on the faraway hill.

"Not very friendly, are they?" he remarked quietly to Orla.

"You always have that effect on people," she retorted with a cheeky smile.

Jacob chuckled as they came to a waist-high stone wall surrounding a churchyard. An iron gate swung off its hinges at the entrance, and weeds had overtaken the garden. The church itself was in no better condition; three of its stain glass windows were smashed, and the badly dented front door looked like it could fall off at any minute.

"Does everyone go to church here?" Orla asked the head robed figure.

"The Church of the Dakew is our way of life. We are sheltered here from the world's increasing cynicism. Religion has taken a back seat to the supposed wonders of technology."

The head robed figure looked sad as he urged the group to keep following him into the church.

"Please, come inside."

Jacob and the others did as he asked. They passed through an unlocked door and arrived at a room by the side of the sanctuary. The head figure bowed in their direction.

"Make yourselves at home. I will inform Father Gambin of your arrival."

Kadesha said, "We thank you, kindly," and then bowed in return.

While Boocka separated a stack of chairs, Jacob helped himself to a chocolate bar wrapped in foil from a cracked plate. He chomped loudly and then noticed the others giving him dirty looks. Before he could apologise, a short, balding Dakew with bushy eyebrows and a scar under his chin approached them from the doorway. He wore white slippers and a grey dressing gown that looked as though someone had dragged it through a field.

"It is wonderful to see you again, Father," Kadesha said.

"Insincerity is not welcome here," Gambin retorted. "It means nothing to me, nothing to the Dakew on this island, and certainly nothing to God."

His face contortioned with rage as he angrily threw the plate of chocolate bars across the room, smashing it off the floor. His sudden outburst made Jacob jump.

"What's your problem?" Boocka growled. "We're here to —"

"To learn the location of the vault," Gambin snapped. "I already know because I spoke with someone who has made this meeting very awkward indeed."

"Ryker?" Boocka exclaimed.

Gambin nodded. "Your man Ryker threatened to have me, and the other colonists killed if I don't reveal the vault's location." He was spitting with rage now and quickly turned to Kadesha. "Tell me, is that how the Revolutionaries conduct their business? By threatening those who disobey them?"

Jacob watched Kadesha's expression turn from shock to anger, and she bowed her head in what seemed like an awkward apology.

"I assure you we knew nothing of this threat," Kadesha said, calmly. "Director Ryker's actions are unacceptable. I promise to bring this matter to the Ambassador's attention upon our return."

Gambin looked unimpressed. "I appreciate your support, but I would rather you not draw any more attention to us than you already have. We live a quiet existence out here, far away from the dramas of outside life. We would prefer to keep it that way."

"I understand. But we must have the vault's location. Something massive has happened."

"Ryker was rather vague in his communication, so I will need answers from you."

Jacob watched as Kadesha pointed towards him and explained the situation. Gambin showed no reaction at first; he just kept staring in disbelief at who was allegedly standing in his church. After what seemed like an eternity, the minister reached into his dressing gown pocket for a pair of thick spectacles and put them on to examine Jacob with childlike wonder.

"Your majesty. Is it really you?" he breathed, tears welling up in his eyes.

Jacob tilted his head away from Gambin's gaze, but the minister moved to a better position and continued to stare, as though enjoying the new animal attraction in a zoo. The intense behaviour made Jacob wonder about the kind of scrutiny he would face if he made it onto the throne. Being king would be very different from his invisible existence on the streets.

"Yes sir, it's me…I think."

Boocka slammed his fist down on the table. "We don't have time for this nonsense. Where's the vault?"

"Boocka!" Kadesha yelled, eyeing him with a mixture of anger and disappointment.

Gambin swung to face the Krokiran. "You, my friend, will be going nowhere near the vault."

"Is that what you think?" Boocka growled.

"King Seth did not want strangers in that vault, and it shall remain that way. Prince Jacob and Lady Kadesha are welcome to go. You and the girl will stay down here."

"Not gonna happen," said Boocka, firmly. "I'm Lady Kadesha's bodyguard. There's no way I'm letting her leave this island alone."

"Nobody has to leave the island. The vault is at the top of Mount Viscera, our highest peak."

"Are you telling me the vault's been on the island all this time?"

Jacob noticed Boocka's left eye twitch and heard his breathing become more intense. It took another intervention from Kadesha to calm the irate Krokiran down.

"Go and take a breather," she ordered.

"But m'lady, I –"

"Go."

Jacob watched Boocka trudge out the door and then turned to Gambin. "How do we get up this mountain?" he asked, hoping the answer involved something unnaturally quick.

"It won't be tonight," Gambin replied. "Far too dangerous to go at night."

"In the morning, then."

"Yes, one of my drivers will take you. His name is Yanseph. You can find him at the mess hall on the other side of the compound. Come back here when you have spoken with him, and I will give you shelter for the night."

"Thank you, Father," Kadesha said.

"There is one more thing," Gambin said bashfully. "Are you looking for a statue carved by Seth?"

Jacob shook his head. "Why do you ask?"

"No reason," Gambin said, his smile returning.

As soon as Jacob and the others got outside, Boocka let rip to Kadesha with his thoughts on Gambin.

"I don't trust him," he raged.

"You don't trust anyone." She laughed. "Now, let's find Yanseph."

The mess hall was nothing more than a big tent. It looked large enough to accommodate every colonist, giving them a place where they could eat and converse together like a proper family. Jacob braced himself for more resistance as they approached the guards at the entrance, but nothing happened. The guards greeted them with a friendly wave.

"Come in," one said, lifting the entry flap to allow them access.

Inside, Jacob saw wooden benches by the side of tables where the colonists sat. A waiter directed the group to a table, and as they sat down, another brought them a glass of water each and a wooden bowl containing lumps of thick, grey sludge.

Jacob felt his stomach rumbling, so he picked up a fork and fiddled with the disgusting meal. The grey sludge was laced with small black balls and smelled foul. He pushed the edge of the fork into one of the balls, and green goo seeped out, almost making him sick on the spot.

"What is this?" he whispered to Orla.

"I'm not sure."

"It looks disgusting."

"You've changed." Orla giggled.

"What do you mean?"

"Think about it. You would have eaten anything when you were on the streets. A few days of being a prince and suddenly, only the very best will do."

"That's not true," Jacob shot back, feeling more than a little defensive.

"I'm only kidding." She chuckled. "Don't take it so seriously."

Jacob forced a smile, but deep down, he knew Orla had a point. He would have gladly wolfed this grey sludge down when he was homeless. It could have been the difference between life and death. Now, he had a choice in the matter. Not wanting to seem ungrateful, he braced himself and then forced a burst black ball with green goo into his mouth. It was chewy, crunchy even, and tasted a lot better than it looked.

"Not bad." He said out loud.

A voice from behind made him swivel in his chair. It was a Dakew who had overheard his comment. She seemed pleased Jacob had tried the dish and urged the others to tuck in. They duly obliged.

"Sonpo always looks worse than it tastes," she whispered.

"Never heard of it before," Jacob admitted.

"We collect Sonpo from the jungle during the day. It's very nutritious."

"Is it easy to catch?" he asked between mouthfuls.

"Oh, it's not an animal," she explained. "It's their droppings. We mix whatever we can find."

Jacob spat the sludge back into his bowl and noted Orla and Kadesha doing the same. Boocka continued shovelling forkfuls between his tusks, seemingly oblivious to what he was eating. Jacob tapped the table to gain his attention.

"What?" he barked, looking unhappy at having his meal interrupted.

"Didn't you hear what the lady said? It's animal droppings."

"Who cares?" he slurped the last of the green goo from the bowl.

Jacob shuddered and then turned back to the lady. "I wonder if you could help us. We're looking for someone named Yanseph."

The lady pointed out a Dakew who was seated a few tables away, laughing and joking with other colonists.

Kadesha said. "I'll go. There is no point in all of us charging over."

Jacob watched Kadesha speak with the driver and could tell from his body language he had agreed to Kadesha's proposal. Finally, they shook hands on the deal, and Kadesha returned to the group.

"He has agreed to take Jacob and I up Mount Viscera."

"Well, that was easy." Orla laughed.

"Is everyone finished eating their cuisine?" Kadesha said in an uncharacteristically sarcastic manner.

Jacob laughed. "Better ask Boocka."

The Krokiran looked unimpressed as he flashed his empty bowl.

"Good," Kadesha exclaimed. "We must get back to the church and rest. Tomorrow will be a long day for myself and Jacob."

Chapter XII

Gunnar Veto found himself standing in the corner of his old chamber, situated on the east wing of Crestmore Castle. As his eyes adjusted to the darkness, he let the memories wash over him; some good, some bad, but all of them fresh in his mind at that moment. This was his home, his sanctuary during his time as one of Queen Fiona's followers. The role was his whole life until the Antantan army overthrew the royals.

The room was exactly as he had left it, right down to the log fireplace, wooden desk, and hand-crafted four-poster bed with an enclosed canopy.

So many memories.

If Veto had the luxury of time, he would have enjoyed the nostalgia a little while longer, maybe even reminisce about the double life he lived from the safety and comfort of his chamber. It was impossible, though. Not when he was so far behind Lady Kadesha and her young protégé, who by now must surely have made significant progress in recovering the Lost ElmKey. That was a scenario he dared not contemplate, and as

Officer Briggs arrived behind him, he gave himself a shake and got down to business.

"Find me some candles," he ordered his nervous subordinate.

Although the moon made only a slight contribution of light through the open yellow curtains, Veto knew his way around the chamber. He pulled a dusty chair away from the desk and then sat in the same spot he had sat in for the better part of three years. Even the celestial glow seemed familiar.

Briggs returned with candles. He lit them and then enquired why they could not use the lamp on top of Veto's desk.

"That lamp has never worked." Veto chuckled, picking up what now seemed like an old friend. "I don't know why I kept it all those years."

"Reminds me a bit of this castle," Briggs said, his breath visible from the cold.

"What do you mean?"

"The President should have razed it to the ground after we took over."

"The President almost did."

"Sir?"

"The original plan involved tearing the castle down but the whole idea never sat right with me. It seemed a bad business decision. Why destroy something with the potential to make you money?"

"Tourism?" Briggs asked, violently shivering in the cold.

Veto nodded. "I lobbied for the castle to remain. Now, it rakes in nearly one billion a year for the Ant-antan coffers."

"Genius," Briggs said, blowing hot air into his hands. "What shall I do now?"

"Start with the letters."

Briggs left and then returned with a brown sack of letters gathered from the perfectly preserved royal chamber. He threw the sack onto the desk, and some letters spilled out onto the floor.

"I beg your pardon, sir, but what exactly are you looking for?"

"We're looking for a place to start." Veto sighed as he picked a letter from the pile. "Maybe something written or received by Seth will shed light on the whereabouts of the Lost ElmKey."

"But our officers already went through Seth's correspondence with a fine-tooth comb. Surely they'd have found something?"

Veto looked up. "Maybe."

"Did anyone check the Queen's correspondence?"

Veto looked up again, annoyed at the constant interruptions. "No point. Seth had stopped trusting his wife and taken complete control of things by then."

"Why?" the confused-looking officer asked.

Veto considered Briggs' question for a moment and then thought back to the state of Fiona and Seth's relationship in the final days before the takeover. Things had escalated to the point where the couple was looking upon each other as the enemy. It had started not long after Veto became a follower. Most couples would argue over important issues–where to buy a house or finding the right time to have a baby. But the king and queen battled over trivial matters. Their relationship then regressed to the point where Fiona began to confide in Veto. That was the whole point of the Antantan plan, of course. But their secret affair was not. Neither was Fiona falling pregnant.

"If only things had been different," Veto found himself saying out loud.

"What do you mean?" Briggs replied.

The temptation to tell Briggs the truth became strong. He trusted the young officer, and desperately wanted to unload his secret onto him. A secret Veto had carried for twenty years.

"It was me who helped baby Jacob escape. I had an affair with his mother."

Briggs had a look of shock at hearing the revelation. "You and the Queen?"

Veto nodded. It felt great to finally tell someone.

"But…she was a Dakew!" Briggs said, disgust written all over his face.

"Yes, but not like the Dakew I was taught about at school," Veto fired back. "She wasn't obsessed with magic, or whatever other nonsense we Antantans get told. Fiona was a warm and gentle soul trapped in an unhappy marriage. I loved her."

"Did she love you?" Briggs asked.

"She said she did, but we could never be together. I begged the President to spare her life, but he refused. That is why I made plans to keep Jacob safe. I couldn't watch the boy die. Not when…he could be my son."

"Y…You're son?"

Veto choked back tears and felt a comforting hand rest on his shoulder.

"Your secret is safe with me, sir."

Veto nodded again. "Go bring another sack."

Briggs saluted his superior. "Yes, sir."

For three eye-straining hours, Veto read over 3,000 letters. His eyes were so blurred and heavy by the end, he could barely keep them open. He was just about to give up when an unopened envelope caught his attention.

Someone must have missed it the first time around.

He read the letter meticulously, letting every detail sink into his brain. A twisted smile crept across his face as the magnitude of its contents became clear. Satisfied with his discovery, he leaned back in his chair and whispered the name. "Gambin."

Veto heard Briggs shuffling over from behind.

"Found something, sir?"

Without turning around, Veto held the letter over his shoulder for Briggs to read. "I have indeed," he told the young officer.

Briggs scanned the contents quickly and then shrugged his shoulders. "I don't get it, sir. It's just a letter from some minister talking about life on an island."

"That minister was Seth's closest friend. He has been missing for a long time. We had no idea he was on the Isle of Charn."

"You think he's still there?"

"I'm willing to bet he is, and I'm also willing to bet he knows something that could help us find the Lost ElmKey." Veto stood up and blew the candles out. "Let's get back to the Shadow-Flare."

He took one last look at the old castle before leaving. It all seemed so long ago now, like the events that transpired in this place happened to someone else. But the pain of losing Fiona remained.

Chapter XIII

The winding roads that led up the mountainside made Jacob's stomach knot, every twist and turn driving his belly into a queasy tailspin that left him with a real urge to vomit. He rolled down the window and emptied the contents of his stomach. As he sank back into the upholstery, he caught Kadesha giving him a sympathetic look.

"Feel better?" she asked.

"I won't feel better until we're out of this truck." He turned to Yanseph. "How much further until we reach the stop point?"

Yanseph bit his lip but did not take his eyes off the road. "We're almost there."

"How long, exactly?"

"About an hour."

"Great," Jacob replied sarcastically.

He stuck his head out the window for fresh air and felt the first drops of rain land on his nose. It had been mostly sunny, but the speed at which the weather changed reminded Jacob of back home, where the seasons flitted in and out like actors taking turns to walk on a stage.

Just over an hour later, the tyres screeched underneath them as Yanseph brought the truck to a halt at the side of the mountain road.

"Wait here," he told the two passengers.

"Where's he going?" Jacob asked, as Yanseph exited the truck and disappeared around the back.

The rain was coming down in sheets now, and the first rumbles of thunder had already made themselves heard from the gloomy sky. When Yanseph returned a few minutes later, he was carrying two royal blue, waterproof storm jackets.

"You'll need these," he said, jumping back into the driver's seat and presenting a jacket to each of his passengers.

"Is this really necessary?" Jacob asked as he yanked the jacket over his head.

Yanseph seemed offended at the question. "The weather changes in an instant up here. Some people go up mountains dressed like they're out for a leisurely stroll in the park. They don't realise how dangerous being under-prepared can be." He disappeared around the back of the truck again and returned with a rucksack. "My canteen is in here. Oh, and a first aid kit and torch. You've already got your canteens, right?"

"Right here," Jacob said, lifting both from the truck floor.

"Excellent." Yanseph opened the rucksack and stuffed the canteens inside. "Now, let's get going."

With Yanseph taking point, the three of them started up the steep trail, following the switchbacks as best they could. The rain had turned the ground into a marsh, so Jacob and Kadesha found themselves stuck in the mud more than once. Yanseph lectured them every time, stressing the importance of proper footwear when hiking up a mountain.

"If he repeats himself one more time…" Jacob muttered under his breath.

Kadesha looked to be stifling a laugh. "That's rude. He's only trying to be helpful."

"He's getting on my last nerve."

Yanseph turned to face them. "Pardon?"

Jacob could feel his cheeks going red. "Oh, nothing. I, er…carry on."

Yanseph narrowed his eyes and faced forward again. "As I was saying earlier, there are many-branched paths shooting off in different directions. Stay away from them. We always follow the designated trail. Wandering off track can cause a loss of bearings. If that happens, you may never find your way back to safety."

Jacob winked at Kadesha. "I'll try to remember that."

She looked unimpressed at his sarcastic comment.

Despite her age, Kadesha never once complained as they trekked up Mount Viscera. She matched her younger companions' step for step. Jacob wondered how she kept herself in top shape but was too afraid to ask in case the question came off rude. If truth be told, he felt tired himself and secretly hoped Yanseph would let them stop for a rest. However, the experienced mountaineer was eager to press on now the rain had eased off, and Jacob's hopes were dashed.

Eventually, they crossed a shallow river and found themselves in a grove of trees standing at the base of a majestic curtain waterfall. It soaked them in foamy spray as it dropped onto the moss-covered rocks in the plunge pool.

"Here we are," Yanseph announced, stopping to rest on top of two closely formed rocks. "The vault lies just behind that waterfall."

Kadesha was looking around in awe. "This place is beautiful."

Yanseph freed himself from the rucksack and then dropped it on the wet ground. "I've been up here more times than I care to remember, but it still takes my breath away."

Jacob barely listened as Yanseph went on to explain how the waterfalls were formed. He could feel his eyes getting heavy as the story dragged on, so he turned to Kadesha and flicked his head subtly in the waterfall's direction, hoping the hint would kick her into motion.

"It has been a pleasure to hear you speak, sir, but I think we should make a move now," Kadesha said, clearly taking Jacob's hint.

"I'll be right here waiting," Yanseph assured them.

Kadesha bowed. "Thank you."

Jacob took the torch from Yanseph and then led Kadesha through the cascading water into a dark, narrow cave. Guided by torchlight, they eased their way through the damp and smelly surroundings, continuing until they reached what appeared to be a larger cave.

It was darker inside the cavernous room, but Jacob heard the ground crunching underneath their feet with every step. The room led to a wider area garnished with stalactites that glowed an eerie pink colour. A circular platform lay at the far end, complete with a metal panel in the centre and two dusty red levers.

"What is that thing?" Jacob asked, his voice echoing in the vastness of the cavern.

"I don't have the faintest idea."

"Well, only one way to find out."

He stepped onto the platform and pulled the lever on the left. Nothing happened. Undeterred, he tried to push it instead.

"It won't budge," he said breathlessly.

"Try the other one."

Despite Jacob's best efforts, the right lever also remained in position.

"Let me try." Kadesha chuckled.

"Sure," he said, stepping aside. "But, I doubt you'll…."

She pulled both levers simultaneously, and the platform detached itself from the rest of the room and began its descent into the unknown.

"An elevator," Kadesha observed, clutching a railing that had sprung up from the edge of the platform.

"I was just about to pull both levers at the same time."

Kadesha raised an eyebrow. "Of course, you were."

There was plenty of time to pass while the elevator made its slow descent, so Kadesha asked Jacob about life in the Capital. He hesitated for a moment, wondering if she really wanted to hear the sorry tale of an orphan struggling to survive on the streets, but her warm smile seemed welcoming, and Jacob found himself telling her everything, from the atrocious living conditions to the feelings of hopelessness day after day. He even moaned about the man from the hunting depot who refused to believe he had killed a Villfaar Dragon on his own.

It was strange to hear himself talk about life in the Capital. Most of those days were spent trying to detach himself from the hardship and emotional turmoil. Such detachment had proved useful at the time, but now, he was starting to feel like those unbearable events happened to someone else. Not an unusual coping mechanism by any means, but it certainly made him question his sanity in more ways than one.

"Life must have been difficult," Kadesha offered.

"I don't want sympathy," Jacob assured her. "What about you? What was it like being the follower of an Elementalist?"

"Interesting," Kadesha replied after a short pause.

Jacob laughed. "It must have been great for Fiona. Having all that power, I mean."

"It could be great," she admitted. "But having great power means great responsibility. Being able to control the elements was a gift, not a tool of destruction. Your mother was always quick to remind us of the dangers of elemental magic."

"Dangers?"

"An Elementalist must generate the power of fire, wind, and water themselves. For example, it would be dangerous to cast any type of water spell by taking the water from a river or sea. There is an old legend about Evren, an Elementalist who ruled over the kingdom of Futoria. One day, her rule was challenged by a dark and twisted entity who was somehow able to command elemental magic as well. Realising this entity was too strong, Evren was forced to channel energy from the world around her to win the fight. Her actions altered the nation's landscape forever and caused great pain and suffering to those affected by the seismic shifts."

"Do you believe that story?"

"It does not matter what I believe. The moral is clear. Casting spells in that manner is dangerous. As is using any kind of terra spell."

"Terra spell?"

"A terra spell is rarely used because it is the only element that cannot be generated by the Elementalist but must be derived from the terrain. This means damage to the world and a higher potential for innocent casualties."

"It sounds a lot of responsibility."

Kadesha nodded. "Indeed, you have a lot to live up to as a king, and not just with magic. Your parents were kind and genuinely cared about the world around them."

"Surely, they weren't perfect?"

She shook her head. "Of course not. Seth was tempestuous and prone to making snap decisions that annoyed your mother. They would clash over trivial matters."

"Did they love each other?"

A smile spread across her face. "I believe they did, yes. Your mother changed the constitution to marry Seth. Until she intervened, it was unlawful for a Dakew to marry a Human. The public saw their relationship as a romantic tale of two lovers struggling to be together and was behind them all the way."

She trailed off, and her smile vanished.

"What's wrong?"

"Your mother always had one eye on the future. Never satisfied with her lot. It's just how she was." Kadesha sighed

Jacob could easily relate to the description of his mother's personality and was delighted they had something in common. Kadesha's startling revelation made him wonder what other aspects of his personality could be attributed to each parent. Who did his resourcefulness stem from, or his sense of loyalty? At least Kadesha could answer those questions.

The elevator came to a standstill, and Jacob stepped off the platform into a room with a lever below what looked like two closed flaps attached to the base of a grey, oval-shaped object hanging from the rocky ceiling.

"That must be it," Kadesha said, coming up behind him.

As soon as she pulled the lever, a black cage with a hole at the base descended slowly from above, and the two flaps sprung open on the floor, releasing a podium that rose to meet the base of the cage. It filled the hole perfectly, and then the cage door swung open to reveal…nothing.

Jacob peered into the cage. "Where are the coordinates?"

Kadesha shook her head. "Has someone taken them?"

"Who else would know the vault's location?"

"Something stinks here," Kadesha said as she reversed the mechanism. "I think we need to have a word with Father Gambin. Maybe he knows where the coordinates are."

Jacob was at a loss for words. He had been so confident about finding the Lost ElmKey that he had not even considered the possibility they would fall at the first hurdle, especially after his bravado with Orla in the armoured truck. She would be devastated if they failed to secure the coordinates. It would mean her hopes of a free Uthovaya would be stone dead. How could he look his best friend in the eye after promising the one thing she desired more than anything in the world, and then failing to make good on that promise? His only hope was that Gambin could shed some light on the matter.

Jacob and Kadesha trudged back to the platform and out the vault, but neither spoke on the way there. Yanseph sat where they had left him, in between two boulders and staring up at the sky. The rain had started coming down again, and as they trudged back down the mountain trail, Jacob realised he would soon have to deal with the winding roads and sickness once more.

Here we go again.

Chapter XIV

It was nightfall by the time Yanseph steered the truck back into the compound, and although Jacob felt weary from travelling down Mount Viscera, the journey had given him plenty of time to trade theories with Kadesha about the whereabouts of the coordinates. The Antantans seemed the most likely suspects, but Jacob could not work out how they knew the vault's location. Unless Queen Fiona had told Gunnar Veto many years ago.

He voiced this idea to Kadesha, but she reacted with outrage to the possibility Fiona could have been anything other than loyal to crown and country. Jacob explained she could have been duped or forced into revealing the location, but Kadesha stood firm. He was unsure if her reaction stemmed from a knowledge of the facts or blind emotion, but either way, he had a bad feeling in the pit of his stomach.

What if the Antantans had already used the coordinates, found the tower, and destroyed the Lost ElmKey? It was the nightmare scenario, and certainly worth considering, even if Kadesha refused to entertain the idea.

"Father Gambin is the most likely suspect," she repeated, offering nothing in the way of evidence for her claim.

"But why?"

"I have no idea." She admitted. "We will soon find out."

Jacob gently steered the conversation back to his mother's potential involvement, but Kadesha's defensiveness reared its protective head again. She demanded they stop speculating until they had spoken to Gambin and the truth could be ascertained.

"What if he doesn't know the truth?" Jacob asked, fidgeting in the back seat.

Kadesha did not reply.

Yanseph brought the truck to a halt, so Jacob jumped out and performed a variety of silly movements to stretch his tired limbs. Kadesha giggled at his antics. It was strange hearing her laugh. He realised she hardly ever did.

Yanseph touched Jacob's shoulder. "Pleasant journey?"

The question had more than a hint of sarcasm.

"Not really. But thanks for the lift. We appreciate it."

"Right then." Yanseph grinned. "I'll just go lock the truck up and head over to the mess hall for supper. Maybe see you over there if you're sticking around?"

"Maybe."

As soon as Yanseph was out of earshot, Jacob turned to Kadesha. "Are we ready to go see Gambin?"

"There has to be something he can tell us." Her tone sounded more hopeful than anything else, now.

The church was shrouded in darkness when Jacob knocked on the front door. The robed figure who had escorted them from the entrance the previous night must have gone to the mess hall for supper because he was nowhere to be seen.

"Why isn't he answering?" Jacob asked, getting frustrated at being kept waiting.

"Try again."

He knocked loudly on the door three times, but once again, there was no response.

"Is he doing this deliberately?" Jacob moaned.

"He could be in the mess hall," Kadesha suggested. "Let's try there."

Just as they turned to leave, the front door opened, and a guard Jacob had not seen before stepped out to greet them.

"Come this way," the guard said, inviting them into the cold nave.

Gambin took forever to come downstairs, and when he finally appeared, he looked flippantly in their direction. "Find what you were looking for?" he asked.

"The coordinates are missing," Jacob explained.

"Coordinates?" Gambin replied in a confused tone. He shook his head and then turned to Kadesha. "What does he mean?"

"There were important coordinates hidden inside that vault."

"I have no idea what you are talking about. Un-less…?" Gambin collapsed onto a chair by the side of the door.

"What is it?" Jacob asked.

"The statue had an inscription on it, a set of random numbers. I didn't think anything of it."

Jacob and Kadesha gave each other a look before Jacob asked, "What statue?"

"It was a simple statue your father carved. He was quite the artist; he said it would be passed down to you."

"What are you talking about?"

"I should have done as he asked, but I thought you were dead. There was no reason to think any of you would ever return to the vault, and the statue was the only item of value."

"Where is it now?"

"I sold it," Gambin replied, refusing to look Jacob or Kadesha in the eye.

Jacob said, "You sold my father's statue? That statue leads to the Lost ElmKey. We may never find it now, thanks to you!"

"We were desperate."

Jacob started to speak again, but Kadesha silenced him, and then knelt in front of the stressed-looking minister, seemingly unable to look him in the eye. "We need those numbers, Father. Please, tell me you re-member who bought it."

"The mayor of Rockwood, a small town in Pavelle. He visited the island while on a cruise. He was a massive fan of the statue as soon as I showed it to him. Said he would pay a lot of money."

"Can you contact this man?"

Gambin shook his head. "No. and I never heard from him again."

"So, that's us in trouble?" Jacob said.

"Not necessarily," Kadesha said calmly. "Perhaps, we should visit Rockwood and see if the mayor will give the statue back?"

Jacob offered no objection, but privately he doubted anyone would hand over a statue they paid a lot of money for. They had no idea if the man was still the mayor or if he even lived in Rockwood anymore. Jacob was surer than ever the coordinates were gone for good, but how could he abandon ship now? Orla would lose hope of a brighter future for Uthovaya, and he had no intention of seeing her broken. He had to see the mission through to Rockwood, at least.

Gambin turned to Jacob. "Before you go, your Majesty, I would like to speak with you in private if I may?"

"I will wait outside," Kadesha announced.

When they were alone, Gambin bowed his head and spoke softly. "I know you might not want advice from me, but you will get it anyway – especially as you are going after the Lost ElmKey. You have inherited a penchant for trusting the wrong people. Just like your mother."

"I trust my companions," Jacob said, angry at the insinuation the others would betray him, especially Orla, who was the most trustworthy friend anyone could hope for.

"I am speaking of Ryker," Gambin explained. "The Revolutionaries have made a terrible mistake getting involved with him. He wants something from you. Men like him always do."

"What do you believe he wants?"

"I don't know, but a strong ambassador would never have allowed Ryker to threaten us. It makes me wonder who is really in charge over there now."

Gambin moved closer and continued, "Trust the right people, Jacob. Don't make the same mistake your mother did."

"I'll try," he replied before bidding Gambin farewell.

Back outside, Kadesha approached him straight away.

"We should find the others and get back to the Veteran as soon as possible."

Jacob nodded, but deep down, he dreaded telling Orla the awful news.

Chapter XV

By the next morning, the Rad Veteran was sailing on the high seas towards Pavelle. Orla had noticed most of the crew were in good spirits, but she could not share their contentment, thanks to news of the statue with the coordinates being sold. It was the kind of setback they did not need. Jacob had said very little, but he seemed downhearted, as if the entire mission was already a failure. The last thing everyone needed was for the future king to give up.

Kicking her legs over the side of the bed, she allowed them to dangle for a moment before dropping to the floor as quietly as could be. Kadesha was lying on the bottom bunk, completely engrossed in a book she had found in one of the cabin drawers. Orla tiptoed past while the boat rocked from side to side like a cradle.

As soon as she stepped out of the cabin, she heard music coming from the captain's quarters at the end of the passageway. The stench of stale smoke and dust was overpowering, almost making her gag as she knocked lightly on the door to Jacob and Boocka's cabin.

Jacob looked terrible when he finally answered; his heavy-set eyes and unkempt hair suggesting he was tired and was trying to get an early night. There was an awkward silence as they stared at one another. The longer the silence went on, the more uneasy Jacob looked. He struggled to make eye contact and repeatedly scraped the sole of his shoe off the floor like a bashful cartoon character.

"You're angry, aren't you?" Jacob asked, breaking the silent tension.

His question took her aback, and all but confirmed something was on his mind.

"What makes you think I'm angry?"

"Because you'll miss the start of university, and it might all be for nothing."

"University isn't important right now. What's important is that we keep our eye on the prize."

"What prize?" Jacob snorted. "We'll probably never find the Lost ElmKey, not if our luck on the Isle of Charn is anything to go by."

"If you don't think we'll succeed, why are you still here?"

Jacob gave her a look that suggested he was shocked at the question. Then he sighed and admitted, "I doubt you'd believe me if I told you."

Orla was intrigued. "Try me."

"OK, but you won't like it." he replied. "The truth is, as much as I've always supported your dream of becoming a politician, I never actually believed you could make a difference."

Eyebrows raised, Orla shook her head, desperately trying to deny Jacob's shocking admission. She wanted to ask a barrage of questions but found herself speechless, devastated by her friend's bombshell – the friend she trusted most in the whole world.

"It's not because I don't believe in you," Jacob explained, quickly. "It's because the Antantans would make sure you never set foot inside parliament. Even if you did somehow gain a voice, they'd have killed you for upsetting the official narrative."

Orla listened intently, wondering why Jacob never said anything before. She had talked about becoming a politician for as long as she could remember, and Jacob had supported her on every occasion. It had all been a lie. All those conversations when she thought he was being supportive; he was only paying lip service to a dream he never believed could become reality.

"I have to go now," she found herself saying in a daze.

Jacob burst from the cabin and blocked her path.

"Hold on," he yelled.

"Let me past. I don't want to speak with you."

"Not until you understand that it's not just about your dream." He fired the words out quickly now, like a verbal machine-gun spraying bullets. "The only reason I'm still here is because this is the *only* way we can take the country back and create a stable future. If I leave now, your dream of Uthovayan liberty will lie in tatters. I can't do that to you."

Orla's stomach somersaulted at Jacob's incredible revelation. It was flattering to know he would continue the mission to spare her feelings.

"I know you want to protect me," she said, softly, "but whether they know it or not, every single Uthovayan is depending on you. I would kill to be that symbol of hope. You must believe we can do this. You must believe we'll find that statue in Rockwood and get those coordinates."

Jacob exhaled breath. "I'll try."

"That's all I ask," Orla whispered. "I'd better go and get some rest."

Jacob scratched his chin and then opened the door, but Orla turned to face him before he could go inside.

"Your parents were arguably the best leaders in Uthovaya's modern history. Ask yourself if they would let a setback like this get them down."

He looked deep in thought and then closed the door gently, leaving Orla alone in the passageway again to consider their conversation. Not many people could say their best friend was trying to save a nation for them. It left her with a warm feeling inside, one she had never felt before, and one she never wanted to end. Was something special developing between them? It was a question that would have to wait because her eyes felt like they would close on her at any minute.

Time for bed.

Orla yawned and then turned on her heels, but the faint sound of music and laughter coming from the captain's cabin made her curious once again. The door was slightly ajar, so she crept along the passageway and peered inside. The captain sat at his table alongside two members of his crew, a bottle of wine in one hand and a fat cigar in the other. There was a deck of cards in the middle of the table.

Orla backed away from the door, but unfamiliar hands wrapped around her waist from behind. She struggled wildly, but her captor carried her into the cabin and then dropped her on the dirty floor beside the captain's table.

"Look who I found outside," her captor slurred. "Reckon, she was spying on you, Captain."

Captain Hudson dropped his cigar into a metal ashtray and then slammed his wine bottle down on the wooden table. He made a subtle hand gesture to Orla's captor, who responded by helping her up.

"Get your hands off me," she yelled, pushing the toothless, tattooed crewmember away.

The captain rose from his seat and approached Orla with a glint in his eye.

"You wasn't spying on me, Miss Paton? Was ye?"

"No, I was not spying on you."

The crewmember who had carried her into the cabin closed the door. Orla felt nervous about the situation she found herself in. She struggled to make eye contact and found herself taking deep, calming breaths. Boocka had warned the group about fraternising with the mercenaries. Some were thieves, but others had committed more heinous acts, including terrorism and murder. These were not your average sailors, and the Rad Veteran was not a cruise ship.

Of the four men, only Captain Hudson had not moved closer to leer. Orla could feel herself shaking but was determined not to give the mercs the satisfaction of seeing her afraid, so she pushed her shoulders back and straightened herself up.

Show no fear.

"Sit down, men." Hudson ordered.

Orla breathed a sigh of relief. "Well, I'd better be going."

"Nonsense," said Hudson. "I insist ye stay. It'll be great to have some lady company for a change." He turned to his men. "Ain't that right, boys?"

A loud cheer went up while the crew clinked jugs of wine together.

"Can I interest ye in an up-n-downer?" Hudson said, returning to the table and holding his wine out in front of her.

She should have made it clear to the pushy captain that the last thing on her mind was socialising with lowlife mercs. But something stopped her. A feeling this grizzled veteran would protect her from the others. His authority was undeniable. Not to mention he was quite the gentleman…for a mercenary.

"Water for me," she replied, taking an empty seat across from the captain.

Another loud cheer from the crew, but this time the captain silenced them and demanded someone bring a jug of water for his guest of honour. When it arrived on the table, Orla inspected the liquid for signs of tampering – a move that made Hudson burst into laughter.

"You and your friends *really* don't trust me, do ye?"

Orla sipped from the jug. "Can you blame us?"

Hudson scratched the back of his neck. "No, but if I was the reading type, I'd say ye can't judge a book by its cover."

"Well, I am the reading type, and let me tell you, sometimes you can."

"It's these ruffians that worry ye, isn't it?" Hudson said, referring to his crew.

Orla said nothing, but the captain continued, anyway.

"They wasn't my first choice, ye know. I'd sooner have my old crew back, but we don't always get what we want in life, do we?"

"What happened?"

He offered Orla a cigar, which she quickly turned down.

"Turn the music off for a minute." he shouted to no one in particular. "About a year ago, we started doing jobs for a Gogglo known as Ulric Raven. He claimed to know the location of the Domdan Treasure and wanted us to retrieve it for him."

"The Domdan Treasure?"

Hudson spoke quicker. "Ye never heard of the Domdan Treasure? It's only the most famous lost loot in the world of Lozaro. Been missing for centuries. Anyway, this Raven character tells us it's buried in Jandalgine, underneath an abandoned outpost named Fort Nebula. He tells us to find it and promises to split the treasure fifty-fifty."

"You didn't?"

"Of course, we didn't. We planned on taking the loot and doing a runner, but a mercenary group called the Red Ghosts ambushed us when we got there. The whole thing was a setup. Turns out, Raven was their leader, and the treasure wasn't buried there at all."

"Why did the Red Ghosts have it in for you?"

"We was the best in the business. The Ghosts were new on the scene and didn't like us getting all the contracts. I was the only one who survived the ambush. Wandered around the Jandalgine wasteland for days. I woulda died if I hadn't got picked up by travellers out that way."

"Fascinating."

He leaned across the table. "I've told you my story. Don't ye think ye should tell me yours?"

"There's nothing to tell."

"Ye sure? Cos you and Jay don't look the type to join the Revolutionaries. What's the deal with that?"

"There is no deal. He's my friend, and I'm here to lend support."

"A friend, eh?" he playfully elbowed one of the crew in the ribs and grinned. "I daresay romance is afoot?"

What is he talking about?

There was no romance between her and Jacob. Or at least she didn't think there was. Up until now, they had remained firm friends, but she had to admit there was a certain spark developing, one that started in Kadesha's safehouse. The surprising heat between them felt slightly awkward but not weird. It was also none of the captain's business.

"It's got nothing to do with romance," she said grumpily. "He needed me with him, so I obliged. That's what best friends do."

"Well, whatever keeps ye busy."

The captain laughed as he counted the cards in his deck and started dealing to everyone except Orla. She could feel herself getting worked up at his smug comment.

"I have a dream of my own, you know," she blasted. "I want to be a politician and help repair the damage done to my country by the Antantans."

Hudson leaned back in his chair. "And yet here ye are, halfway around the world supporting yer supposed friend instead. Ye won't do much good for yer homeland all the way out here."

The absolute cheek of this man.

"Well, I think I'll be going now." she announced, standing up and pushing the chair away with the back of her legs. "Got a long journey ahead of us."

160

"Fair enough, Miss Paton. Remember, if ye need any help, ye only gotta say the word."

Orla was confused. "Help us how?"

"We're going to Pavelle to find something of yours, right? I know a lot of people in Pavelle. Could make things easier."

"And why would you want to do that?"

"I'll do whatever it takes to help Jay complete this mission."

Orla thought about his comment for a moment. "Do you know what I think?" she said, standing up from the table. "I think you're full of it."

Hudson looked surprised and burst out laughing. "Do ye now?"

"You don't want to help; you only want to know what's going on and get your money from Ryker. I wouldn't trust you if you were the last person left on this planet."

A commotion at the door disrupted their chat. Boocka burst into the room and was heading straight for Hudson. The crew members tried to halt the Krokiran's advance, but he rag-dolled them with ease and slammed his fists down on the table.

"What's going on?" He glared at Hudson as if to say, this girl is under my protection, so leave her alone.

Hudson calmly turned to Orla. "Remember what I said, Miss Paton. If ye need help, ye know where I am. Oh, and live yer own life, not someone else's."

Back outside the captain's quarters, Orla sensed a frosty atmosphere between herself and the disappointed Krokiran. He gave her periodic looks of contempt while they walked down the hall, clearly annoyed she had put herself in danger by fraternising with the captain and his understudies. She could hardly blame him, not when he had told of the dangers many times before. An apology would not appease him.

"Take this." Boocka said, quickly handing her a small pistol from his satchel.

Orla took a closer look and then turned away, repulsed by the sight of the weapon. "I told you, no guns."

"We're on a dangerous mission. At some point, you'll encounter a situation where using a gun is inevitable if you or someone you care about is to survive. Take it."

Orla huffily snatched the gun.

"I'll teach you how to use it over the next few days," Boocka promised.

"Boocka."

"What is it?"

"Thank you for sticking up for me back there." She gave him a warm and well-deserved hug.

"Er, no problem," he replied sheepishly.

In that moment, she was sure they had an understanding.

Chapter XVI

The next few days saw the Rad Veteran battered by a storm the likes of which Jacob had never seen. Even an experienced seadog like Captain Hudson, who was now spending more time with the group, claimed never to have encountered such bad weather before. On the third day, the Veteran sailed through the eye of the storm, braving fifty-knot winds and twenty-foot waves that tested the tired old vessel to its limits. Jacob hid below deck with the others as nature's raw power threatened to capsize the ship.

Tragedy struck when a drunken crewman tried to show off by going to the top deck. He never returned. Hudson believed the man fell overboard and warned everyone else to stay below deck until the storm passed. More bad luck followed as Quiet-Flu spread amongst the crew, flooring everyone except Boocka, who had an inbuilt tolerance against the common virus. Orla was hit the hardest, suffering symptoms ranging from nausea and dizziness to chills and sweats. She was also the only patient to lose her voice completely, falling victim to Quiet-Flu's serious assault on the vocal cords. Jacob feared she would end up like so many others and be left permanently mute.

After a few more days, Orla showed signs of improvement, but any hopes of a change in fortune evaporated when Kadesha learned from Ambassador Bellis that all the Charn colonists had been dumped in a mass grave, each one executed with a bullet to the back of the head. The shocking news left everyone devastated, and Jacob feeling guilty. It was obvious the Antantans were behind their execution, and with the Shadow-Flare confirmed to be on its way to Pavelle, finding the Lost ElmKey was a less sure thing than it had ever been.

As they prepared to dock at the tiny port of Denizen, Jacob decided to pay his recovering friend a visit, partly to keep her spirits up, and partly to discuss his plans going forward. He wanted to fight. Fight for his lost childhood, fight for Mr. Janmano and the people of Uthovaya, fight for what was rightfully his. He no longer wanted to be just Jacob. He wanted to be Jacob Crestmore and live up to the family name.

Knocking lightly on the cabin door, he waited a few seconds before stepping inside to find Orla sitting on the edge of the top bunk, eating chocolate from a wooden bowl. She was fully dressed for the first time in days, wearing a pair of baggy trousers and a white, short-sleeved shirt.

"Hope you don't mind me coming to see you?"

"Not at all," she croaked. "As long as you don't mind me sounding like a CrellFrog?"

"Hey, at least you look better," he lied, trying not to stare at her tangled hair and pale face as he leaned against the bunk bed frame.

Orla looked pleased with his comment, but her face fell again when she caught sight of herself in a small hand-held mirror.

"Are you kidding me? I'm as white as a ghost."

"Nonsense," he replied with an impish grin. "You look strong enough to take on the entire Antantan army."

"I might have to," Orla quipped, her dry comment turning the playful mood into something more serious. "Although I haven't had much of a chance to practice with my new gun."

"Gun?"

She reached under the pillow and pulled out a small pistol.

"Boocka thought I should learn to use it. He said it's impossible for him to protect us all.

Jacob felt awful. It was bad enough Orla had to give up university, but the fact she had been forced to take on a weapon to protect herself went against everything she stood for.

"I've been thinking about what you said," Jacob whispered, hoping their conversation would take her mind off the gun.

She handed him a piece of chocolate, but he shook his head and watched her eat it instead.

"You were right," he told her firmly. "My mother and father would turn in their graves if I went on half-heartedly or gave up. I promise to do everything in my power to find the Lost ElmKey and restore the dimensional gateway. Then we'll get rid of the Antantans and make Uthovaya great again, make it a better place for everyone to live. I won't rest until I'm back on that throne…or until I die trying."

He waited nervously for a response to his passionate speech, but Orla simply popped the last piece of chocolate in her mouth and gave what looked to Jacob like a forced smile. The awkward moment only lasted a few seconds before a knock at the door from Boocka, interrupted them,

"There you are," he said. "Lady Kadesha wants us all up top."

"Be right there," Orla replied.

Jacob thought he had misheard.

"You're coming, too?" he asked, tying the Dynasty Staff to his back with bits of string.

"Of course."

"But you're not fully recovered yet."

"I'm not staying here with the mercs, that's for sure." She climbed down to the floor and then stuffed the pistol into the back of her trousers. "Are you coming or not?"

Kadesha's briefing lasted only a few minutes and concentrated on the need to be cautious now that the Antantans were almost certainly headed to Pavelle in search of the statue. Jacob agreed with her words of wisdom. The last thing they needed was running into the Antantans. It was imperative they reached Rockwood as quickly as possible.

"Could the Antantans get to Rockwood before us?" Orla asked.

"I cannot deny the possibility," Kadesha replied glumly. "The Pavellians will assist the Antantans in any way possible. Their respective leaders made a pact years ago to always support one another in business and in war."

"They tried to get Krokira in on their little pact too," Boocka added. "But we told them it wasn't happening."

Jacob said. "Aren't you afraid they'll just invade Krokira to get you onside? The might of the Antantan army might be too much, even for the Krokiran Special Forces." Boocka threw his head back and roared with laughter. "You've never been to Krokira then?"

Jacob shook his head. Krokira had always been a mystery to him, as it was to most who had never travelled to the country. Very little about Krokira had been recorded in history books down the years.

Boocka explained, "Krokirans hibernate for three months during the winter to survive the harsh conditions. Those damn Antantans would freeze before they knew what hit them."

"What if their attack came in a different season?" Jacob asked.

Boocka laughed again. "That would be a fair fight. They wouldn't stand a chance against the KSF."

The boat docked at Denizen Port a short while later, and the group made their way down the gangplank. It was a lifeless place, reminding Jacob of the harbour back home; the industry had been stripped away, leaving only rusty machinery and weather damaged boats. There were three old sheds, and each one looked like a slight wind could blow it down any minute. The windows on the harbourmaster's house were boarded up, and weavel rats scuttled in and out from small cracks in the stone.

"Not exactly a welcoming sight," Boocka moaned.

"Show some respect," Kadesha warned, scolding her bodyguard with an acidic tongue.

"Sorry, m'lady."

A stroll through the town revealed unexpected deprivation and poverty. The residents looked unhappy, they were thin and haggard, wearing rags for clothes and begging for food and money. Jacob felt bad for them but cheered up when Kadesha revealed she had brought bags of fruit and chocolate from the Rad Veteran. The desperate locals thanked her constantly as they accepted her kindness.

"This is horrible," Jacob whispered to Orla.

"I don't understand these levels of poverty," Orla replied. "Pavelle's main export is prime, the most useable source of energy on the planet. It powers everything from home appliances to vehicles and weapons."

Kadesha had obviously overheard their conversation because she passed the bags of fruit and chocolate to Boocka and wandered over to join them, a sad look on her face.

"The capital city of Vala sucks up most of the money. Everyone else has to fight for the leftovers."

"That's not right," Orla said angrily.

"Certainly not, but it remains a sad reality for these poor souls."

They chatted with the locals before pushing on towards Denizen station, where Jacob noticed a small number of green bipedal lizards maintaining the tracks. All of them looked malnourished and wore blue, short-sleeved overalls.

As Jacob got closer, he noticed they had visible sores on their scaly arms, and their olive-coloured snouts sagged in the most unnatural way.

"Those poor lizards," Kadesha whispered.

"Who are they?" Jacob and Orla asked simultaneously.

"They hail from a once-thriving island off the coast of Northern Pavelle known as the Republic of Snarkol. It sank beneath the waves after a volcanic eruption about sixty-five years ago. The survivors sought refuge here, hoping for care and acceptance, but instead, they found no sympathy for their predicament. Most were drafted into the Pavellian Cybernetic Army and turned half-machine against their wishes. The rest work low-paying jobs to make ends meet."

"Treated like second class citizens," Jacob said, shaking his head in disgust.

He felt a deep sadness at the plight of the Snarkeen and thought of those back home, suffering under a brutal regime that saw them as nothing more than chattel, to be used how they see fit. It made him wonder how many other poor souls were out there, struggling against the tide.

The train to Rockwood was not due for another half-hour, so they hung around the station, waiting patiently on the broken benches scattered along the length of the crumbling platform. As he waited for the train, Jacob could only think about how he could prove to Orla he had changed. It was time to start acting like a leader, someone everyone could turn to in times of trouble, no matter the situation.

"What are you thinking about?" he heard Orla ask from the seat beside him.

"Nothing," he lied.

"You're awfully quiet."

"And you still don't look well," he retorted, noticing she was paler than before.

"I'll get some rest on the train."

"OK, here it comes now."

The conditions inside the train carriage were awful. A variety of disgusting bugs shared the badly worn seats with passengers, and the floor was stained with puddles of urine. Jacob wondered if he would make it to Rockwood without being sick.

"I'm cold," Orla said, shivering beside him on the seat.

"Take my jacket," he insisted, removing the dirty brown coat, and covering her up with it.

"Thanks," she replied, resting her head on his shoulder.

Less than a minute later, Jacob realised she had fallen asleep.

"Dream us some good fortune," he whispered, as he pushed strands of hair behind her ear.

Jacob and the others stared out the window in silence for the entire journey, travelling eastwards past the mountains, and through Plendor Valley, passing several stations and small towns in the process. Orla had still not woken up as the train pulled into the dilapidated shack that doubled as Rockwood station, so Jacob shook her gently.

"Wake up, sleepyhead."

"Are we here already?" she replied, stretching out on the chair.

"We sure are." He grinned. "Feeling better?"

Orla nodded. "I do feel much better, actually."

"You look a better colour at least."

Rockwood was only a short distance away, but instead of finding a sleepy little town, they found nothing but derelict buildings, burnt-out cars, and machinery poking out from large craters in the ground. No birds flew overhead, giving the ghost town a creepy feel.

"What the hell's happened to this place?" Boocka exclaimed.

There was an abandoned playground in the town centre, but the missing swings, broken seesaw, and lopsided roundabout would have silenced the innocent laughter of any children trying to play there. Not that there were any children around. Jacob sat on the only available swing, but the seat broke, leaving nothing but two dangling chains, and Jacob sprawled out on the dirt.

"You OK?" Orla asked, giving him a hand up.

"I'll be a lot better when we figure out what's going on. We should start searching the buildings to see if anyone's still here."

Kadesha nodded. "Boocka and I will take that side of the town. You two check out the other side."

The first house on the left painted the unsettling picture of a normal life suddenly disturbed by an unexpected incident. Cutlery and plates had been laid out at the dinner table, and several chairs were upturned, as though someone had left in a hurry. A mouldy baby's bottle lay on the floor, and a headless teddy took the place of a child in the red and yellow highchair.

"I'll check upstairs," Jacob heard Orla say.

"Be careful."

Jacob investigated the first level further while Orla was upstairs. He noticed no valuables whatsoever and wondered about the other houses in the town. *Had it been a mass robbery?*

"Jacob," Orla called from the floor above him.

"Yeah?"

"I think you better come up here."

Creeping upstairs, he wondered whether he wanted to know what Orla had discovered. It would no doubt be something horrible if downstairs was anything to go by. Still, he continued to the top landing and found Orla in one of the three bedrooms, looking at a bullet-riddled wall. On the floor was a circle of what looked like dried blood. A chill shot down Jacob's spine, and he wondered if whoever caused the gruesome scene was still nearby. He looked over his shoulder and then back again, half expecting someone to jump out at them.

"We should check the other houses," he whispered in a shaky voice.

After searching every house, Jacob and Orla returned to the playground where Kadesha and Boocka were already waiting, their dispirited body language already answering Jacob's question of whether they had found anyone on their side.

"There's still one more we haven't tried," said Boocka, pointing at a larger building in the centre of the town. A sign proclaimed it as the town hall. Or at least it was before it had sloped into a giant crater.

"The statue should be in there," Jacob replied.

The reception area inside was a mess, broken flooring, upturned furniture, and broken glass everywhere. It was impossible to walk around due to the slope of the floor, so Jacob suggested he slide down to the next room.

"Be careful," Orla said firmly.

He moved across the broken floor, gripping the edge of each cracked tile as he eased himself down the dangerous slope to reach a counter that had been halved in two. There were three shelves behind the counter; two were empty, but one had a dirty map of the town hall. Jacob took a quick peek and noted the mayor's office lay at the far left of the building.

He manoeuvred himself away from the counter, and then slid down the marble flooring towards the faraway wall, using his feet to cushion himself as he skidded into it. Then, he heard the unmistakable sound of engines roaring from somewhere outside.

"What's that?" he called to the others.

"Better not be what I think it is," Boocka replied, rushing outside to look.

Jacob's heart thundered in his chest as he waited for Boocka's update.

"It's the Shadow-Flare," Boocka yelled.

"Jacob, get back up here," Orla cried. "The Antantans are here."

Trying to keep calm, Jacob stepped across the wall towards the door leading into the next room.

"Not until I've searched for the statue."

"Don't be an idiot," Boocka growled.

"Just go and hide," Jacob shouted. "I'll come and find you when I'm done."

"That don't even make sense," the Krokiran shot back. "How the hell you gonna find us?"

There was no time to respond, so Jacob watched his friends exit the building. He was all set to move into the next room when Orla re-appeared with a worried look on her face.

"I promise I'll be fine," he said. "Go before they find both of us."

His words obviously snapped Orla to her senses because she nodded and then ran outside again. Jacob swung himself through the doorway, rolled into the next room and grabbed the door handle to stop himself from sliding further. The mayor's office was on the far-left side, but before Jacob could scramble across, he heard voices coming from behind him and peeked around the doorway to see two Antantan soldiers standing where his friends had been just moments ago. Each carried an assault rifle and seemed to be assessing whether the building was safe.

Jacob decided it was risky to wait any longer, so he pushed into the mayor's office where he found another broken desk, collapsed filing cabinets, and a white pedestal lying amongst piles of rubble. There was broken glass scattered all around it and a sign that read, *King Seth Crestmore–Statue of an Unknown Tower*.

Jacob's excitement came with the merest suggestion of disappointment. He had found a link to the statue but not the statue itself. It was tempting to look on the bleak side again, but now he had the strength and courage to ignore any potential setbacks and instead concentrate on the positives.

Manoeuvring out the back window, he dropped to the ground and found himself inside the crater, surrounded by dirty puddles and machinery. The only way back up was an unsafe-looking ladder on the opposite side. He trudged through the muck, finding each step heavier than the last, but was forced to spin behind a large digger when a group of Antantan soldiers appeared at the top of the ladder and then started climbing down in single file.

Panicking, he swung back around and headed back into the sloping building where he worked his way back up to the main entrance. Outside, Antantan soldiers patrolled the streets. Jacob could see the Shadow-Flare grounded on the outskirts of the town.

His thoughts immediately turned to the whereabouts of his friends. It was doubtful they were in one of the buildings because the soldiers were searching every one of them. It was then Jacob caught sight of the person directing the troops. It was Gunnar Veto. The man who killed Mr. Janmano, the man who betrayed his mother and father. He was dashing back and forth between the troops on the street, barking instructions, and generally looking more stressed than he had been in the ballroom.

Finish him.

The thought struck Jacob quick and unexpectedly. Veto would not be expecting an attack. He would be vulnerable, just like Jacob's parents when Veto gained their trust and then cruelly shattered it. Jacob felt the bile move into his throat as he brought the Dynasty Staff to the front of his body and readied himself to attack the evil man standing in front of him. Suddenly, Veto turned around to speak with someone, forcing Jacob to dive for cover before he was spotted, and roll away to the side of the closest building. He got back to his feet and moved on, keeping low to avoid the soldiers inside from seeing him through the shattered window. He reached the back door and promptly ran into another two soldiers standing beside a dumpster. Both looked as startled with his presence as he was them.

"Halt," one said, raising his weapon. "Identify yourself."

Chapter XVII

Jacob stood frozen to the spot, his mind working over-time for a solution. He had to say something, anything to convince the soldiers to let him pass without inci-dent...*but what*?

"I-I'm on a field trip," he stammered. "The rest of my university classmates are around here somewhere. I'll just go find them."

"Not so fast, Mixling scum," the mouthy soldier barked. "I'm calling for backup."

The soldier had just brandished his communica-tor when a bola came from nowhere, tightening it-self around his neck and sending him crashing to the ground, dead. The other soldier did not have time to react before a second bola tangled around his neck and strangled him too. Confused, Jacob turned to find a dark-haired boy running towards him. He was barefoot with brown rags for clothes and looked about thirteen years old.

"Thanks," was all Jacob could mumble.

"Help me put their bodies in this dumpster. Hope-fully, the rest won't notice two of their men missing."

Jacob did as the boy asked and then closed the dumpster lid.

"Follow me," the boy said.

"I need to find my friends."

"Your friends are at my place. I took them there to hide them from the Antantans."

The boy led Jacob away from the town and into an empty field. A trapdoor was hidden in the long grass.

"Down here," said the boy, pulling the trapdoor open and urging Jacob to go first down the rusted ladder and into the dimly lit box room.

Down below, Jacob could make out a few small crates piled on top of each other, and some rolled up blankets. There were pots of dirty water everywhere. A single empty bookshelf sat against the opposite wall, and two dirty mattresses lay in the middle of the floor. Orla and the others came out from the shadows with a little blonde girl. She looked a few years younger than the boy, and her clothes were in slightly better condition.

"I'm so glad you're safe," Orla said, hugging Jacob so tight his eyes felt like they would pop out of his skull.

"Likewise," he replied, freeing himself from the hug.

The young girl flashed a toothless smile and then ran over to Jacob and Orla. "I'm Coco," she announced confidently. Then she pointed at the boy. "That's my big brother, Devin."

"Hi, Coco. Hi, Devin. I'm Jacob."

She giggled and then ran over to lie on one of the dirty mattresses. Boocka was beside Jacob in an instant, demanding to know if he had found the statue.

"No, but it was definitely here."

"Do you mean King Seth's statue?" Devin interrupted.

"Yes."

"I'm afraid the men took it. Just like they took everything else."

Coco shrieked in terror and then jumped off the mattress. "Bad men?" she yelled, bursting into tears.

Devin immediately ran to his sister and brought her tightly to his body in a protective embrace.

"It's OK, Coco. Those bad men will never find us. I promise."

As Jacob watched the kids embrace, he once again wondered what happened in the small town of Rockwood. Where were the other townspeople? Why were these two kids the only ones left?

Boocka stepped in. "Any idea who these men were or what they wanted?"

"All I know is they were businessmen," Devin explained. "They came and told everyone large amounts of prime had been discovered underneath the town. Everyone was given two days to move."

"Then what happened?"

"The men weren't pleased when the adults refused. They started killing everyone." He paused and stared towards the other side of the room, as though reliving the horrible events. "I think my mum was killed, too. She left us down here and went to get her gun. I followed her back to the house and heard gunshots, but I never saw her again."

Jacob thought back to the gunshot holes in the wall from the first house and instinctively bowed his head in sorrow.

"What about your father?" Orla asked.

Devin swallowed hard. "He died not long after Coco was born. It was just us and Mum after that."

"I'm sorry," Orla said.

Jacob saw her turn away, probably hiding her tears from the kids.

"How did you survive all this time?" Orla asked, without turning back around.

Devin put a protective arm around his little sister. "I go out hunting for food and water. This place ain't much, but it keeps us sheltered."

Jacob said, "About the men who came. Is there anything you can tell us about them? What they looked like maybe?"

Devin looked deep in thought. "They were Human, wore dark sunglasses, and drove fancy black cars. Not the old-fashioned kind, but the newer ones that hover. Each had a symbol on the side. A sort of red inverted M shape with an I beside it."

"Anyone recognise that symbol?" Jacob asked.

Orla and Boocka shook their heads, but Kadesha seemed deep in thought.

"I will contact Ambassador Bellis on the way back to the Rad Veteran," she said. "Perhaps, she can be of assistance."

"What about the kids?" Orla replied. "We can't just leave them here."

"What else can we do?" Jacob interjected. "We can't take them with us. It's too dangerous."

Kadesha said, "We passed a children's refuge centre in one of the towns on our way here."

Devin suddenly became defensive, clenching his fists and pulling his sister behind him.

"I won't go," he yelled angrily. "And neither will Coco. We've lived very well out here and don't need help from anyone."

"We do not have any other option," Kadesha insisted. "At least you will be safe there."

Jacob gently approached Devin and tried to persuade him. He was resistant at first but eventually came around to the idea of a comfortable and warm bed every night.

"It does sound good," he admitted, turning to Coco. "As long as we're together, nothing else matters."

Coco laughed and then turned to Jacob and the others. "My big brother knows best."

Boocka was first to open the trapdoor and look outside for any Antantan activity.

"They're gone," he said. "Let's get back to the train station. The sooner we leave, the sooner Lady Kadesha can contact Bellis and find out who these mass murderers are."

Chapter XVIII

Back on the Rad Veteran, Orla rapidly paced the passageway, stopping only to glance at the captain's cabin door every now and again, as she contemplated a course of action, she would have never thought possible. Kadesha had contacted Ambassador Bellis as soon as they returned from Rockwood and learned the MI symbol the children had described, stood for Merrick Industries. It was apparently a well-known company. The owner, a Pavellian man named Jullien Merrick, was a powerful prime baron who lived in Vala. Orla had never heard of him, but Bellis explained Merrick was known as a ruthless businessman. He would be unlikely to give up the statue.

The bad news had left them at a dead-end with nowhere to turn. Now, as Orla took a deep breath and knocked on the captain's door, she hoped her decision would be the right one, and the others would understand why she took this course of action. Why she needed to ask for his help.

The captain's white shirt was unbuttoned when he answered the door, exposing a ripped torso to a surprised Orla. Embarrassed at catching him in a state of undress, she blushed and looked at the floor as she addressed him.

"I… I was hoping you and I could have a little chat?"

"What about?"

"Something important," she said, still staring at the floor. "Er, could you make yourself decent?"

"Sure. Come inside." He closed the door and buttoned up his shirt. "So, what can I do for ye?"

"I can't believe I'm about to ask this," she said, pacing the room like a caged animal.

Orla felt sick whenever she thought about the consequences of revealing sensitive information. Boocka had warned everyone not to trust Hudson, and here she was ready to do the opposite.

"It was a mistake to come here," she cried, trying to open the cabin door and escape.

Hudson looked befuddled as he slowly guided her into the centre of the room.

"Yer here now," he said gently. "Why don't ye tell me what the problem is?"

Spinning on the spot, hair flying wildly behind her, she wiped her brow and looked the captain straight in the eye.

"Do you remember what you said to me the night I came to your cabin?"

"Sure do; live yer own life, not someone else's. I meant every word."

Orla rolled her eyes. "Not that. The other thing."

"What other thing?"

"You must remember?" Orla said, aware of the desperation in her voice.

Hudson looked deep in thought. After a short pause, he folded his arms and then tilted his head to the side. "Refresh my memory."

There was a hint of devilment in his response. It took Orla a few seconds to realise he was toying with her. Perhaps, he enjoyed the fact she had come begging for help so soon after dismissing the chances of ever needing his assistance. Even so, she swallowed her pride, took a deep breath, and hoped Hudson was the forgive and forget type.

"You said if I ever needed help, I could come to you."

"Doesn't sound like something I would say."

"Knock it off," Orla blasted. "We're running out of time here. Can you help us or not?"

"Possibly," Hudson replied, pulling a cigar from his breast pocket, and taking a seat on top of the table. "I'd need to know what ye need help with for a start."

"We're looking for a priceless statue. It was made by King Seth Crestmore of Uthovaya."

"That's what this whole trek has been about? A statue?"

Orla urged him to focus as she explained further. "There's an inscription carved into the base. Coordinates to a tower hidden in the Tavara desert. It's of immense importance to us and the people of Uthovaya. I can't say any more than that."

Hudson looked sceptical, so Orla chose her next words carefully. Revealing Jacob's heritage to the captain would be a dangerous move. It was information he could use to his own advantage.

"I'm telling the truth," she insisted. "The statue was left on Charn, but it was then sold to the mayor of Rockwood. We believe he is dead and that a man named Jullien Merrick gained possession of the statue shortly after."

Hudson puffed away on his cigar, just watching Orla for what felt to her like an eternity.

"I've never had any dealings with Merrick," he admitted. "Dangerous guy by all accounts."

Orla rolled her eyes again. "Will you help us or not?"

"What do ye want me to do?"

"Get the statue back."

But Hudson was barely listening. Instead, he stared into space. Orla took a few steps forward and waved her hand to get his attention.

"Hello, anyone home?"

"I was miles away." Hudson laughed. "OK, leave it with me. I'll see what I can do. No promises, though."

"Is that it?"

Hudson nodded. "Shut the door on yer way out."

After following the captain's instructions, Orla stood alone in the passageway and tried to make sense of what had just happened. The captain had been so blasé about their need to find Seth's statue, she wondered if he had any intention of helping them. He had not shown much interest in her explanation, never mind her pleas. Maybe he was holding out for something in return.

She was still thinking about their exchange when she went looking for the others and found them holed up in Boocka and Jacob's cabin. Nobody had bothered to turn on the light, so all three sat in darkness, barely speaking to one another, and looking clueless on how to proceed.

"Where you been?" Boocka asked bluntly from a single seat in the corner of the room.

"I went to speak with Captain Hudson."

Jacob, who had been lying on the top bunk, suddenly sat upright. As did Kadesha from the bottom bunk.

"What did you want with him?" Jacob asked.

Orla paused. She had no idea how they would react to Hudson being brought into the loop, armed with information he was never supposed to have in what now seemed like a futile attempt to get him to help. She assumed their response would be negative but decided to come clean.

"I asked Hudson if he could help us get the statue."

"You did what?" Boocka hissed.

"How could you be so careless?" Jacob blasted. "Father Gambin said don't trust the wrong people. Hudson couldn't be anymore untrustworthy."

Orla steeled herself for more flak as she defended herself. "I stand by my decision."

"What if that no-good mercenary sells the information?" Boocka snapped.

"There isn't any information to sell. The Antantans will already know we're after the statue, and I didn't tell him Jacob is the rightful king, or what the coordinates on the statue would lead to."

Kadesha walked slowly up to Orla until their faces were inches away from each other.

"What about Operation Creeper?"

Orla shook her head. "I left that part out."

Kadesha breathed an obvious sigh of relief. "Well, that is something, I suppose."

But Boocka refused to back down. "I gotta sort this out," he said, marching towards the door.

"Sort what out?" said a familiar voice.

Orla swung around to find Captain Hudson leaning against the doorframe. He eyeballed Boocka, and then swaggered across the room to Orla.

"I know someone in Vala who should be able to help us get your statue," he announced confidently.

Orla could scarcely believe Hudson was agreeing to help them. He seemed so disinterested back in his cabin.

"Are we really gonna trust this man?" Boocka roared. "He's a liar, a thief, and most likely a murderer. Why would he do anything that benefits us?"

Hudson turned towards Boocka. "I want my money, and that can't happen unless Jay completes his mission and gets back home safely."

An uneasy silence took over the group. Orla desperately wanted to jump for joy at the possibility they could be back on track but knew the others had concerns. It was Kadesha who made the first move. She approached Hudson and held her hand out for him to shake, Boocka and Jacob looking on in stunned silence.

"If you could help us, we would be truly grateful."

Hudson's nodded response was subtle, barely noticeable unless someone was looking for it.

"I'll be coming along this time." Then, he turned and grinned at Boocka. "I bet yer excited about that."

Hudson departed the room, leaving Boocka seething, and Orla struggling to stifle a laugh.

Less than an hour later, Orla and the group, along with Hudson, arrived at Denizen town train station, intending to buy tickets for the train to Vala. Problems arose almost immediately when they learned the train no longer went as far as the capital. The station attendant explained there was not enough demand to justify putting on a train.

"Nobody wants to come to a place like this, and nobody can afford to leave," he admitted. "The furthest we go is Benjola."

"What now?" Jacob asked as the group gathered outside the station.

"We could travel by Gudhopper," Hudson suggested. "There's a depot in Benjola."

"What the hell's a Gudhopper?" Boocka asked Kadesha

"A Gudhopper is a large creature that was once a popular mode of transport. They became less common as technology improved and other forms of transport became available, though. I didn't know they were still in use."

"I'm not sure I like that," Boocka replied.

Orla noticed Hudson had another glint in his eye and wondered exactly what the cheeky merc was planning. It was fascinating to be in the presence of someone so dynamic. Hudson was probably used to thinking on the spot. How else could a merc escape all the dangerous situations they found themselves in?

"Don't worry." He winked as if he could see her thoughts. "It'll be an experience."

I bet it will.

They headed back in Rockwood's direction, but Orla could not help thinking about Coco and Devin as the train whizzed past the children's refuge centre. She had no doubt the kind volunteers would look after them, but what about their future? Would losing their parents and fight for survival scar them for the rest of their lives like it had Jacob?

Orla had been so obsessed with the suffering in Uthovaya; she had not considered people in other countries could suffer too. She felt like a veil had suddenly been lifted, allowing her a proper look at the injustice of the world. It was a world she felt ashamed to be part of, and one that needed fixing, if a fix was even possible.

They stepped off the train at Benjola station, right in front of a mother and father hugging their two children. The touching scene made Orla instantly think of her own parents. She missed them terribly. Her restlessness gave way to a sadness that proved difficult to hide as she and the others continued following Hudson to the Gudhopper Depot.

"Care to talk about it?" she heard Kadesha whisper.

"How did you know?" Orla replied in wonderment.

Kadesha slowed down and urged Orla to do the same. It was an obvious way to get some privacy.

"I know you and I haven't really spoken much, but I can still help."

There was something about Kadesha's friendly manner that made Orla want to confide in her, so she spoke freely about her recent thoughts.

"I'm starting to wonder if I've missed the bigger picture," she admitted.

"How do you mean?"

"I was so wrapped up in Uthovaya's political situation that I didn't realise just how horrible life can be in the wider world. Why did I bother striving to become a politician, when I could have helped those in need without being one?"

She took a deep breath as the answer to her own question hit hard.

"Vanity. I wanted it to be me who made the difference."

Kadesha took a moment before she spoke. "You cannot beat yourself up over this. Motives are rarely unselfish, even if we tell ourselves otherwise."

Orla let Kadesha's words sink-in. "Then, I shouldn't feel bad?"

"Of course not. You can still help those in need, even if your reasons aren't entirely selfless."

"But how? Uthovaya already has its saviour waiting in the wings. I look at the suffering in Rockwood, those poor kids, and think who is on a mission to help them? Then there's the poverty everywhere else. It's just as bad here, if not worse than what we see in Uthovaya."

They walked in baby steps now, the others getting further and further away.

"You cannot help everyone in need," Kadesha explained in a soft voice. "That is the sad reality of the world we live in. There is too much bad and not enough good."

"It shouldn't be that way."

Kadesha responded with a sigh. "No, it should not,"

The others had realised they were far away now and were calling on them to hurry up.

"Are you going to be OK?" Kadesha asked.

Orla was unsure if she could answer Kadesha's question. There were too many emotions swirling around her mind. She needed to re-evaluate her goals in life, do what should have been done in the first place: help the less fortunate in a more direct manner.

The Uthovayans would flourish under Jacob's rule, so Orla knew she was needed elsewhere. Her developing feelings for him would only get stronger, but telling him the truth would surely lead to rejection and embarrassment. Why ruin their beautiful friendship? No, it was far better to start afresh, she told herself.

"I will be OK now," she said, suddenly feeling optimistic about her future.

After re-joining the others, the Gudhopper Depot came into view. Made entirely of wood, the building was a complete circle stabilised by support bars driven deep into the ground. The thatched roof had seen better days, and the front door hung off its hinges.

The depot looked much the same inside. Several wind chimes hung from the ceiling, and because the front door could not be closed, they made a never-ending, but less-than-melodious jingle. A large aquarium took up the entire left-hand wall, but the tank was empty and smashed, with a dirty and damaged carpet offering hints at where the water went. There were two female members of staff behind a worn-out counter, wearing blue and grey uniforms and straw hats. The one on the right had a nametag that said Kathryn, while the other one was named Idris. Kathryn looked a million miles away, but Idris smiled at the group as they made their approach.

"Hi. How can I assist you today?" she asked in a polite and friendly manner.

"We're looking for passage to Vala," Hudson replied.

"OK, sir." She disappeared under the counter, and then re-appeared with a large white folder and a pencil. "Number of passengers?"

"Five."

"No problem," she said, writing the information down in the folder. "That will be 20 nova, please."

All eyes turned to Kadesha, who paid the fee with the ever-dwindling allowance given to them by Ryker and Bellis. Idris took the money, placed it inside a drawer under the counter, and then turned to the other staff member.

"Can you take our customers to the stables, please, Kathryn?"

Kathryn barely mustered a grunt in response. Looking a little embarrassed, Idris turned back to the group and laughed nervously.

"Kathryn is new here. I'm training her up, you see."

"Ah," the group replied in unison.

"Why don't I take you round to the stables?"

There were two stables at the back, both made from a heavy metal. Idris pointed to a rectangular platform and explained how it was a launch point for the Gudhoppers.

"Are these things safe?" Jacob enquired.

"Things?" Idris snorted, her look of horror obvious. "The Gudhopper is not a thing. She is one of the most beautiful creatures in the world. Standing at over 40 feet tall when upright, but as fast as anyone could imagine."

Orla shot Jacob a look, and he responded by holding his hands up to signal acknowledgement for his poor choice of words.

"Sorry," he whispered sheepishly.

Idris continued, "The Gudhopper was once the most exotic form of transport in Pavelle. Too expensive for anyone but nobility, a ride on the Gudhopper was nothing but a pipe dream for commoners. That all changed around fifty years ago when they became affordable for the masses."

"Why did they become affordable?" Orla asked.

"More efficient methods of transport became available. Suddenly the upper class could travel in luxury. Even common folk had options."

Idris flicked a switch beside one of the stables, and the door slid upwards, allowing a blue-tinted, smooth-skinned creature to toddle out on all fours. Orla could only marvel at the creature's beauty.

"Meet Rochana." Idris beamed. "She has muscular hind legs to help with jumping vast distances and a long thick tail to help with balance. Both feet have padded soles to prevent shock damage when landing on rough terrain."

As Rochana traipsed forward, she swung her massive head towards the group, letting off a loud roar as if saying hello. Then the creature lay on her stomach with all four legs spread out, inviting the group to climb onto her back, where Orla noticed a see-through bubble inside, with restraints set for five people.

"Oh, before I forget…" Idris rummaged around in her pocket and produced five red pills. "You'll all need to take one of these."

"What are they?" Boocka asked, eyeing the pills with suspicion.

"Stabilisers."

"Why do we need stabilisers?"

"You'll have a very unpleasant experience without them. The Gudhopper covers vast distances with a single leap. Stabilisers suppress the sensation of movement, so you won't get sick or feel dizzy."

"Good enough for me," Hudson laughed. He stepped forward and threw a pill down his throat.

Boocka faced Kadesha. "Well, I'm not taking one of them. You shouldn't either m'lady. They could be anything."

Idris insisted the pill was safe, but Boocka refused to entertain her assurances.

It took the combined efforts of Orla and Kadesha to make Boocka see sense and finally let Kadesha take the pill and have one himself. Each of the group took turns getting into position on the Gudhopper's back, and Idris strapped them in one by one. When the safety checks were completed, Idris coaxed Rochana onto the launch pad, bid the group goodbye, and wished them luck.

Lying on her front beside the others, Orla felt the sensation of being lifted into the air as Rochana stood on her hind legs and then burst from the launch pad, galloping across the fields at a speed that made Orla dizzy. The dizziness did not last long, and as the pills took effect, she was able to relax while Rochana leaped across rivers and towns, speeding towards their destination.

Chapter XIX

Veto's patience was wearing thin.

After failing to secure the statue at Rockwood, he had hit upon the idea of visiting the Pavellian Prime Minister to see if the powerful leader could shed any light on the statue's whereabouts. What he had not banked on was the president's insistence that Gex go with him. Now, as they sat outside the PM's office in Vala, Veto wished he could be anywhere else but stuck beside Gex, who was staring straight ahead, rapping four fingers on the vacant chair beside him.

Every now and again, Veto caught him sneakily glancing over, as if looking for a reaction. This childish behaviour convinced Veto he was trying to be annoying on purpose. If he was being deliberately bothersome, his stupid plan was working.

Tap, Tap, Tap.

Don't say anything, Veto urged himself.

Tap, Tap, Tap.

Keep calm. He mustn't know it bothers you.

Tap, Tap, Tap.

The PM's secretary, a pretty Human with glasses and dark hair, coughed to get their attention and then smiled when they looked over. Veto was glad for the distraction.

"The prime minister won't be long. His meeting has run later than expected." Both nodded in response.

"Would you like some refreshments in the meantime?"

"We're fine." Gex barked. "Just the PM will do."

Veto thanked the lady for her offer. He was deeply embarrassed at his superior's response, no doubt fuelled by Gex's hatred of so-called common people. The Vice-President made no secret of his disdain for the lower classes; having to speak with a lowly secretary would be crushing his soul. It was an abhorrent and arrogant attitude. Veto's mother was a seamstress and his father a factory worker. He had met people from all walks of life while serving in the Antantan army. Veto had little time for elitism.

"This is intolerable," Gex moaned as they sat back on the chairs.

"What do you suggest we do, give up on the Lost ElmKey completely?"

"Of course not." Gex fired back. "I just cannot be bothered hanging around here."

Veto knew there was no point in conversing further. It was times like these that convinced him Gex should never have been appointed Vice-President. His negotiation skills were non-existent, and he lacked the imagination to change his strategy. Threats, intimidation, and violence were all he knew. Unlike Gex, Veto was smart enough to know when a softer approach was required.

Not that he had used a soft approach back on Charn. Torturing Father Gambin to learn Jacob and Kadesha's next destination was essential. The man of the cloth had proved surprisingly tough but eventually even he gave up and spilled his guts. Afterwards, Gex wanted every colonist executed. Veto had argued against the decision because, unlike the terrorists being groomed at the Dance for Liberty, the Dakew colonists posed no threat and were being murdered solely because of Gexs' prejudice. Despite Veto's pleas, his superior refused to budge, and the islanders were executed by firing squad and then buried in a shallow grave.

"Excuse me?" Gex shouted to the secretary, still sounding exasperated at all the waiting around.

"Be with you in a moment." she smiled, before going back to a conversation she was having on a communicator.

Suddenly, Gex leapt up, leaned over the desk, and snatched the communicator from the secretary's hand.

"She will call you back." he told the stranger on the opposite end.

Then he turned the communicator off and tossed it back to the secretary.

"Are you planning on keeping us waiting all day?" he raged.

"Sir, as I've already told you, the prime minister is in a very important meeting and cannot be disturbed."

"That is not our problem. Call him out right now or I will go in and get him myself."

"I wouldn't do that, sir. Our security team is programmed to shoot on sight."

The words had barely left her mouth when two cybernetic soldiers blundered their way over to the desk, aiming cyber-rifles at Gex and Veto. Their vacant expressions, pupilless eyes, and bald, scaly, scarred heads creeped Veto out. There was something about the way they moved, too; It was…. unnatural.

"Step away from the desk." one of the soldiers ordered, in a voice that sounded like a mixture of lizard and machine.

There was a buzzing noise from the intercom, and then they heard the prime minister instructing his secretary to show the visitors into his office. She responded by sending the soldiers away and using her keycard to open double doors that led into the PM's office. It was spacious, filled to the brim with paintings and statues of the prime minister. All four walls were emblazoned with campaign posters and on the grey desk was a photo of him holding an ugly baby. Behind the desk sat the man himself, short and barrel shaped and gazing at them over the top of a noticeable wart on his nose.

"Let me do the talking." Gex whispered, a little too loudly.

"Fine, but don't screw this up."

The ginger haired Pavellian did not extend a hand to greet them, nor did he get out of his large black swivel-chair. Instead, he ordered his secretary out of the room and asked both men to take a seat.

Veto studied the prime minister with the intention of spotting a weakness. His record in power made it clear this was not an incompetent man. In the fifteen years since his election, Prime Minister Nelson Colmer had ended the long Pavellian recession that saw its reputation as a superpower take a serious battering. He had also brokered an arms deal that sold weapons to Byglonish rebels fighting against their Minturon masters. It was a long and bloody war that had only recently been the subject of a ceasefire. The PM was a man who could get things done.

"Gentlemen." He said in an obviously unfriendly tone. "I trust you are here to offer an explanation for the events at Rockwood?"

Veto looked at Gex in confusion.

"Explanation?" Gex parroted.

"Your president sent troops into Rockwood without authorisation, a move that indicates he no longer views Pavelle as an ally, but as a nation he can bully."

Veto could understand the PM's frustration. He had broached the subject of authorisation to Gex before they entered Pavellian airspace but as usual the Vice-President had outright dismissed his concerns. Now, they would need to placate the clearly miffed PM before they could ask for his help – something Gex would likely be incapable of doing.

"I suggest you voice your complaints to the President." Gex said. "We could not wait for permission on this occasion. This is a matter of national security, so I assure you we had no other choice."

The PM looked less than impressed at the response. "I assure you I will speak with the President as soon as possible."

"Good, then maybe we can get back to why we are here?"

"Give me the details." He replied sharply.

Gex grinned. "With pleasure. An important artefact has ended up on Pavellian soil. An artefact we desperately need to stop an uprising in Uthovaya."

"And this artefact is in Rockwood?"

Gex nodded. "It was bought by the mayor of Rockwood. A priceless statue with numbers inscribed on it. We found evidence it was kept in the town hall but its whereabouts are currently unknown, along with the mayor."

"What happened to the town?" Veto asked.

The PM now had a concerned look on his face. "The details are being kept under wraps by Jullien Merrick."

"The prime baron?"

"Yes. When his company discovered Prime underneath the town, we turned a blind eye to anything that happened after that. Even the government cannot touch Merrick. But given his interest in art, it's possible he has your statue."

Veto turned to Gex. "It's time we paid Julien Merrick a visit."

The PM shook his head and countered, "If he does have the statue, he won't just hand it over."

"Can't you pull some strings?" Gex pressed.

"Cross a man with Merrick's influence on the media? I cannot get involved. Not if I want to stay in power."

Veto could see his hopes of beating Jacob and the others to the statue starting to fade. The last thing he needed was another failure. The President would not be so forgiving this time around.

"So, there's nothing you can do?" Veto asked in disbelief

"I'm afraid not."

Gex stood up from his chair and urged Veto to do the same.

"Wait." The PM said meekly. "I might be able to locate the statue through unofficial channels. If my contact confirms Merrick has it, I will allow you to send in a small squad. No uniforms, no insignia. Nothing that can link back to this meeting. I will be in touch when I have the information."

Veto nodded and thanked him sincerely.

After leaving the PM's office, Veto felt quietly confident Merrick would have the statue in his possession and that they could somehow wrestle it from the prime baron's grasp.

"We'll need a squad on standby." Said Veto to his superior.

"Forget about that." Gex replied without breaking his stride. "This is a perfect opportunity to test our new division – The Phantoms."

"I thought The Phantoms hadn't finished training."

"I received word from the president this morning, they're ready to be deployed."

"Are you sure it's wise to use them at such a crucial time? It will be their first mission, after all. Maybe, it's best if I take a squad?"

"Nonsense." Gex replied flatly. "No one stands a chance against them. They have been trained well. The best-of-the-best. Soon the statue will be in our hands and any hope Kadesha and Jacob have of finding the Lost ElmKey will be dead in the water."

Chapter XX

Jacob did not know exactly how long they had been travelling for, but he guessed it was a good two hours at the very least. Being strapped to the back of an animal had proven even more uncomfortable than it sounded, and by the time Rochana had slowed to a crawl, he was itching to get his feet back on solid ground.

Jacob was first to disembark when Rochana came to a halt at the station. She lay on all fours beside the launch pad, allowing an elderly man with one eye to unfasten their restraints and lead the group safely to the ground.

"Good evening, my friends. I trust your journey was comfortable?"

"Very much so," Kadesha replied. "It has always been a dream of mine to travel by Gudhopper."

A smile spread across the man's face. "We're sure proud of them. Particularly, Rochana. She's the eldest dontcha know?"

"Fascinating," Kadesha remarked.

Jacob left them talking and made his way over to Orla. He had noticed she seemed quiet since they left the Rad Veteran.

"You seem a little distracted," Jacob said gently. "Everything OK?"

"I'm fine," she insisted, playfully punching his arm. "Anyway, we've got bigger things to worry about right now."

"I guess so," Jacob replied, although his suspicions remained.

As soon as Kadesha had finished talking to the man with one eye, they made their way onto the bustling streets of Vala. Jacob marvelled at the size of the buildings, massive skyscrapers ascending to the stars, and towers with windows so large he could make out office workers going about their business. He had never seen so many Fast-Wheels and fancy cars, some traditional and others hovering above the road. It was like peering into the future.

"This is all wrong," Orla said to no one in particular.

"What?" Jacob asked.

"The difference in living standards between Vala and Denizen is obscene."

Boocka said, "Never mind all that now. Remember, Bellis called and said the Shadow-Flare is here. Keep your eyes peeled."

"Will you relax?" Jacob countered. "It's not like they're going to stumble across us."

"How do you know? The authorities could be looking for us as we speak,"

Hudson said. "As much as I hate to agree with Ol Mr. Paranoid, this time he's right. We can't travel through the main streets. They're far too open."

Taking a sharp turn into an alleyway, they found a young Pavellian boy standing beside two quadruped reptiles who were fast asleep. He had harnessed both to an old wagon with ripped seats. The dishevelled boy wore a crumpled white t-shirt, brown trousers, and a dirty brown cap, and was standing behind an upturned box with a sign marked, "Pay Here for Travel."

"Hey," he called to the group as they hurried past. "Hey, you guys."

"Just keep walking," Hudson ordered.

"Why walk when you can travel in style?" the boy shouted back with a confident tone.

Jacob thought the boy sounded like someone who sold newspapers. He was half-expecting him to shout, "Extra, Extra, read all about it."

Kadesha was first to stop and approach him. "Do you live around here, young man?"

"Do I look like I live here? I stay in Quideel, a small town outside the city." He pointed at the sleeping reptiles. "And these two Micadillo are my pets. They can carry you anywhere in the city for a nominal fee."

Kadesha smiled. "Is that so?"

"It sure is, lady. I guarantee to get you there swiftly and safely, and I've never had no complaints. Ask any of my customers."

"Who are your customers?" Orla piped up.

"Those who can't afford to pay the steep public transport prices, but now and again, I get customers like you."

Jacob exchanged a confused glance with Orla.

"What do you mean, customers like us?" he asked.

"You know what I mean," said the boy, looking around to ensure no one was listening, "those who want to keep a low profile."

Boocka said, "What makes you think we're keeping a low profile?"

"I don't know. A hunch, I guess. Now, wadya say we get down to business?"

Jacob turned to the others. "It makes sense. Be quicker than travelling on foot."

Hudson shrugged his shoulders. "As long as he keeps to the back streets, I don't see a problem."

The boy jumped excitedly. "I guarantee you won't regret this. Now whereabouts are you going?"

"Do ye know Fagan's?" Hudson asked.

"Pub on the eastside? Yeah, I know it. Hop into the cart, and we'll be on our way."

"How much?" Kadesha asked, getting the funds ready.

"Five nova."

When she handed over the coin, he placed the money in a small bag, and they all climbed onto the mount.

"Is everyone aboard?"

"We're ready," came the group's response.

"Then hold on to your hats."

He had barely finished speaking when the reptiles took off. Jacob felt his stomach churn immediately. He could have done with more motion pills from the Gudhopper Depot. The Micadillo pulled them through the backstreets, only venturing onto the main streets when needed.

Twenty minutes later, the Micadillo brought the cart to a halt outside Fagan's. Jacob spotted a tough-looking Snarkeen at the front door. He had scars all over his face, and gaps in his mouth where his teeth had once been. After thanking the boy, they exited the cart and made their way over to the pub entrance. The Snarkeen greeted them with a look of suspicion but reluctantly allowed them to enter the pub.

It was smoky inside, no doubt the result of four or five regulars puffing on pipes in the corner. The bar started near the entrance and wound away round the side of the room to a smaller enclosed area. Animal heads hung on the walls, and the floor was stained and sticky.

Orla screwed her face up. "This place isn't very clean."

The barman overheard and snapped, "If you're not happy, then go someplace else."

Jacob feared trouble was about to kick off, but the situation cooled when Hudson approached the barman with a wide grin.

"Be careful with her, Fagan. She's tougher than she looks."

"Do my eyes deceive me?" Fagan exclaimed. "Zach Hudson, standing in my bar. I heard you'd been killed in Jandalgine."

"Worried I couldn't pay my tab, eh?" Hudson replied, pushing fifty nova across the bar.

Fagan laughed as he counted the money and then put it away. "So, what brings a rotten, no good seadog like you back to Vala?"

"Junt Kidd," Hudson replied. "Know where he is?"

The barman narrowed his eyes. "Wadya want with Junt?"

"Let's just say he owes me."

"Ha, who doesn't Junt owe? He doesn't come in here much now. Last I heard he was living in some big house up west."

"You got an address?"

"No, but there's someone who can get it. One of his boy's drinks in here. Usually, appears around an hour before closing."

"We'll wait then," Hudson replied.

"As long as you buy drinks, I don't care what you do."

Fagan disappeared to serve another customer, leaving the others standing at the bar.

"So, what now?" Jacob asked. "We just hang around until this friend of Junt's comes in?"

"Got it in one, Jay," Hudson teased. "Let's grab ourselves a cold one and relax."

Kadesha found a table, while Hudson bought drinks. Jacob saw his chance to speak with Orla in private, find out why she had suddenly clammed up. Was she still unwell, or had something else happened to make her so distracted?

"Can I talk to you?" he asked Orla as she sat with the others.

"Uh-oh, sounds serious."

"It is serious."

"Oh. What's up?"

"Not here."

He coaxed her to a separate table where they both sat across from one another.

"Our company not good enough?" Hudson joked from across the other side of the bar.

"Clearly not," Jacob snapped.

Orla tapped him gently on the arm. "That's a bit harsh."

"Sorry, but we're trying to keep a low profile, and he's shouting in the middle of the pub."

"He's only having a laugh. Remember, if it wasn't for Hudson, we would still be on the Rad Veteran, scratching our heads."

"I know. Forget about him for a second. How are you feeling?"

"OK, I guess. Apart from missing my parents and having my eyes well and truly opened."

"Your eyes opened to what?" Jacob asked, reaching across the table to hold her hand

She pulled it away immediately and then leaned back in her chair. The swiftness of her reaction shocked him.

"What's wrong?"

"Nothing, I…it's just…nothing."

"It's obviously something."

"Please can we change the subject? How are you feeling?"

Jacob shook his head. "Never mind how I'm feeling. There's something you're not telling me."

An awkward silence lasted much longer than Jacob could stand, but finally, Orla leaned forward and accepted his outstretched hand, forcing a look that barely qualified as a smile.

"I felt a bit out-of-sorts after we met those kids back in Rockwood," she admitted.

"Yeah. Those poor kids."

"Not just those kids. The other kids in Pavelle, too. Look at the boy who brought us here? That's no life for a child. It got me thinking about a future away from the Capital. Somewhere I can really make a difference."

Jacob was surprised his best friend was planning to leave the country without helping him turn things around.

"But what about the people of Uthovaya?"

"There was a time when I thought of nothing else, but that time has passed."

Jacob was confused, so he shrugged his shoulders and gave her a wide-eyed stare, hoping she would get the hint and explain further.

"I was jealous of you," Orla blurted out, much to his surprise.

"Jealous of me?" He tried to contain his laughter. "Nobody could possibly be jealous of me."

Orla's chuckled response seemed forced. "You have to understand how much of a shock it was when I learned your real identity."

"A shock for you?" Jacob interrupted, shooting her a look of hard scepticism.

Orla chuckled for real this time. "OK, that sounded selfish, and don't get me wrong, I'm glad you learned the truth about your parents, but your fight was supposed to be my fight."

Jacob took half-a-second to understand what she meant. "You're talking about your university dreams, right?"

"Yes and no," Orla admitted. "I've realised those dreams were more about my own personal glory. Uthovaya is going to be in great hands when you become king. You won't need me hanging about. I've got to find those who do need my help, even if the thought of leaving you behind makes my heart break."

Jacob swallowed hard, took her hand, and leaned in close enough to see his reflection in her eyes. He felt her hot, sweet breath on his face.

"Then stay with me," he whispered.

"I can't do that," she replied.

"Why?"

"Because it wouldn't be right."

"What wouldn't be right"

Orla squirmed in her seat and struggled to make eye contact. She seemed embarrassed, or at the very least, unable to confide something important to him.

"Just forget I said anything," she said firmly.

"No, you're hiding something from me. Tell me what's wrong so we can work it out. Then you can stay and help me be the king Uthovaya needs."

"You already *are* the king Uthovaya needs," she said, flashing a smile. "And do you know why?"

He shook his head.

"Because you are Jacob Crestmore."

Hudson interrupted them by asking if they wanted another drink, so Jacob leaned back to process everything he and Orla had spoken about. There had to be a way to keep her in the Capital. She was no longer just his best friend. There was something more. He was sure of it now, even if Orla showed no interest in anything other than friendship.

"Let's go join the others," he insisted.

Although Jacob had plenty on his mind, he enjoyed himself in the pub, having a laugh with the locals and letting his hair down. It was a rare opportunity for everyone to relax, free from the worry of such an important mission. Finally, the man who knew Junt's address appeared. Hudson spoke with him privately upstairs. When the captain finally came back down to the bar, he had persuaded the man to take them to his boss.

Junt's place was a plush house on the corner of a fancy street. There was a Bondurian guard stood outside, trying, and failing to keep an automatic rifle out of sight. His stony expression did not change as Jacob and the others followed Hudson towards him. Like every Bondurian male, his skin was rough and a royal blue colour.

"What kind of person needs a guard outside their front door?" Jacob asked Hudson.

"Junt has more reason than most to keep himself protected. He once broke into the Antantan's most secure military base, stole secrets, and then sold them."

"I heard about that," Jacob noted. "It was Viper's Fist who rescued him from a prison bus and saved him from being executed?"

"That's a touchy subject," Hudson replied, marching up to the Bondurian guard. "Am looking for yer boss."

"He's not taking callers right now. Come back later."

Jacob watched Hudson to see how he would react.

"It's important," Hudson explained.

The guard shook his head and then repeated the line about his boss not accepting callers. Hudson nodded and then started to shout Junt's name repeatedly, much to the guard's annoyance.

"Shut your mouth," the guard raged, his finger twitching on the trigger of his automatic rifle.

"Tell him Captain Hudson's here to see him."

"I told you he's not accepting callers."

Jacob noticed Hudson reach for his weapon, but Orla stepped in and calmed the situation before issuing the guard with an ultimatum.

"If you don't get your boss out here, my friends will keep making a scene," she warned, turning to Jacob and the others, urging them to join her in a chorus of Junt's name.

Their rabble-rousing only lasted a few seconds before the guard reluctantly opened the door and called for his boss.

"What is it?" came a low voice from somewhere inside.

"There's a Captain Hudson here to see you, sir."

No response.

"What shall I do, sir? Him and his friends aren't taking no for an answer."

"Send them in."

The group trudged inside, up the hall, and into the main room of the house. It was a poorly lit room, but Jacob could make out the outline of a Snarkeen sitting on an overstuffed chair. He wore a black jacket with wavy red lines, and his grey t-shirt was tucked inside a pair of tight, dark trousers.

As soon as they stood in front of him, the door closed with a thud, and the room filled with light, revealing a quaint living space with a ripped purple carpet. Above the seated figure were two crossed swords inside a golden frame.

"Well, this is a surprise!" the Snarkeen exclaimed.

"Hello, Junt," Hudson replied.

"What can I do for you?"

"Got a problem I was hoping ye could help me out with. We're trying to find a priceless statue. It may have fallen into Jullien Merrick's hands."

Jacob saw Junt's expression change at the mention of Merrick's name.

"What is it with everyone and this statue?" he moaned.

Jacob wondered what he meant, but Hudson beat him to the punch by demanding an explanation for his off-the-cuff remark.

"You're not the first to ask for my help on this," Junt admitted.

"The Antantans?" Hudson confirmed quickly.

Junt nodded. "A friend of mine got in touch a few hours ago, said the Pavellian government were looking for information on a statue that Merrick might have. When I pressed him further, he admitted the Antantans were also involved."

"Is this friend reliable?"

"He's never been wrong. I put my ear to the ground and learned the statue was indeed taken from the mayor of Rockwood's office by one of Merrick's lackeys. It was then passed onto the baron himself."

Jacob interrupted. "We need your help getting that statue back,"

Junt roared with laughter. "Gathering information is one thing but breaking into Merrick's mansion and stealing from him is another."

Orla pointed an angry finger in the Snarkeen's direction and growled, "So, you're a coward?"

"I'm no coward, sweetheart. I'm one of the most dynamic individuals in this country. Look around you; I'm the only Snarkeen who isn't working a dead-end job, or had my brain sucked out to become one of those mindless Cybernetic soldiers. You think that's an accident? I'm useful, and those at the top know all too well how much of an asset I can be."

"So why won't you help us?" Orla shot back.

"Because I don't have a death wish. You'll have to find someone else to do your dirty work."

Hudson stepped forward. "You owe me big time, Junt. If it wasn't for the Fists, ye'd have been hung in front of a baying mob of Antantans. We risked our lives to spring you from that prison bus."

"You were well paid."

"But we wasn't, was we? Not compared to the money you made selling secrets from Goldfront Military Base."

"That's not my problem. You shook on the deal with my associates."

Hudson looked deep in thought for a moment. "Then maybe I'll take you to the Antantan authorities. I'm sure they would love a reunion with the man who's still selling their military secrets."

"You wouldn't."

"Try me."

Junt sighed loudly. "OK, OK, I get the picture. Merrick's having a party tomorrow night. I'll think of a way to get you in."

"Good man."

"We'll need to be careful, though. The Antantans are planning on stealing the statue at the exact same party. In fact, I've heard they're sending in the heavy team. Some special unit known as the Phantoms."

Chapter XXI

Standing in front of Junt's full-length mirror, Jacob could hear Orla sniggering at his attire from the other side of the room. Not that he blamed her. Being dressed in a tailcoat with high-waisted trousers was bad enough but wearing a magician's top hat seemed like overkill. He had never felt so ridiculous as he huffed and puffed away from the mirror to throw himself down on a single padded chair.

"This doesn't feel right." he moaned, crossing his arms to show his displeasure.

Orla chuckled as she made her way over to the mirror. She looked like a goddess in her white, long V-neck dress with stiletto heels.

"You certainly have changed." She laughed. "First the food on Charn wasn't good enough, and now these clothes aren't to your fancy."

"Don't be silly," he shot back. "It looks ridiculous is all. Surely, I'm not expected to wear this out in public?"

"I'm afraid you are."

"Even the magician's hat?"

"Especially the magician's hat." She grinned.

Kadesha came into the room, took one look at Jacob, and then noticeably stifled a laugh.

"Have you finished?" he asked, half-joking, half-serious.

Kadesha let out a chuckle. "Yes, I have now. Thank you."

"You won't be laughing when this suit gives me away at Junt's party. I can't pull the posh look off."

"Nonsense," Orla replied, rubbing dust off his hat. "I have every faith you'll work your magic."

Kadesha and Orla burst out laughing at the same time.

"You're both enjoying this a little too much. If I didn't know any better, I'd say this was a set-up."

A heavy slap on the back almost sent him flying, and he turned to find Boocka giving him the once over. He too, looked ready to melt into fits of hysterical laughter.

"Relax," the Krokiran snorted. "Do you think we'd endanger the mission just to make you look ridiculous?"

Boocka's comment got Jacob thinking about the mission in question. Jullien Merrick was having a swanky party, so the plan was for Orla and Jacob to infiltrate the mansion disguised as a couple who owned an obscure museum. From there, they could give Boocka and Hudson access to recover the statue. It was a plan fraught with danger; one wrong move could jeopardise the entire mission and put them at serious risk.

"Are you ready yet?" Jacob called to Orla.

She twirled in front of the mirror and took a bow in front of an imaginary audience. Just when she seemed ready to step away, she locked herself in place for another admiring glance.

"I love this dress."

"Well, at least someone's happy with what they're wearing," said Jacob.

"Oh, shush," she laughed. "Can you hand me those fascinators over there?"

Jacob found three sitting alongside each other in the room's corner. He passed them to Orla, who tried each one about six times before settling on the third option, an elegant mesh number with ribbons and a feathery headband.

"This will be great," she said excitedly.

Great was not how Jacob would describe the challenge facing them. Stupid, maybe? But definitely not great. The only information they had on Merrick and his mansion came from Junt and his extensive network of contacts, but what assurances did they have he was telling the truth? They barely trusted Captain Hudson, never mind the Snarkeen he recommended to hatch this risky plan.

Making matters worse, the stories about Merrick made Jacob uneasy. He was apparently an art lover who had a penchant for living the highlife. A brilliant businessman, he made a living buying and selling paintings, then struck lucky when he inherited land bursting with prime. He could turn on the charm when required but had a ruthless streak, never hesitating to destroy anyone who crossed him.

Junt had shown the group an article with quotes from Merrick's former butler, in which the ex-employee alleged his boss liked to indulge in sick and twisted torture sessions inside his mansion. The irate Merrick then sued the newspaper, causing it to fold with the loss of two hundred jobs. Merrick's heavy-handed actions meant his business rivals were subject to intense scrutiny, while he himself escaped it. More than once, journalists had been accused of hacking communicators on his say so. Merrick was a dangerous man, indeed.

Captain Hudson appeared, his confident stride attracting everyone's attention as he powered to the centre of the room. He took one glance at Jacob's head attire and then craned his neck in a jokey attempt at sizing up the top hat.

"Not you as well?" Jacob replied, folding his arms in disgust.

Hudson ignored the comment and then rubbed his hands together.

"Listen up," he ordered. "We're going over the plan for getting in and out one more time."

Orla rolled her eyes. "We've been over this plan a million times already. Jacob and I are Donovan and Liszla Endolmen, husband and wife owners of Uthovaya's smallest museum. We mingle with the other guests for a while, eat some food, have a drink, and then Jacob disables the door alarms."

Hudson nodded. "Letting me and Boocka sneak in through the Generator Room."

"Where you'll make your way to the bottom floor," Orla continued. "Jacob and I will meet you down there. We find the statue, and then make our escape outside to Junt and Lady Kadesha, who will be waiting in a getaway truck with our weapons."

She did a little jig to celebrate knowing the plan by heart.

But Jacob was concerned. "Are you sure we won't get busted doing this? I hate to rain on the parade, but none of us knows anything about art. What if someone asks questions?"

"Improvise," Hudson said flatly. "Ye have brains, right? Use em?"

"Great." Jacob whispered to Orla, "We're in more trouble than I thought."

A noise startled them, but it was only Junt coming into the planning room. He made his way over to the centre table and laid out a crumpled set of blueprints. Jacob looked closer as Junt smoothed out the edges. It appeared to be a complete layout of Merrick's mansion. There were two floors above ground level and three below.

"Listen up, Jacob. You need to get here," he said, jabbing at the paper with his clawed right hand. "As long as you make it to this room without anyone seeing you, there should only be one guard guarding the room. He'll be armed with a compact pistol and a telescopic baton. Take him out, and you'll have access to the alarm controls on the terminal."

Jacob peered closer to the plans. "The guard might be a problem."

"Hudson said you're a hunter. I'm sure you can handle it,"

"Can I take my staff?"

"There's nowhere to conceal a weapon. Merrick's men will search you at the front door. Me and Kadesha will bring you and Orla's clothes and weapons when we come pick you up in the truck"

Lady Kadesha had not spoken since they started going over the plan, but she made her way over and tapped Junt on the shoulder. The Snarkeen looked annoyed at the interruption as he turned to face her.

"Problem?" he grunted.

"Your plan sounds risky. I don't want the boy put in danger."

"Your boy is breaking into Jullien Merrick's mansion. Danger comes with the territory."

Kadesha shook her head. "We will find another way."

"There isn't another way."

Jacob urged them both to stop. The last thing they needed was to waste time thinking up another plan. Not with the Antantans circling around the statue as well. He would find a way to take the guard out, no matter what it took.

"I'll be OK," he insisted, hoping Kadesha could not see through the lie as it left his lips.

"I do not like this," Kadesha said, turning to Jacob. "But, I promise we will send in the cavalry if Merrick captures you."

"Can we get on with this now?" Junt asked impatiently. "Once you've dealt with the guard, go onto the terminal and use this." He handed Jacob a small, blue microchip. "It will disable all alarms and give you access to the network. Don't forget to unlock the doors, too. You'll find the controls in a folder marked Miscellanea."

"Where am I supposed to hide the microchip?"

"Under your tongue," Junt replied, sticking his own forked tongue out.

"Wait, a minute," Boocka piped up, approaching Junt aggressively and eyeballing Hudson at the same time. "How will we know when the alarms are down?"

Junt took a deep breath. "There's a blue light at the top of the generator room door. When it turns off, that's your signal to go. There will be guards, so watch yourselves. Remember, Merrick has a collection of storage rooms for his artwork. The statue will be in one of them." He handed Hudson a piece of paper with a series of numbers written on them. "Some doors will be keypad-protected. These are the correct codes in order of the doors you'll encounter."

Jacob was impressed by Junt's thoroughness. Hudson's decision to involve his old friend was looking like a stroke of genius. Assuming the information was accurate, and he was trustworthy, of course.

"Remember, you only get one shot at this," Junt said, turning his attention back to Jacob and Orla. "If anyone suspects you're not who you say you are…"

"Game over," Jacob finished.

As everyone chatted amongst themselves, Jacob wandered to the corner of the room, closed his eyes, and took deep, calming breaths. The mission to infiltrate Merrick's mansion was about more than gaining possession of the statue. It was also a chance to prove he could handle the pressure and responsibility associated with being a leader.

Jacob had always considered himself a follower, but that would change when he became king. Uthovaya needed a strong leader, and he was determined to give them one, even if the plan to reach the throne was fraught with danger. He was still contemplating those dangers when he and Orla arrived at the mansion and got a first-hand look at Merrick's tight security.

There were cameras with small guns monitoring every inch of the grounds, ready to open fire on anyone who deviated from the designated footpath that led to the front door. Guards stood to attention everywhere Jacob looked, all wearing bulletproof vests, navy caps, and dark sunglasses. They were armed with machine-guns and telescopic batons and communicated using light communicators stored in the breast pockets of their navy armoured jackets.

"Those guards look like they mean business," Jacob whispered as they casually walked towards the mansion.

Orla nodded while taking a quick peek in their direction. "You can bet Merrick hires the best security in the business."

"I keep thinking they're watching us," Jacob said, out the corner of his mouth.

"It's your imagination. Remember, eyes straight and keep walking."

"Easy for you to say. You're not wearing a magician's hat."

"There's nothing wrong with the hat," Orla snapped.

A series of crackles and pops from above stopped them in their tracks and drew their attention to the night sky, where a dazzling display of fireworks illuminated the mansion gardens.

"I could watch this all night," Orla admitted, taking Jacob's hand, and nuzzling into his shoulder.

As they watched in silent awe, Jacob wished the world around them would suddenly freeze, trapping them in the picturesque scene forever. He wanted to forget the infiltration mission, ignore the noisy fireworks drowning out his thoughts, and concentrate on the here and now with the woman he had fallen in love with. It was an all-too fleeting dream because right on cue, two guards passed by, reminding him of their dangerous predicament.

"Best to keep our mind on the job," he whispered. "The last thing we need is to get busted before we walk through the door."

Joining the end of the queue at the main entrance, the first thing Jacob noticed was a doorman with a clipboard, and a second one searching every guest before he allowed them to enter.

Showtime, thought Jacob, as he bowed his head and covertly pushed the microchip into his mouth and under his tongue.

"Do I sound normal?" he asked, Orla.

She nodded. "Let's hope Junt got our names on that list like he promised."

"We'll need to get outta here in a hurry if he hasn't."

"Not a chance in these heels."

A middle-aged Human doorman greeted them when they reached the front of the queue. He was at least twenty stone of solid muscle with a pug nose that had obviously taken quite a pounding over the years. He looked the sort of person who hated his job and wanted to be anywhere but standing on Merrick's doorstep.

"Names?" he barked.

"Donovan and Liszla Endolmen," Jacob replied, trying to sound calm and posh with a small microchip under his tongue.

The doorman grunted again and then flicked through the pages on his list, eyeing the fraudulent couple with a beady eye while he did so. His suspicious glances made Jacob fear the plan had been rumbled, but after a tense few minutes, the doorman pointed to Orla.

"You're first to be searched, ma'am."

Orla cautiously moved towards the searcher, an elderly Human male with fuzzy brown hair and a fresh scar across his right cheek. He was rough, thorough, and uncompromising, even shining a torch into Orla's mouth in his search for incriminating evidence. It was a move that panicked Jacob enough to feel like running away. He had to envisage his feet being planted in the ground to stop himself from grabbing Orla's hand and taking flight. All he could do was hope the searcher missed the microchip under his tongue. Or even better, not look there at all.

As soon as the searcher finished with Orla, he beckoned Jacob over and ordered him to spread his legs and hold his arms out.

"Take that ridiculous hat off," the searcher ordered.

Jacob flashed Orla a smug smile as he removed it.

Unimpressed with Jacob's antics, the searcher threw the hat on the ground and then patted him down, rifling through his pockets like a common thief.

"All clear?" Jacob asked, more in hope than anything else.

"Not yet," the searcher replied, flicking a button on his torch. "Open your mouth."

He froze on the spot. There was no time to escape if they got caught.

"Pardon?" he mumbled.

The searcher gave him an ice-cold stare. "I said, open your mouth."

As Jacob opened his mouth, and the searcher shone the torch inside, he waited for the order to lift his tongue. It never came. Instead, the searcher flicked the off switch and nodded to the doorman with the clipboard.

"He's clean."

"You can both go on through," the doorman said, trying to hand Jacob his hat back.

"Keep it," was his humour-filled reply.

The main hall was spectacular. Hundreds of guests had gathered on the black and white tiled floor, sipping champagne, and waiting for the host to appear on a balcony at the top of a wide flight of stairs. A red carpet ran up the steps in the centre of two diamond-encrusted bannisters. Jacob glanced around and marvelled at the collection of statues and artefacts littering the hall. He also saw beautiful paintings, crystal glass pieces, and even ancient pottery with complex illustrations of a time gone by. The world's largest diamond was the main attraction. It sat on top of a pedestal and was protected by red lasers capable of causing extreme damage to potential thieves.

"How much money does this guy have?" Orla breathed.

"He must be the richest man on the planet," Jacob whispered back.

Suddenly, Jacob felt someone crash into him, nearly knocking him to the floor in the process. As he steadied himself, he realised the culprit was a drunken Dakew.

SEAN CLARKE

She offered no apology and staggered away in the direction of the buffet.

"How rude," Orla said loudly.

"Don't say anything," Jacob begged. "We're supposed to be keeping a low profile."

She calmed down quickly, and Jacob breathed a sigh of relief his normally hot-headed friend had managed to control her temper. A waiter handed them a glass of champagne each, and they conversed between sips, trying to speak as posh as possible.

"Gooood eveeeening," Orla crowed in a ridiculously over the top, posh tone.

"That's not right," Jacob replied with a grin. "Let me try. Gooooooooooood eveeeeeening."

They burst into fits of laughter that only ended when the guests broke into a round of applause. Jullien Merrick had appeared above them on the balcony. He had piercing blue eyes, high cheekbones, and a shock of black hair.

Orla elbowed Jacob in the ribs.

"Ouch. What was that for?"

"I didn't expect him to be so…handsome."

"He's not handsome," Jacob scoffed, hoping Orla would be oblivious to the jealousy ripping out of him.

"Aw, are you feeling left out." Orla grinned and then pinched his nose. "Don't worry; Merrick isn't as handsome as you."

Jacob tutted and turned his attention back to the host who was raising a glass to his guests, as a burly looking assistant placed a microphone underneath his square chin.

"Good evening, ladies and gentlemen." He spoke in a soft, off-balance Pavellian accent. "It's an absolute pleasure to see you all here tonight."

Jacob and Orla joined the guests in another round of applause as he continued.

"I've hosted many of these parties, but tonight will be the best one yet. Enjoy yourselves and feast, not only on the tasty food but on the beautiful pieces in my collection as well."

A third round of applause greeted Merrick as he made his way down the steps into the thick of the action, where a flurry of well-wishers immediately swarmed him, desperate to speak with the man of the moment. Jacob struggled to comprehend how anyone with morals could wish to be friendly with the guy. Not if the stories about him were true, anyway.

Orla said, "He seems quite the gentleman."

Jacob shook his head and started towards a Remman wearing a tuxedo who was locked in conversation with a Human couple.

"What are you doing?" Orla whispered.

"I'm socializing. We have to act natural, remember?"

He waved his hand to the waiter, who immediately brought a tray of light snacks. Jacob and Orla munched on them while working the room, socialising with Dakew, Humans, Remmans, Bondurians, and other Mixlings. Jacob even saw a few Gogglos doing the rounds.

After half an hour of mingling, Jacob was satisfied they had socialized enough and started the process of finding a meeting point for when he returned from disabling the alarms – *If* he returned.

A large statue of a Stingtross did the trick. The predatory bird's large wingspan helped keep them partially hidden in the corner, giving Jacob time to work up the courage to move onto the next phase of the plan.

"Are you gonna do this or not?" Orla whispered as they stood underneath the right wing of the Stingtross.

"Don't rush me," he shot back, tapping his foot nervously.

Orla exhaled a breath. "Boocka and Captain Hudson will be in position by now."

"I'm going, I'm going."

"Be careful. Remember, the Antantans could be here."

"Well, if they are, I haven't seen them."

Orla laughed. "They wouldn't exactly announce themselves. Just keep your eyes peeled. "

"Ssshhh."

Jacob headed for the exit to the mansion hall but was stopped before he reached the door by the same rude lady who had bumped into him earlier.

"Do I know you from somewhere?" She slurred her words as she spoke. Clearly, the champagne had gone straight to her head.

Jacob rolled his eyes at the obvious conversation starter, but what could he do? He couldn't cause a scene, not here anyway. Hoping to slip away quickly, he gave the lady a courteous nod and tried to go around, but she anticipated his movements and blocked his path again.

"I said, I know you from somewhere."

"I don't think so," he said emphatically. "I don't go anywhere."

The lady threw her head back and laughed. It was an obnoxious effort that convinced the anxious Jacob she had alerted the entire room to his presence.

"I know I've seen you before because I never forget a face. My friends are forever telling me I'm wrong about these things, but I never am. So, tell me, whereabouts are you from?

"Well…"

"You're from up west, aren't you? That's where I'm from. Do you like it up there? I'm thinking about moving further down this way because sometimes it's nice to shake things up, don't you think?"

Jacob struggled to get a word in as the lady harped on. He glanced over to Orla, who was standing beside the statue with her arms folded, looking bemused. Fearing she would come over and make a scene, he bid the lady goodbye, but she cut him off once again by running a finger up and down his chest in a seductive manner.

"I see your wife's not with you," she whispered, the lust dripping from her voice. "Whadya say you and I find an empty room and get to know each other a little better?"

Jacob had no idea how to respond to the lady's advances. He was about to mumble the first thing that came to mind when he saw Orla approaching with an obviously fake smile.

"Excuse me," she said through gritted teeth. "Could I have my husband back for just a moment?"

The drunken lady apologised repeatedly and then staggered away to annoy someone else. Jacob breathed a huge sigh of relief and thanked Orla for coming to his aid.

"I didn't think she would ever leave."

"It's a good thing I came along when I did. She'd have dragged you off to her lair."

"Close call then?" he chuckled.

"You need to get to that computer terminal now. Boocka and Hudson will think something has gone wrong."

Jacob said nothing before he exited through the side door, keeping low to avoid detection. He found himself in a dimly lit hallway with a seating area and various large vases spread alongside both walls. The sound of chattering guards coming his way forced him to duck behind one. The guards passed without incident, continuing their conversation until Jacob could no longer hear what was said.

Moving into the next hallway, he passed a variety of locked rooms that no doubt held Merrick's secrets. Finally, he came to a silver door marked "Danger, Keep Out!"

One glance through the small round window confirmed the security guard Junt had told them about. He sat with his back to the door, amongst a hodgepodge of coloured monitors, multi-coloured wires, and discarded sweet wrappers.

Jacob spat the microchip into his hand and then placed it into his pocket. Taking deep breaths, he rapped on the door several times, forcing the sluggish guard to his feet. He spun around, angrily gesturing for Jacob to back away from the door. Jacob put a hand to his ear in response, hoping the guard would come closer.

With an annoyed scowl, the guard pulled the door open and started explaining that this was a restricted area. Jacob did not reply. He threw himself headfirst into the guard's stomach, pushing him backwards and slamming them both into the wall next to the terminal. The guard recovered quickly, and dug his right elbow into Jacob's upper back, dropping him to the floor in agony.

"Big mistake, boy," the guard bellowed, rolling Jacob over and driving a boot into his gut

The guard produced his compact pistol, but Jacob was way ahead, spinning on his back to kick the gun away. It hit the ground and skidded underneath the terminal. Still winded, Jacob bounced up, but the guard smacked him back down with a quick punch to the face.

"Stay there, boy."

The guard released his telescopic baton and slammed it towards Jacob. Agility learned from hunting allowed him to roll away at the last second. Jacob then jumped to his feet and speared the guard back into the wall, knocking him unconscious.

Jacob collapsed to the ground, struggling to get his breath back. There was no time for a rest, though; he could hear the familiar chatter of the guards making their way back along the hallway. Quickly, he crawled towards the door and closed it, hearing the locking mechanism click as he did so. He lay on the floor and listened until the guards passed by.

After a few minutes, he dragged himself towards the unconscious guard's gun, but it was lodged underneath the terminal and not budging anytime soon. He gave up and pulled the microchip from his pocket, pushing it into the terminal and then hunting for the folder named Miscellanea. Within two minutes, he had found it.

"Gotcha."

Chapter XXII

Satisfied he had done his job properly, and Boocka and Hudson could now sneak into the mansion to steal the statue, an out-of-breath Jacob stepped past the unconscious guard and hurried back to the busy hall where he expected to find Orla waiting patiently by the Stingtross statue. She was nowhere to be seen.

"Maybe, she's in the ladies' room," he whispered to himself, slightly unsure of his own theory.

He tried to remain calm beside the statue, his eyes darting around the room in search of Orla. There was still no sign of her twenty minutes later, and Jacob began to fear something was wrong. He did a quick sweep of the hall but returned to the statue without success. Next, he canvassed some other guests, enquiring if any had seen the young blonde he arrived at the party with, but none could remember Orla being there, let alone explain where she had gone.

What if Merrick or his men have captured her?

Taking a deep breath, Jacob sauntered through the guests to a position where he could see Merrick's balcony, suspended high above the hall. Sure enough, Orla was seated beside the prime baron, holding a glass of champagne, her head darting from side to side in obvious panic as she gazed down at Jacob and the other guests.

Jacob wracked his brains for a way to get Orla away from the deadly situation. He was panicking as well now, unable to think straight for worrying about Orla's safety. Someone tapped him on the shoulder, and he whirled around to find two burly, Human guards eyeballing him.

"Can you come with us, Mr. Endolmen?" one said.

"That depends," Jacob replied.

"On what?"

"On where you're taking me."

"It's not a request, Mr. Endolmen. Either you come with us voluntarily, or we will force you. It's your choice."

"Well, I guess I'd better come voluntarily then."

Jacob stayed quiet as the guards escorted him through the crowd of bewildered guests and up the steps towards the balcony, but his mind raced with horrible possibilities. Junt had planned the operation out perfectly, but at no point had they discussed a backup option if Merrick demanded they join him for drinks. The situation was getting more and more dangerous.

"Ah, Mr. Endolmen," Merrick said, waving his hands in the air excitedly. "Make yourself at home. Your good lady Liszla was just telling me all about you."

"Good things, I hope." Jacob smiled, taking a seat across from Merrick and Orla.

"Of course, old boy."

Merrick clicked his fingers, and a waiter scurried from nowhere with a glass of bubbly for Jacob.

"I hope you don't mind me bringing your lovely wife up here. She seemed so lost down there by herself."

Orla cleared her throat and turned to Jacob. "I told him you were feeling sick and had been in the bathroom for a while."

Her calculated lie took a second to register. "Ah, yes. I'm feeling better now."

Merrick chuckled. "Well, that's good news, at least. Mrs. Endolmen tells me you both run a small museum in Uthovaya?"

"It's great," Jacob replied. "Keeps us busy, doesn't it, darling?"

Orla coughed and then almost choked on her drink. "It sure does," she spluttered.

There was an awkward silence, leading Jacob to believe their plan had been uncovered. Merrick seemed to be sizing them up, trying to work out if they were genuine. Or maybe it was Jacob's imagination? This was crunch time for the plan. If Merrick asked no more awkward questions, they might just get away with it. The key would be short answers that got straight to the point, leaving as little room as possible for any follow-up questions.

"Are you enjoying the party?" Merrick asked.

"Very much so. You have some impressive pieces in your collection,"

Jacob wished he hadn't opened his mouth because Merrick started waxing lyrical about some of his rare finds, and his enthusiastic tone suggested he genuinely believed Jacob was a lover of rare pieces like himself and would love nothing more than some verbal ping pong on the subject. As he prattled on, Jacob faked a few laughs at his art-related jokes, hoping Merrick wouldn't ask if he knew any himself.

"Have a look at this," Merrick said, pointing to a painting on the faraway wall. "It's the most impressive piece in my entire collection, painted over 2000 years ago. It would have ended up in an art gallery in Antantis, had the owner not believed it was a fake. Thankfully, I knew better and paid next to nothing for it."

"That's amazing," Jacob replied.

Merrick looked pleased with the compliment. "Oh, stop it. Everyone in the art world knows that story. You don't need to pretend you have never heard it to impress me."

Bracing himself, Jacob stood up with his drink in hand and sauntered across to look at the painting of what looked like a giant robot towering over a small town. He had never seen or heard of it before, but he had to say something or risk blowing the whole charade.

"I recall reading about that," he lied, adopting a posh voice for effect. "Did the Antantans ever find out the truth?"

"They never did," Merrick replied, giving him a cheeky wink in the process. "More champagne?"

Jacob held his empty glass up. "That would be lovely."

Merrick clicked his fingers again, and the waiter left the room, returning a few moments later, carrying a silver tray with a bottle of expensive bubbly on top. Merrick ordered him to refill the glasses and then raised his own high in the air.

"A toast, to your wife's good health, Mr Endolmen."

Everyone chinked glasses together.

"So, Mr. Endolmen...."

"Please, call me Donovan."

"Donovan. I wonder if you remember a deal, we completed with your museum a few years back?"

Jacob glanced awkwardly towards Orla and guessed the look of blind panic on her face matched his own. Merrick seemed smug as he waited for a response.

Had he worked out the truth?

"Are you sure you're not thinking of another small museum in Uthovaya?" Orla asked feebly.

"No, I'm quite sure it was yours," Merrick replied in a low voice. "There only are two museums in Uthovaya: the national and Lydney House. I assume you own the latter."

"Er...yes. I trust the deal was well handled?" Jacob said, hoping to ride out the storm on a wave of ignorance.

"We had no complaints."

"I'd expect nothing less." Jacob gulped the entire glass of champagne down.

"Trouble is, I don't remember you," Merrick said. "The lady running the museum was a Mrs. Joltan, and her husband died ten years ago."

Jacob could feel Merrick's stare almost penetrate his body.

"We only took over last year," Orla piped up.

Jacob nodded. "Y-Yes, that's it. We only took over last year."

A third guard hurried into the room, cutting the conversation short. Jacob's sigh of relief only lasted a few seconds, until the guard informed Merrick he needed to speak with him urgently.

"Sir, there's been a disturbance downstairs. Two intruders have broken in."

Jacob remained silent, but he knew the guard was talking about Boocka and Hudson, who would now be on their way to recover the statue. He tried not to look in Merrick's direction, as though the very act itself could prevent their plan from coming undone.

"That is most unfortunate," Merrick said. "Deal with the problem quietly. I don't want the guests panicking."

"Understood, sir."

Orla stood up, and brazenly asked, "Anything we can do?"

"I think we've played this little charade long enough," Merrick said calmly. "Guards, seize them."

There was no time to react as one guard grabbed Orla from behind, wrestling her away from the chair towards the door.

244

"Let me go," Jacob heard Orla shout.

A second guard approached Jacob, holding his gun out just a little too far in front of him. The careless approach allowed Jacob to explode from his chair and throw his left arm out to knock the pistol out of the shocked guard's hand. As it skidded across the balcony floor, Jacob followed up with a swinging right hook that caught the guard square in the jaw and left him staggering backwards onto the sofa.

"Stop!" Orla's captor shouted to Jacob. He was pushing his gun into Orla's forehead. "Take one more step, and I'll blow her brains out."

Left with no choice, Jacob dropped the gun and raised both hands in the air. The floored guard bounced back to his feet, reclaimed the gun, and pistol-whipped his young adversary to the floor. Pain exploded through Jacob's head, and dizziness overtook him.

"Stop it!" Orla screamed, fighting to get free.

Merrick simply laughed. "Get him up."

Jacob felt himself being pulled back to his feet as Merrick looked on. He grabbed Jacob by the scruff of the neck and dragged him across the balcony to the painting he had earlier boasted about.

"This painting is worthless. My late mother bought it for me as a gift. She obviously knew as much about art as you and your supposed wife."

"Maybe, I got mixed up…" Jacob trailed off as he realised it was pointless to keep lying.

Merrick laughed and let Jacob go. "I don't know what you're after, but whatever it is, you're not getting your grubby hands on it."

The guard who hadn't moved to seize either of them stepped forward.

"What shall we do with them, sir?"

"The two of you take him downstairs and find out everything he knows."

The guard nodded, then his colleague asked about Orla's fate.

"I'll get someone else to take her to my quarters," Merrick said with a twisted smile. "I have big plans for the so-called Mrs. Endolmen."

Jacob could only imagine the depraved and psychotic impulses that lay buried underneath Merrick's fake gentleman persona. He tried to struggle against the guards, but they were too strong and dragged him down the steps through the crowd of shocked guests. Next, they pulled him into an elevator in a hallway opposite Merrick's balcony and pressed the button to go two floors down. Once downstairs, they yanked him through a lifeless corridor and through a metal door into a room filled with barrels of alcohol, built within a soundproof shell. Jacob looked around and recognised torture devices. There was a rack, stocks, and a wooden horse.

Despite Jacob's precarious situation, Orla was his only concern. He had already made peace with the fact he could die trying to bring stability to Uthovaya but had no intention of allowing Orla to make the same sacrifice. He needed to escape somehow and rescue her from Merrick's clutches.

"Welcome to the boss's torture room," one guard said, ruffling Jacob's hair in a strangely playful manner. "We're going to have some real fun in here."

"I doubt it'll be the kind of fun I can enjoy," Jacob countered, trying to make light of his dire situation.

"Shut up," was the guard's response. "You're going to tell us why you've broken into the boss's home."

"Well, I hope he's paying you by the hour because you'll be waiting a long time for the answer."

A sudden, stinging backhander to the jaw knocked Jacob sideways. He was just about to deliver another wisecrack when the sound of voices and footsteps from outside spoiled his fun.

"What's going on out there?" one guard asked.

"I don't know, go check it out," said the other.

"You check it out."

"Why does it always have to be me? I'm –"

"Look, I'll go check it out," Jacob interjected. "You two wait here."

"Nice try," the first guard replied.

Suddenly the voices grew louder, and the door burst open. Jacob instinctively threw himself to the ground and rolled behind some barrels. Two quick swooshing noises followed bursts of gunfire, and then a couple of thuds preceded a profound silence. Peering around the barrel, Jacob saw the guards lying dead on the floor.

Three assassin types carrying swords and dressed entirely in black with masks on were searching the room. One looked in his direction, but Jacob pulled his head away before he was spotted.

"We must be close," Jacob heard one of them say. "Let's continue searching floor by floor."

"Agreed. Contact...." The man's voice trailed off as the assassins left the torture room.

Jacob rolled away from the barrel, careful to make as little noise as possible. Then he crept to the open doorway and peeked around the corner. The assassins were huddled around a communicator, speaking to someone whose voice Jacob recognised from the ballroom and from Rockwood.

Gunnar Veto.

"I want those coordinates," Jacob heard Veto say. "Search every floor until you find that statue. Do I make myself clear?"

With the assassins otherwise occupied, Jacob slipped through the hallway back to the elevator and pressed the button to take him to the bottom floor. There was nobody in sight, so he hurried along the corridor in search of Boocka and Hudson. He had almost given up when Boocka leapt out from behind a pile of crates.

"Where's Orla?"

"That psycho Merrick took her to his quarters," Jacob replied in a rush.

"How the hell did that happen?"

"Does it really matter? Who knows what he'll do to her if we don't get there first?"

Hudson appeared and said, "We need to find the statue first. Nothing is more important than you and the mission."

"You really are a mercenary, aren't you?" Jacob spat. "Do what you like, but I'm not leaving Orla alone with that scumbag."

Hudson narrowed his eyes and then brought out his pistol. "Ye don't even have a weapon, Jay. You'll be dead if ye go charging around the mansion alone."

"And you only get paid if I come back alive. So, stop babbling and help me get Orla to safety."

"I can't do that," said Hudson, pointing his weapon at Jacob. "Ryker wants the mission completed as well. The quicker we get the statue, the quicker we go help the girl."

Jacob turned to Boocka for support but only got silence in return. It was obvious the Krokiran agreed the mission had to come first. With nowhere else to turn, and with Hudson holding a gun to his head, Jacob realised he would need to co-operate.

"Let's get this over with," he snapped, feeling nothing but disgust for the two warriors in front of him.

Hudson nodded and then turned the gun away from Jacob. "Stay behind us, and we'll take any guards out."

"We've got another problem," Jacob interjected. "I just ran into a group of Antantan assassins with swords.

It's a good bet they're the Phantoms that Junt told us about."

Boocka's nervous glance at Hudson worried Jacob greatly.

"Let's get a move on then," Hudson ordered, sprinting around the corner.

"Wait up," Jacob and Boocka replied in unison.

The next corridor was shorter than the first, but a minigun mounted on the wall protected a door at the end. Its robotic pre-programmed movements had not yet caught them, but Jacob knew it would be instant death should it do so.

"This could be tricky," Boocka said as the trio took refuge behind another pile of crates.

"We'll need to destroy it," said Hudson, and then he turned to Boocka. "Want me to do the honours?"

"Be my guest."

Hudson adjusted his scarf and then released his two pistols, waiting until the minigun turned away before taking aim and firing. It exploded into bits, and only the remains clung to the wall. Boocka ran to the keypad and pushed the four digits that Hudson insisted was the correct combination. There was no response.

"What's wrong?" Hudson said as he joined the Krokiran by the pad.

"I don't know. It's as if…."

BING!

The keypad turned green, and the door swung open, allowing Jacob to follow them into a room full of computer terminals.

"I'll guard the door," Boocka announced.

"Check the system. Number 5," Hudson shouted to Jacob, pointing to a terminal in the right-hand corner.

Jacob touched the keyboard, and strings of folders with codenames flashed up on the monitor.

"Which one is it?" he asked, eyes frantically scanning up and down the screen.

"That's the one." Hudson pointed to a file marked U//n//n…. T//a//r//. "Basement Floor, Room 2A."

Rows of unopened crates greeted them when they arrived in room 2A, stacked floor to ceiling, and marked by different colours and symbols.

Boocka said, "The statue is in one of those boxes. Be caref –"

Hudson suddenly blasted all three to pieces. Through the clutter, Jacob saw the statue on the floor.

"You idiot," Boocka snapped. "What if you had destroyed it?"

"Well, I didn't so quit moaning."

Jacob passed it to Boocka to place in his satchel. "Let's get up to Merrick's quarters. Which floor is it on?"

"The top one," Hudson said confidently.

Boocka snorted. "How the hell do you know?"

"Because I saw it on the map, obviously."

"Well, you better be –"

Jacob jumped between the pair. "Will you two knock it off? We don't have time for this."

Gunfire from behind sent them each spinning in separate directions, diving for cover behind anything they could find. Jacob steadied himself and saw two of Merrick's guards, blocking the exits. One of them had a communicator in his hand and was calling for backup, claiming to have the intruders trapped.

"What now?" Jacob cried, as more bullets were fired into the room.

"I dunno," yelled Boocka. "But we need to be away before backup arrives, or we'll never get out."

"Any ideas?" Jacob shouted to Hudson.

"I've always got ideas," he said with a grin.

It only took Hudson a few seconds to explain his plan, but Jacob was immediately unsure of its quality. It was bold, risky, and not achievable without a huge slice of good fortune. Nonetheless, he figured they had no alternative.

"Whenever yer ready," Hudson whispered to Jacob as he slid one of his pistols towards him.

"We can't trust this merc," Boocka cried. "He'll shoot us the minute our back is turned."

"We don't have a choice," Jacob replied, picking up Hudson's gun.

Jacob and Boocka slid their weapons in the direction of the door. There was a silence before one guard could be heard scurrying to retrieve them.

"Come out," another ordered.

"We will," Jacob called back. "But don't shoot. We're unarmed."

"Just get out here with your hands up."

"Don't try any funny business either," added another.

Jacob took a deep breath and nodded for Boocka to go. They both ventured into the open at the same time.

"Wait, where's the other one," said a guard. "Someone's still in there."

Suddenly, Hudson rolled into the middle of the doorway and fired two perfectly placed shots into the chest of both guards with his remaining pistol. They stumbled backwards and then sank to the ground.

"Great shooting," said Jacob.

"I told ye the plan would work." Hudson beamed

"Let's find Orla now," Jacob said.

Boocka nodded. "There's bound to be security searching every floor now. We'll need to fight our way to Merrick's quarters."

"Suits me fine," Hudson agreed, spinning both pistols and then re-holstering them.

Jacob said, "Try to avoid the Phantoms if we can. The last thing we need is a fight to the death with them."

Hudson growled. "If we have to go through them, we will."

Chapter XXIII

Orla could not stop shaking, as the horrifying reality of being imprisoned in Merrick's quarters hit home. She felt like the walls were closing in, trapping her with a total psychopath, whose intentions towards her were too grim to contemplate.

She suffered a violent shiver and then scanned her surroundings for what must have been the fifth time since the guards locked her in. The room was an exercise in ostentatiousness; there was a four-poster bed with a white canopy, a collection of unusual ornaments lined up on a bookcase with no books, and wall-mounted animal heads running the length of the entire right side of the room. The décor exploded with vibrant colours, creating a dizzying effect that gave Orla a headache. Clearly, she mused, Merrick was a man who owned his eccentricities.

She took a few steps forward but almost tripped over the soft, animal skin-rug beneath her feet. A polished wooden table broke her fall. There was a spread fit for a king on top. Fancy morsels, exotic snacks, and even an ice-bucket containing a half-submerged bottle of champagne.

"I need to get out of here," Orla said out-loud.

A computer terminal on top of a crescent-shaped desk caught her attention. Hurrying across the room, she touched the screen, and the monitor lit up, showing a single folder entitled Escape Door Lock. Hope swelled inside her for one brief shining moment, but the folder was password-protected, and all hopes of an escape were quickly dashed.

Deflated, she paced the room, allowing her thoughts to drift towards Jacob and the possibility of him still being alive. Terrifying visions of him being tortured and writhing in agony, left her angry, helpless, and unable to concentrate. The visions were relentless and disturbing, like a restless spirit driving her to the edge of insanity.

The double doors flew open, and a grinning Merrick appeared, leaning against the doorframe. He had changed from his business suit into a scarlet robe with red slippers. Were her situation not so serious, Orla would probably have laughed at the fluffy red ribbons above the toe.

"Sorry about the wait," he breathed, locking the door. "I had to slip into something more comfortable."

His comment tested Orla's gag reflex, but she managed to retain the contents of her stomach. Somehow composing herself, she quickly stepped back from the man holding her hostage. It was all she could do to put some distance between them.

"Why so edgy?" Merrick asked. "I thought we could have some fun."

"What about your guests?"

"Pfft, guests? Every year I throw this bash, and every year it's the same result; a room full of parasites who eat and drink me out of house and home. They are only here for what they can get from me, conversing about the most mundane things, laughing at each other's pitiful jokes, and pretending their failing businesses are making them a mint. Deep down, they all hate each other."

"Then why did you invite them?"

"Some of them, I didn't. Look at you and your husband?" He shook his head and exhaled loudly. "You have no idea how boring these parties can be. Most of the time, I wish I was somewhere else.

"I think I know the feeling," she replied, looking around the room she had no hope of escape from.

"Are you not comfortable?"

Orla snorted at the question. "I've never been so uncomfortable in my entire life."

"Relax. You're in good hands here."

"What about my husband?" Orla replied. "

Merrick sighed as he poured champagne into each glass. "We both know he isn't your husband, Mrs. Endolmen…or whatever your real name is. I find your presence very convenient."

"How so?"

"Well, I happen to know the Antantan President's airship recently landed in Vala, and suddenly you and your acquaintance break into my mansion. It doesn't take a genius to work out who you are."

Orla bit her lip. "You think we're Antantans?"

He handed her a glass of champagne. "I think you are, but I can't work out why you'd have a Mixling with you. I thought the Antantans hated Mixlings."

She stopped herself from speaking. Giving out information now was pointless. Far better to let Merrick think he knew the truth than let him know any of the facts.

"So, we have established who you are, but we haven't talked about why you're here. Care to share?"

"If you let my friend go, I will tell you," she replied, hardly thinking the words through.

Merrick shook his head. "I can't do that."

"Why not?" Orla replied.

"Because he broke into my home," Merrick snapped. "He deserves to die."

"And me? I broke into your home, too. Are you going to kill me as well?"

"I'll be gentle with you." Merrick grinned. "You look amazing in that dress."

His deep blue eyes were wild with excitement as he jumped off the bed and leaned in to stroke her hair. Orla froze at first. It was like his touch had turned her entire body to stone. Slowly, she found the strength to push his hand away and take a few steps back.

"Don't be nervous," Merrick whispered.

He pulled his sleeve up to reveal a communicator and then twisted the outer casing three times. A squared area of the floor parted, and a hot tub ascended from below. There was a second bottle of champagne chilling by its side.

"Care for a dip?" Merrick asked, kicking off his slippers.

Orla watched in horror as he untied his robe and let it slide to the floor. He was only wearing a pair of unflattering red swimming shorts underneath. The sight of his pale, almost nude body made Orla feel queasy, and she moved across to the bookcase to sit her glass down, still glancing around for a miracle escape route to present itself.

"I'm fine where I am, thanks."

"Ah, come on. It will relax you."

"I haven't brought my swimming costume."

It was the first thing that entered Orla's head, but she sensed her refusal would not go down well with the creepy prime baron. He was undressing her with his eyes while licking his lips in anticipation.

"There's no need for one." He clapped his hands three times, and the lights dimmed. Then he moved beside her again.

"I want you," he whispered breathlessly.

"Don't be silly," Orla laughed; it was a nervous laugh that made her wish she had reacted differently.

"Kiss me."

"Not a chance," Orla cried, rushing away from the bookcase. She tried to open the door again, as though some unseen force would have unlocked it while she and Merrick were talking.

"There really is no escape," Merrick warned as he crept towards her.

"You come anywhere near me, and I swear I will break your jaw."

He was standing in front of her now. She took a step back but felt the door against her back. Merrick lunged forward, trying to plant his lips on hers.

"Get away from me."

She slapped him hard, and he recoiled while holding his cheek. Orla expected an angry response, but it never came. He seemed pleased by her actions, grinning wickedly as he put both of his hands on her waist. She ducked underneath his arm and bolted to the crescent-shaped desk on the other side of the room, but Merrick laughed maniacally and gave chase, forcing her in a different direction, where she tripped and landed on the bed.

He was on top within seconds, tearing at her dress like a wild animal. Everything became hazy. Her screams were silent, and the pressure on her chest unbearable. She gripped the covers of the bed for dear life, unable to think straight, as she realised what was about to happen. Tears rolled down her cheeks, and time seemed to slow down.

SEAN CLARKE

"It'll be a lot easier if you don't struggle," Merrick said, smothering her with unwanted kisses. "I always get what I want."

His breath reeked of stale smoke and champagne, and as he tried to kiss her again, she got a hand free and aimed a well-timed punch that sent him stumbling back across the floor, clutching a bloodied nose. He took seconds to recover, and as he checked himself in the mirror, his face twisted into something darker.

"Look what you did," he screamed. "You'll die for that."

Orla jumped off the bed as he swung a punch in her direction, but she ducked underneath the hit and then sank her teeth into his other arm. He stumbled back in agony and thundered a second punch that sent her spinning to the floor. Dazed and in pain, she felt Merrick grip her hair and drag her towards the hot tub, where he dumped her into the water backwards and headfirst, her legs up in the air.

She felt his weight come crashing down on her from above, pinning her and making it impossible to lift her head above the surface. The mass of bubbles disoriented her and stung her eyes. She thrashed and kicked in a desperate attempt to move the great lump trying to drown her. He was staring at her with wide-eyes through the glassy water, his bone-chilling calmness betraying the severity of the situation.

Orla's lungs screamed for air, and her life flashed before her eyes, evoking memories of happier times with Jacob. Energy spent, and unable to hold her breath for much longer, she stopped struggling and prepared to accept the inevitable – a watery death in Merrick's mansion.

Chapter XXIV

A surge of adrenaline coursed through Orla's body, as though her mind had given her an extra shot at survival. Merrick had shifted most of his weight to the right side, meaning Orla could lift her right hand above the surface of the water. She felt the outline of an object on her fingertips; the bottle of champagne in the ice-bucket.

Using the last of her strength, Orla smashed the bottle into her attacker's left cheek. The force of the blow knocked him sideways, instantly removing his weight from her tired body. She pulled herself to safety, taking large and grateful gulps of air. Merrick lay dazed at the side of the hot tub, so she scrambled away from him, hoping to find something else to fight with, but her adrenaline evaporated, and she crashed to the floor in a fit of dizziness.

Helpless and exhausted, she watched Merrick rise and make his way towards her. There were bits of glass lodged in his blood-soaked cheek, and his look of murderous intent made Orla quiver with fear. He looked nothing like the handsome businessman from the party.

"I will kill you," he raged.

"I wouldn't do that if I were you," Orla said breathlessly.

"Oh?" He grinned, bending over to put his injured face close to hers. "And why not?"

She kicked the back of his heels full force, and he jumped around in agony, tripping over the animal-skin rug and then crashing face-first onto the floor beside her. Sensing her chance to escape, she got to her feet and ran for the double doors, trying to prise it open with her fingertips. It was no use. Merrick was vertical again and methodically making his way towards the bed. He slid his hand underneath and retrieved a large knife. Orla shuffled away from the door, but there was nowhere left to run. She was almost out on her feet now, soaking wet and gasping for breath as Merrick came towards her with the deadly weapon. Despite the imminent danger, Orla's thoughts turned towards her mum and dad, and the consequences should she die in Merrick's mansion. They would probably spend the rest of their existence in agony, wondering what happened to their little girl.

This is the end.

There was an almighty crash as the double doors exploded open, and Boocka rushed into the room towards Merrick. The baron swung the knife, but Boocka was too quick. He dodged the silver blade and then head-butted Merrick, knocking him unconscious. Jacob then came into the room, swiftly followed by Hudson. Orla's hands trembled and her legs wobbled as she cried out in relief. The nightmare was over.

"What did he do to you?" Jacob asked, lifting Orla's bruised chin, so her eyes met his gaze.

"I'm fine," she croaked, turning away to catch sight of a gaunt and dishevelled stranger in the mirror. It was frightening to see herself so battered and bruised.

The tears came thick and fast as her bravado melted away, leaving nothing but the emotional distress of what had transpired in the room with Merrick. She felt Jacob pull her in close, and then the softness of his lips on her aching forehead. It felt nice, comforting somehow.

"I thought I would die," she sobbed.

"But you didn't," Jacob assured her.

Hudson loudly cleared his throat to catch their attention, and Orla released herself from Jacob's warm embrace.

"We should get going," Hudson said. "We've got what we came for."

"I think he has a secret escape route," Orla explained, her voice still shaky. She pointed to the desk at the back of the room "It's password-protected on that computer terminal."

Hudson looked at the others and then shook his head. "How are we supposed to get out without the password? Looks like Junt didn't think of everything."

"Maybe I shouldn't have knocked Merrick out?" Boocka replied sheepishly.

Hudson laughed at the comment. "It's a bit late now."

"I don't see you offering any ideas," Boocka fired back.

Jacob jumped between them. "Give it a rest, you two."

The sound of moaning diverted their attention to the floor, where Merrick was slowly but surely regaining consciousness. He pulled a small device from his pocket, opened the top, and clicked the button.

"My guards will be here any moment," he said groggily.

"Shut up," Hudson barked. "What's the password for your terminal?"

"You think I'd tell you?"

Merrick's eyes were blazing now, and purple veins popped out of his neck. Everyone gasped when he spat in the captain's face. Hudson calmly wiped the spit away and then much to Orla's surprise, shot Merrick in the right leg. The businessman screamed and writhed in agony on the wet floor.

"Y-you…you shot me."

"The next one will be right between the eyes if ye don't start talking."

"You wouldn't dare kill me," Merrick grunted in an unsure tone.

Hudson turned to Orla. "He thinks I won't kill him. What do you think?"

Orla studied the injured Merrick. The cocky, arrogance from before had gone, and in their place was a man terrified of losing his life. Orla imagined he bore the same look she did when Merrick held her below the surface of the hot tub water. In that moment, any sympathy she had for the billionaire disappeared.

"The password!" Orla demanded, pointing at Hudson's gun as a reminder of what would happen should he fail to comply.

Merrick sighed. "845tyzk."

"See, that wasn't hard, was it?" Hudson quipped.

Raised voices from down the hallway interrupted them. Boocka ran to the door for a look.

"Merrick's guards are heading straight for us," he said quickly.

"Me and Boocka will deal with the guards," Hudson said to Orla and Jacob. "You two get our escape route sorted."

Gunfire exploded, as Boocka and Hudson traded shots with the guards out in the hallway. Orla reached the terminal before Jacob and quickly typed Merrick's code in. There was a pinging noise, and then a bookcase against the wall slid to the side, revealing a secret tunnel lit by lights along the ceiling.

"Hurry up, you two," Orla screamed.

"Bit busy at the moment," she heard Hudson reply over the top of more gunfire. "Go ahead, and we'll catch up."

Orla raced to the end of the tunnel with Jacob at her side, running straight to a ladder leading to an access door below. As they climbed down, Boocka and Hudson came tearing through the tunnel behind them.

"Get that access door open," Hudson yelled.

It was the first time Orla had ever heard the captain sound like anything other than a cool customer. His sudden panic left her feeling even more jittery than she already had been. If the captain was worried, then the rest of them should be as well.

"Did you take care of the guards?" Orla asked as she pushed open the access door.

"The guards were easy," Hudson replied. "It's the Phantoms we need to worry about."

Looking up, she saw three assassins clad entirely in black. Each carried large swords and were looking down from above.

"Get through that door," Hudson ordered,

Orla scrambled down the ladder with Jacob not far behind, and seconds later, they were standing in the gardens of Merrick's estate but could see Junt and Kadesha waiting beside a red multi-terrain truck on the other side of the fence. Boocka and Hudson emerged and closed the access door behind them, but there was no time to breathe, because the Phantoms burst through it seconds later.

"Move!" Hudson yelled.

"Can't you shoot them?" Orla cried.

"Already tried but they blocked the shots. Their swords are bulletproof."

More bullets narrowly missed them, this time from guns attached to the turrets monitoring movement in the garden. Orla struggled through a hole in the fence and reached the truck.

"Get in the back," Junt ordered. "Kadesha's already in the passenger seat."

"Where's our weapons?" Orla heard Jacob shout.

"There's a pile of crates, back there. Your weapons are in the top one."

As Orla and the others got in the open-top cargo area, she noticed the Phantoms had changed direction. They seemed to be heading for Merrick's garage. She understood why when a vintage motor driven by Merrick's guards burst through the doors, heading straight for the Phantoms. One flipped away, but the car mowed down the other two and then smashed through the front gate. Orla watched the remaining one run for the garage, perhaps searching for a car of his own?

Junt pulled the truck away, but the guards were now in hot pursuit. There were four in total – one driving, another in the passenger seat, and two in the back. The guard in the passenger seat leaned out his window, firing wildly in the truck's direction.

"Get behind the crates," Boocka roared.

Quickly, and somewhat clumsily, Orla reached up to push the top crate over, and the pistol and Dynasty Staff spilled onto the floor beside them. Shots rang from the front of the truck, and Orla realised Junt was leaning out the window to fire his pistol at the chasing car. He moved back inside but then re-appeared seconds later, casually taking out the guard in the chasing car's passenger seat.

"That's how it's done," he screamed.

"It sure is," Boocka screamed back. "Now it's our turn."

He winked at Hudson, and both exploded from their hiding place, shooting madly at the driver who kept low to avoid being hit by the bullets smashing through the windscreen. As the guards in the back retaliated, Hudson and Boocka ducked behind the crates again, only emerging when an opening presented itself. Boocka dispatched the guard in the left passenger seat, while Hudson took out the one on the right.

The truck turned onto the first of many country roads. At first, the road was straight, but it twisted and turned the further they drove into the countryside, making it even harder to hit the driver of the car pulling up the rear.

"Get this guy off our tail," Junt called from the front.

"We're having some trouble with that," Hudson shouted back.

"Fine. I'll do it myself. Hold onto your hats"

Junt spun the wheel hard to his left, and the truck crashed through a wooden gate into a field and then bounced around on the uneven terrain. The clever manoeuvre befuddled the driver of the other vehicle who missed the turning point and instead, entered the field at the next gate. His slow reaction gave the group time to regain their composure. By the time the car caught up and rammed the truck from behind, Boocka had a clear shot at the driver and dispatched him through the windshield with ease. The driverless car then spun out of control and into a ditch.

"We're free!" Orla screamed in delight as Junt brought the truck to a standstill in the middle of the field.

"Don't celebrate too soon," Hudson replied, pointing to a new threat on the horizon.

A second vintage car was coming up fast; it was driven by the last Phantom who had obviously stolen it from the garage.

"Start the truck!" Jacob cried.

The truck roared into life, but the car was alongside them in seconds, allowing the assassin to climb out the window of the moving vehicle. He steadied himself on the roof and then jumped across the gap between vehicles to the cargo area, landing in the middle of the group and taking Hudson out with a spinning heel kick. Hudson fell backwards into Boocka, sending them both crashing through the pile of crates. Orla aimed a kick in the assassin's direction, but he caught her foot in mid-air, and then spun her around, throwing a heavy punch to the back of her head in one quick movement that left her in excruciating pain. She landed on her back but twisted herself around. Helpless, she watched the attacker draw his sword, but Jacob reacted quicker, blocking the fatal strike with the Dynasty Staff. The two struggled for a moment, but Jacob fell back, and the assassin raised his sword again, ready to end his resistance.

Without thinking, Orla grabbed her pistol and pulled the trigger, shooting the off-balance assassin through the chest. He stood with a shocked look on his face for half-a-second and then fell off the back of the cargo area, bouncing and rolling along the dirt as the truck sped away.

"I can't believe I just did that," Orla whispered as she dropped the gun.

"You had no choice," said Jacob. "It was him or me."

Orla was in a trance when she nodded back, too busy thinking about Boocka's words when he gave her the gun back on the Rad Veteran.

"We're on a dangerous mission. At some point, you'll encounter a situation where using a gun is inevitable if you or someone you care about is to survive."

Those words were all Orla could cling to, in order to soften the fact, she had taken another life; the kind of heinous act she had never envisioned herself capable of. The sight of the lifeless Phantom falling from the truck would always be there, haunting her forever.

"Good job, guys," Junt cried from the front. "It won't be long until we're at the airport."

Orla and Jacob shared a confused look. "Airport?"

"My friend owns a Sky-Darter. He's gonna fly you to your destination."

"Just what I need to cure my fear of heights," Orla mumbled, sarcastically.

Half an hour later, the truck came to a halt in the middle of a large field beside the hulking Sky-Darter. A Human pilot wearing a red-striped jumpsuit waited patiently by the aircraft's side.

"Well, here we are," said Junt, leaping out the driver's side of the truck.

Kadesha said, "We can't thank you enough."

"Think nothing of it."

Junt helped Boocka load everyone's clothes and weapons onto the Sky-Darter.

"Be careful with that," Jacob heard Boocka cry as Junt disappeared into the cargo hold with his trusted satchel.

"Sorry," Junt replied, looking a little too suspicious for Orla's tastes.

Jacob and Orla changed out their party clothes and then took their seats beside each other. There was an unquestionable excitement amongst the group as they waved Junt goodbye from the dusty windows, but Orla struggled with the thought of being up in the air.

"I can't do this," she said, gripping the arms of the seat for dear life.

"Think of something else," Jacob replied.

"Like what? The Sky-Darter crashing and all of us dying?"

Her own words freaked her out so much she automatically tried to stand up, but Jacob urged her back down, promising the flight would not be that bad if she didn't look out the window or think too much about being high-up in the air.

"Easy for you to say."

"Let's talk about something else," Jacob soothed, as the engines started up. "Your parents, maybe?"

Orla felt a twinge of sadness. "I miss them," she admitted. "The prospect of seeing them again was the only thing that kept me going back there. I know Dad's not perfect, but he's the only one I've got."

She was suddenly aware of how insensitive her comment was to Jacob, someone who had never known his real parents, but her apology was met with a subdued shaking of the head.

"Don't worry about me. I'm fully concentrated on reclaiming the throne."

"King Jacob Crestmore still doesn't sound right." She laughed softly. "Are you sure you're ready for this?"

"You asked me the same thing once before," Jacob replied as the aircraft lifted into the sky.

"Did I?"

"Back in Oakhedge. Just before we went into my old house. The place this journey started. I'll tell you now what I told you then…"

Orla beat him to the punch. "You're ready as you'll ever be."

Chapter XXV

Gunnar Veto paced the empty corridor of the Shadow-Flare like a caged animal. He had sent his young protégé, Officer Briggs, to keep a distant eye on Merrick's mansion in order to provide updates on the Phantoms bid to recover the statue, but had heard nothing since the last update over two hours ago. The lack of communication made him nervous, and the longer it lasted, the more he wondered if something had gone wrong with the plan.

Buzz, Buzz, Buzz.

Veto pulled the communicator from his breast pocket, expecting Briggs' face to flash up on screen. No such luck. He was instead confronted by an image of Gex staring back at him.

"What do you want?" Veto said, barely glancing at the screen.

"Is this a stupid question competition? Obviously, I want an update on the Phantoms. You're two hours late."

"If I had any information, you would be the first to know."

Gex narrowed his eyes. "You mean that idiot Briggs hasn't reported back yet?"

"Not a word."

"This is your fault, Veto."

"How the hell is this my fault? You're the one who wanted to use the Phantoms. I wanted to go in myself. If they've failed, then it's on you."

"I had no choice but to use them. I can't rely on you. Your list of failures is as long as your arm." A wry smile spread across his face. "Well, the one you have left, obviously."

Gex then ended communication, leaving Veto to stew over his superior's final dig. He could not dwell on the remark for long because Briggs was now marching towards him with a worried look on his face.

"Where have you been?" Veto barked. "I've got Gex breathing down my neck."

"Sorry, sir. My communicator was playing up."

"Well, where's the statue? What's happened?"

"You're not going to like it, sir."

"Tell me," Veto replied, dreading what Briggs would say.

"The Phantoms are dead."

"Dead?" Veto felt the anger rising like a nasty bout of acid reflux.

"I spoke to some of the guests after they left the mansion. They told me a couple was taken away by the guards in the middle of the party."

"What couple?"

"Not sure, but that's not all." Said Briggs. "From my vantage point, I noticed a group escaping from the mansion. They were being chased by our Phantoms and Merrick's own guards."

Veto was confused now. "Who were these people?"

"I can't say for sure, but one of them was a Krok-iran."

Veto felt disappointment and frustration in equal measure because he knew fine who the Krokiran was–Kadesha's bodyguard, Boocka, who was no doubt protecting the boy as well.

How had they learned the statue's location in the first place? Father Gambin had unknowingly sent them on a wild-Gudhopper chase to Rockwood, a town that was nothing more than rubble, yet they had ended up at Merrick's mansion. How did they make the connection? The Pavellian Prime Minister came to mind, but Veto had more pressing matters at hand.

"Are you quite sure the Phantoms are dead?" Veto said, probing Briggs for more information. "Tell me everything you know."

"Two of them were hit by a car."

"What about the other one?"

Briggs lowered his head. "We found him further away, sir. Gunshot wound."

Veto felt sick at the news. Jacob Crestmore and Kadesha would be on their way to find the Lost ElmKey by now, probably gloating at scoring another victory over the great Gunnar Veto. Enraged at losing control of the situation, he pulled the communicator from his pocket and threw it against the corridor wall, where it smashed into thousands of tiny pieces on the floor. He was about to tear into Briggs, but the officer's terrified expression softened Veto's attitude. Briggs had always been loyal and supportive. None of this was his fault.

"What now, sir?" Briggs asked.

"How should I know? We continue the search, somehow."

Briggs' sudden serious expression did not go unnoticed by Veto.

"Have you actually thought about you'll do if you catch up with Jacob?" the officer asked, tentatively.

It was a good question. Veto had never considered the possibility of how to handle seeing Jacob. He could not bring himself to kill the child during the initial coup, nor hand him over to the President. Not without knowing for sure about his parentage. Even if Jacob was not his son, Veto did not want to lose the last connection to Fiona. Reluctantly, he pushed Jacob to the back of his mind.

"Just concentrate on the job at hand," Veto said crossly. "Do we have any leads on them at all?"

"Sorry, sir. None whatsoever."

Fatigue had ravaged his mind and body, but Veto needed time to assess the situation? Create a clear plan going forward.

"Things can't get much worse," he admitted.

"I wouldn't be too sure about that, sir."

"What do you mean?"

Briggs gestured to the right, so Veto swung around to find Vice-President Gex storming towards them, a look of exasperation etched on his face.

"Get back to work," Gex ordered Briggs.

"Right away, sir," Briggs replied, saluting the Vice-President, and then making himself scarce.

Gex turned to Veto. "Well?"

Veto shook his head. He knew excuses would not work on this occasion. He had the race for the Lost ElmKey in the bag but somehow managed to finish second. Once the President learned of his latest failure, he would either be put out to pasture or worse.

"They escaped," Veto said under his breath.

"Pardon?"

"I said they escaped."

"Why am I not surprised?" Gex sneered.

"Never mind trying to score points. Jacob and Kadesha are on their way to get the Lost ElmKey. We must stop them."

"And how do you propose we do that?" Gex replied sharply.

Veto sighed. "I have no idea."

"Well you better think of something fast. The President will not be happy if you come up short again. He is fed up with this never-ending saga and expects it to be over."

Veto gritted his teeth. He felt a sudden urge to teach this insufferable man a lesson, end the fool's arrogance with direct application of electrical current from his doctored arm, but he resisted. Now was not the time for division within the ranks. They had to work together if Jacob and Kadesha were to be caught.

"I'm open to suggestions," Veto whispered, practically choking on his own words.

The sound of Briggs calling from the other side of the corridor interrupted the conversation. He was racing back towards them with an excited look on his bright red face.

"Sir, sir," he cried breathlessly.

"I told you to get back to work," Gex snapped.

Briggs turned to Veto. "Someone is here to see you."

"I don't have time for visitors," Veto snapped.

"You will want to make time for this one. It's the Snarkeen who broke into Goldfront Base."

"Junt Kidd?" Veto said in a daze. "Here, on the Shadow-Flare?"

Briggs nodded with excitement. "He claims to have information that might be of benefit to you. Information about Jacob and Kadesha."

"Let us see this visitor," Veto said.

Briggs led them both to a private room, where Junt Kidd lazed across a lounger with his feet up on the table. He was calm and collected. Too calm and collected for Veto's liking, especially considering his status as one of the most wanted individuals in Antantan history.

"Ah, Vice-President Gex and the famous Gunnar Veto." Junt grinned. "I told…" He clicked his fingers as if trying to remember the name. "Officer Briggs, I only wanted to see the top man, and what does he do? He brings you two instead."

"Shut your mouth," Gex barked, before walking across and pushing Junt's feet off the lounger. "You stole a lot of secrets from Goldfront. I hope for your sake you have something good to give us?"

Junt cleared his throat, and then gently pushed Gex away from the lounger so he could put his feet back up again. Veto should have been enraged at his audacity but watching Gex become annoyed made him happy.

"As I said, I'll only speak with the President," said Junt.

"And I told you earlier the President isn't here." Briggs countered.

Gex waved Briggs away. "Wait outside."

"Yes, sir." He left, closing the door behind him.

Veto moved forward. He was standing over Junt now, ready to pounce at the drop of a hat. He could tell Gex was thinking along similar lines by his body language, leaning forward with both fists clenched.

"You told Officer Briggs you have information about Jacob and Kadesha. I hope for your sake, it's something good."

"Would I be here if I didn't?" Junt said smugly. "You're looking for a key of sorts."

"How —"

"I helped Jacob and Kadesha escape from Pavelle with a set of coordinates. They're heading to a tower where this key is located."

Almost spitting with rage, Veto pulled Junt up by his collar, swung him around, and threw him against the wall for Gex to burst forward and hold him in place.

"We already know that." Gex barked, releasing a pistol from his holster, and pushing it into Junt's chin. "So, it looks like the end for you."

"I wouldn't do that if I were you," Junt replied, squirming wildly as the gun was pressed into his chin.

"And why not?"

"Because I know exactly where this key is." Junt spluttered, trying to flash a toothy smile. "I snuck a look at the coordinates when I helped load their luggage onto my associate's Sky-Darter."

"Give us the location," Gex ordered.

"I won't just hand the information over."

"Is that a fact?" Gex replied, pushing the gun further into Junt's chin.

Veto urged Gex to back off. There was no time to torture Junt. Surprisingly, Gex listened, allowing Veto free reign to bargain with their visitor.

"What do you want?" Veto asked reluctantly.

"Immunity from prosecution," Junt fired back without missing a beat. "I leave here a free lizard. You never come looking for me again."

"Is that it?"

Gex exploded again. "Not a chance this thief leaves here alive."

"Seems a win-win situation to me," Junt said calmly. "You get the coordinates, and I stop looking over my shoulder."

"You really think you can walk away?" Gex blasted. "After what you did?"

Veto wondered whether the Snarkeen could be trusted. There was nothing to stop Junt from taking his prize and disappearing off the face of Lozaro. It seemed silly to entertain the idea of a deal, but they were desperate and had no choice but to agree to his demands.

"Clock is ticking," Junt said with a cheeky grin.

After Veto and Gex spoke in private for a few moments, it was decided to go ahead.

"You've made the right decision," Junt said, producing a communicator and handing it to Gex. "I will send the coordinates to this communicator once I'm safely away and receive my official pardon from the president."

"If you betray us…"

"A deal's a deal," Junt said with a serious expression. "I'll be on my way now."

Veto left and started for the communications room to contact the President about granting Junt immunity. Their leader was certain to be wary about the deal but would come around if it helped them find the Lost ElmKey and stop Jacob and Kadesha in their tracks. If Junt was true to his word, Veto was in no doubt the tide had turned.

Chapter XXVI

Jacob woke up with a startle, unsure of his whereabouts, and still feeling groggy. He unclipped his seatbelt and then looked around, remembering he was in the Sky-Darter heading for Tavara. He yawned loudly and stretched, noticing Orla still fast asleep beside him. Kadesha was in the back row, deep in discussion with Boocka. Hudson was in the front row, but Jacob could not tell if he was sleeping or resting his eyes.

"Are we nearly there?" Orla said as she came to.

"No idea," Jacob replied softly. "How did you sleep?"

"Better than I ever imagined on an aircraft." She unbuckled the seatbelt and twisted her body around until she was kneeling on the seat facing Boocka and Kadesha. "Has anyone contacted Ambassador Bellis and told her how close we are to the Lost ElmKey?"

"There was no answer from the Ambassador," Kadesha replied with a heavy sigh. "So, Director Ryker was the next best thing. He has promised to send a Pulse-Fighter to pick us up."

Jacob could almost see the wheels turning in Orla's head.

"I thought all aircraft were being prepped for the launch of Operation Creeper?"

Boocka jumped immediately. "That's exactly what I said. Seems strange to me."

"Very strange," Orla replied, turning to Jacob. "What do you think?"

"Maybe, they're ready for flight now?"

"Maybe?" came her instant reply. "I just don't trust that man."

"Join the club," said Boocka.

Jacob could understand the concern. They were so close to the end now. The last thing they needed was unforeseen events popping out of nowhere, either slowing them down or preventing them from getting the Lost ElmKey altogether. Even with their destination looming, he refused to believe it would be that simple.

"Something's bound to go wrong," he said glumly.

Orla laughed. "How many times have I told you to look on the bright side?"

"Enough for me to stop listening," he replied with a cheeky smile.

"No need to be so cynical, your Majesty."

"Don't call me that."

"Why not? It won't be long till everyone does. I might as well get into the habit. I draw the line at curtseying, though."

"Curtseying?"

"Yes, you know, curtseying." She stood up and curt-seyed in an over the top manner, before sitting back down on the seat. "You'll never catch me doing that. Well, apart from that one time just there."

The tannoy crackled, and Jacob heard the captain's voice informing his passengers to put their seatbelts back on because they would be landing at Fendosco International Airport in the next few minutes. The airport was in Fendosco City, the Capital of Tavara.

"You OK?" Jacob asked Orla, suddenly noticing she had turned pale.

"I....think so," she replied, bending over to stare at the floor.

"What's the matter?"

"Nothing, I er...I could have done without the sudden reminder we're on a Sky-Darter."

"Nearly there now. You've done well."

Orla sat back in her seat. "I have, haven't I?"

The landing was bumpy, but Jacob had no time to worry. He was far more concerned with Orla, who spent the entirety of the landing muttering prayers under her breath and rocking back and forth. When the Sky-Darter finally came to a stop, the colour seeped back into her face.

"That was easy," she said.

"Sure was." Jacob grinned, humouring her for a moment.

Boocka found a batch of old clothes in one of the storage compartments and came up with the idea of using them to fashion headgear for protection from the sun and sandstorms. Hudson point-blank refused to take his scarf off, but finally relented when Orla pointed out how childish he was acting and how warm it would be as they travelled through the Tavara desert towards their destination.

"Everyone ready?" Jacob asked.

Orla said, "Don't forget your staff."

"Way ahead of you," he replied as he tied his mother's weapon to his back with string.

The searing Tavara heat hit Jacob as soon as he stood at the summit of the airstairs. His face felt like it was on fire, and the stifling air seemed to choke him as sweat poured down his forehead and dripped off the tip of his nose. It was easily the hottest weather he had ever experienced, a fact he relayed to Orla as the group hurried through the busy airport to the main street, where they bought water for the journey.

"It's going to be a struggle to cope," Orla admitted, wiping her brow with the back of her hand.

They traipsed through the busy streets; dodging Tavarian market traders eager to sell their latest gear from a variety of stalls. Almost everyone wore light clothes like multi-coloured robes and headscarves. Most Tavarians were Human, but Jacob noticed some Remman traders going about their business as well, not to mention a Gogglo dragging passers-by towards his stall and flashing various bits of gold jewellery.

"What's our plan of action?" Orla asked no one in particular, as they pushed through the crowds of enthusiastic bargain-hunters.

Kadesha said. "Director Ryker contacted a lady who has promised to sell us Sabchews. We won't reach the tower without transport."

"What's a Sabchew?" Orla asked Kadesha.

"Birds who cannot fly. Their specially adapted feet enable them to move through the desert at fast speeds."

"But they're the stupidest animals you ever saw," Hudson chimed in.

"How far until we reach this lady?" Orla asked Kadesha.

"Not much further."

The lady in question was very helpful. She took payment for three Sabchews as each one could carry two passengers on their back. Jacob shared with Orla, Boocka shared with Kadesha, and Hudson took one of his own. Before they left, Kadesha programmed the co-ordinates from the statue into her communicator and then bid the lady goodbye.

The Tavara Desert was a desolate wasteland of never-ending sand and more sand, stretching far into the distance and only occasionally interrupted by dunes scattered across the landscape. They trudged across the barren wilderness, Jacob doing his best to ignore the geographical monotony in every direction. Instead, he focused on making sure the others were coping with the punishing conditions. Orla seemed fine, whistling through the sandy nightmare like a native who had braved the elements a thousand times before. Kadesha tired easily, but her loyal bodyguard kept her spirits up.

After a few hours, Kadesha needed to stop and rest, so Boocka hung a sheet across two large rocks to keep everyone out of the sun's direct rays.

"Drink?" Orla asked Jacob as they lay under the sheet, her throat all croaked and dry.

Jacob nodded and took possession of the canteen, letting the delicious drops of water settle on his tongue in the most satisfying manner. Before long, he was gulping at the liquid. Orla snatched it back, cruelly ripping the sweet taste away from him.

"Easy with that."

"What?"

"It has to last, remember?"

"Sorry."

While they rested, Jacob looked around at the others and wondered what they were all feeling as they closed in on the Lost ElmKey. If truth be told, he was unsure of his own feelings on the matter. It had been a long and dangerous journey, but worth it at the same time. He had made new friends and seen a bit of the world – certainly more than he would have gotten had he stayed in the Capital. He had learned something about himself, too. Finding an inner strength, he did not know he possessed

It was the latter that got him thinking about Orla and her wish to move somewhere else. Was it the right move? He was unconvinced if truth be told. Orla could still be a massive help to the Uthovayans. Maybe, she would come around if he came clean about his feelings? Then again, maybe she would reject him outright and leave their friendship in tatters? He mulled both scenarios over until his eyes became heavy, and he drifted off to sleep.

As soon as everyone woke up, they travelled onwards through the desert, making quick progress on the Sabchews. Finally, they arrived at the desired coordinates but found only sand and more sand, with no evidence of the mysterious tower that had been sketched in Fiona's journal.

"Shouldn't it be here?" Orla asked.

"Maybe Mum got the coordinates wrong?" Jacob offered.

"That better be a joke," Hudson snapped.

Jacob was irked at his response. "Do you see me laughing?"

Suddenly, there was an almighty rumble from below them, followed by a short tremor that nearly knocked everyone off their feet.

"What the hell was that?" Boocka yelled.

More rumbling and then sand began to fly everywhere as a tornado sprouted from nowhere and rose into the sky, before turning into a giant structure that looked like it was made of solid gold.

Jacob was too speechless to say anything, but he could see Hudson and Boocka with their mouths agape. Only Kadesha seemed at ease with the magnificent tower in front of them.

"Of course." She pointed at Jacob "The tower only appears in the presence of someone from the magic bloodline. No wonder it has remained hidden here."

"How do we get in?" Jacob asked. "There doesn't seem to be an entrance."

"We should try around the back," Kadesha suggested, taking possession of Boocka's satchel with Fiona's journal and the statue inside.

The entrance was indeed around the back, a small door big enough for one entrant at a time. Kadesha went first, with Jacob following, but before the rest could enter, a sudden orange force-field appeared, blocking anyone else from getting inside.

"What's going on?" Orla cried, touching the force-field, and receiving a light shock for her troubles.

"Looks like it locks when someone from the magic bloodline enters," Kadesha said, turning to Jacob. "You should have gone in last."

"What?" Boocka growled from the other side of the force-field. "No way am I letting you go in there alone, M'lady."

"I will be OK."

"But –"

"You cannot protect me forever. Prince Jacob is with me. We will be fine."

"I'll take care of Lady Kadesha," Jacob promised.

Boocka hung his head. "I'm just doing my job."

"I know," Kadesha soothed. "And you have done your job very well. You have saved me more times than I care to remember, but this time I must venture into the unknown without you."

"I understand."

Jacob turned to Orla. "Well, this is it," he said, wishing the force-field wasn't keeping them apart.

"I guess so," she replied, offering a limp wave. "You come back safe. Do you hear me?"

Jacob nodded and turned back to Kadesha. "Let's do this."

They walked in single file with Jacob wondering what lay ahead. He hoped it would be easy to find the Lost ElmKey, but a nagging voice inside told him differently. There was danger ahead; he was sure of it.

The first room of the structure was dark, and it took a while for Jacob's eyes to adjust. In the centre of the room appeared a glowing stone that formed a second when Jacob stepped on it. Kadesha got the hint and stood on the second one. There was a whooshing noise as everything around them disintegrated. The atmosphere no longer felt real and seemed to flip over. What was once below, was now up above. Only the two floating stones kept them from falling into the abyss. Kadesha steadied herself, but a rising wind sent her off balance. She teetered on the brink as Jacob tried to grab her, but a second gust of wind blew them off the stones, and plummeting into the unknown.

Chapter XXVII

Bruised and battered from the fall, Jacob dragged his aching body off the ground and steadied himself against a shoulder-high pillar protruding from the soft dirt. A sharp pain in his chest accompanied every step he took, but he knew there was no time to dwell on bruised ribs. Not when Lady Kadesha was lying somewhere, possibly injured and in need of help.

Pushing the pain to the back of his mind, he scanned the squared room and found stone walls on every side. Kadesha was slumped against the brickwork of the opposite wall, a line of blood trickling from her forehead. Jacob staggered across the room, his initial fear dying down when Kadesha began pulling herself up.

"Are you OK?"

He knew it was a silly question. They would have died had the ground not been so soft.

"That was a strange turn of events," Kadesha said, using Jacob's arm as leverage to get back on her feet.

"What happened?" he asked, looking up from where they had fallen. "One minute, we were at the top, and now we're at the bottom."

"The entire structure seemed to flip," Kadesha replied, wincing as she touched the cut on her forehead.

"You OK?"

"I will live."

Jacob nodded and returned to staring at where they had fallen from. "It's a long way back up."

"We do not want to go back up," Kadesha replied bluntly. "We want to keep going through the tower."

"Check my mum's journal. Maybe there's something in there that can help."

"I already have. Fiona wrote about this room but not how to get out of it."

Jacob ran his hand along the stone wall, feeling for something that could offer a hint on how they could escape the sealed room; a lever, a loose brick, anything that could get them moving through the structure. Exasperated, and still nursing sore ribs, he gave up and lay back, staring up at the darkness.

"What's that?" he moaned.

"What?" Kadesha replied.

Something was digging into his spine. He rolled over and scraped away some of the dirt that had been under him. There was a small button buried in the soft ground.

"Could it be a way out of here?" he asked.

"Only one way to find out."

Jacob was sceptical. "What if it's something that makes our situation worse?"

"I struggle to think how our situation could be any worse," Kadesha chuckled. "Then you do the honours?"

"OK."

Using the ball of her right foot, Kadesha applied pressure to the button. Nothing happened. She tried again, practically stamping on it this time. A slight scraping sound accompanied the wall to their left before it slid away to reveal a doorway that led to a spacious room lit by flaming torches.

"Who put those torches here?" Jacob asked.

"I have no idea," Kadesha admitted. "I wonder if they were created as part of the structure."

Jacob turned around and found himself staring at a red mist swaying back and forth in the stuffy air. It had appeared from nowhere and moved like it possessed a mind of its own. Upon seeing the mist, Kadesha reached out to touch it, but it shot away into the next chamber.

"Follow it," yelled Jacob.

Kadesha checked the journal when they arrived in the next room, but there was no information on the mist that had led Jacob and Kadesha inside. The map of the tower showed there were three floors in total; Jacob and Kadesha were still on the bottom.

"What does that say?" Jacob asked, pointing to a strange scribble on the middle floor section of the map.

"Centre of the tower," Kadesha said as she took a closer look.

A set of stairs lay to the far right of their current position, and they climbed to the second-floor chamber. It was damp with a collection of small puddles. Jacob caught sight of his reflection in the murky water, and his appearance morphed before his very eyes. First, his brown hair turned grey, and then laughter lines and wrinkles ravaged his young face, progressing until his skin withered away and fell off, leaving nothing but a skull staring back at him.

He gasped, jumping back from the unsettling sight.

"Are you OK?" Kadesha asked, walking to him.

"I…the-the reflection!" he stammered, pointing towards the puddle.

Kadesha took a closer look. "There is nothing there."

"Impossible!" Jacob cried as he walked back to the puddle and saw his normal reflection. "I looked older. Like I'd aged rapidly."

"It must be an illusion. A test of our strength to keep going."

"Pretty convincing illusion."

"I understand it must have been terrifying, but we cannot let anything stop us."

Jacob trusted Kadesha's judgement but wondered if they could be in physical danger. It was all very well dealing with psychological tricks, but something capable of causing physical harm was a different story.

A high-pitched shriek broke the silence, and something landed behind them with a thud. Whirling, Jacob found a gigantic red insect with black spots covering its body. It had four hairy legs, vicious fangs, and two quivering antennae. Another one clung to the ceiling to his right and then clumsily dropped to the ground beside them.

"Where did they come from?" Jacob cried, backing away from the unsettling creatures.

Kadesha said, "I think they are illusions made by the tower."

"So, we run?"

"Why? They cannot hurt us."

The Ant who fell first spat a gloopy green acid in Jacob's direction, but he ducked, and the acid splatted against the wall behind him, eroding a small part of it in the process.

"Are you sure about that?" he cried to Kadesha.

"Now that you mention it...no."

"Run."

They bolted through the chamber, barely stopping to look at their surroundings. The insects scuttled behind them, spitting acid that missed Jacob by inches. After turning a corner, Jacob and Kadesha found themselves standing in front of what seemed to be an infinite drop.

"Trapped," Jacob yelled in panic, as he heard the insects scuttling closer.

"Over there," Kadesha said, pointing to a small ledge protruding from the left wall. It ran across the drop and ended on the other side, beside another set of stairs leading upwards.

With Kadesha in the lead, they moved sideways like crabs across a sandy beach, while the insects spat globs of acid from the pit-edge. One hit part of the ledge below Jacob's feet, eroding the rock and sending him crashing through it. His heart nearly stopped, but he threw a hand-out at the last second, holding on for dear life as he dangled above the bottomless pit. Kadesha's anguished cries echoed through the chamber as another glob of venom almost found its hanging target.

"Pull yourself up," Kadesha screamed, trying to move backwards across the ledge to reach him.

"I can't," he yelled back. "Never mind me, just get to the other side."

Jacob did not look down as he dangled because he was certain the shock would send him plummeting to his death. Getting hit with acid was also a non-starter, so he shimmied along the ledge, gritting his teeth as the weight of his body tested the meagre muscles in his skinny arms.

The insects were frenzied now, running towards the edge of the pit before turning back and repeating the movement. Jacob braced himself for another round of poisonous glob, and sure enough, it came thick and fast, splattering the wall inches from his face.

"Come on," he heard Kadesha call from the safety of the pit's opposite side.

A sudden sheer will to survive gave him an extra kick, and Jacob shimmied faster, luckily avoiding more globs of venom before pulling himself to safety, just as the entire ledge crumbled into the bottomless pit. The insects on the other side still spat acid, but the distance was too great, and Jacob breathed a sigh of relief as he led Kadesha up the next set of stairs.

"Over here," he said, pointing to a narrow doorway at the top. It led to a box-room with a statue of a female Dakew that stood the entire height of the room. There was a gap in the ceiling above, leading to the next floor.

"That's conveniently placed," Jacob remarked.

"Very," Kadesha concurred.

Jacob arched his neck to look at the gap in the ceiling. They could reach it by scaling the Dakew statue and standing on top of its head. The only question was whether Kadesha had the energy for it. She looked tired. It was clear the journey had taken a lot out of her.

"Will you make it?" he asked.

"Make it?" Kadesha chuckled. "I'll be up there before you."

He shook his head in disbelief as she moved away and began to scale the statue.

What a lady.

"I think you better come and see this," she shouted down.

Jacob took a short run and leaped onto the statue's right knee, using small dents in the surface for something to grip to. He scrambled up the body, across the right arm, and onto the nose, using it as a ledge to reach the head. Once up top, he dragged himself through the gap and found himself in a well-lit room full of statues, with six tiers on either side and a set of golden steps in the middle. There was a pedestal at the top of the steps, but whatever lay on top was outside his line of vision.

Kadesha gasped. "The ElmKey is up there."

"Are you sure?"

"Your mum seemed convinced it would be," she replied, flashing the journal pages again.

"So, we made it?" Jacob said excitedly.

He felt like a kid in a sweet shop. There was a time, particularly after the events on Charn, where he struggled to believe their attempts to find the Lost ElmKey would be successful. Now, he stood on the brink of its recovery, wishing his mother was around to see him retrieve the artefact she had written so much about in her diary.

"Wait a minute!"

Jacob turned around and saw what had caused Kadesha's outburst. The mist from before had returned. It floated around the room like a lost soul searching for a body and then absorbed itself into the statue of a monstrous creature with an elongated head and two horns. Within moments, the statue turned into a living entity, and the monstrous creature burst from its position, emitting deafening roars that seemed to shake the tower itself.

"Do you think it's mad we've busted into its home?" Jacob asked, pulling the Dynasty Staff from his back, and adopting a fighting stance.

"He sure looks it."

The creature flew across the room on its hind legs, knocking the Dynasty staff from Jacob's hand with its right horn. Jacob kept his balance, but the creature's thick tail caught him on the head, and he crashed to the ground, leaving him at its mercy.

"Over here," Kadesha called as she came into the creature's line of vision, frantically waving her hands to gain its attention.

The creature sped away from Jacob in hot pursuit of Kadesha, who was hurtling towards stairs that led to the tower's top tier. She raced up them and rolled through a gap between the wall and floor, out of reach of the creature's searching claws.

Jacob got to his feet and recovered the Dynasty Staff, just as the creature turned around and sped across the room again. This time, Jacob dived away at the last second, and the monstrous entity slammed against the wall, knocking a flaming torch to the ground. The creature recoiled in pain as the fire died, but it recovered quickly and then stormed ahead to smash Jacob with another tail swing. Winded, Jacob struggled to the stairs and rolled to safety alongside Kadesha.

"Did you see that?" Kadesha asked, excitedly.

"See what?"

"The way it reacted when the torch went out? It seemed to cause it pain. We need to put the rest out."

Another roar that sounded like it would bring the entire tower down exploded around them. Then the creature rushed towards the stairs, scrambling up and gnawing and pawing to reach the two invaders who had gate-crashed its home. Jacob felt smoke-filled breath on his face and saw the creature's blood-red eyes up close.

He needed to get out to reach the torches. But how?

"Use the staff!" Kadesha cried.

Jacob poked the creature straight in the eye, and it straightened up for a moment in what was probably equal parts shock and agony, giving Jacob time to run out and jump over the edge of the tier. He landed and executed a perfect roll, grabbing the nearest torch in the process and then racing up the stairs to safety on the other side. Once again, claws came within inches of finding their target, but Jacob dropped the torch and stamped it out. The creature writhed in agony, allowing Kadesha to retrieve another torch from the other side of the room and extinguish its flame. They continued taking turns until only a single torch remained, and the creature had returned to its harmless mist form, floating aimlessly around the room.

Jacob dusted himself down and joined Kadesha at what he presumed was The Lost ElmKey, sitting on top of a pedestal. It was a purple orb with three red lines appearing to float in a watery substance.

"I cannot believe we found it." Kadesha beamed.

Jacob reached forward and placed his hands on the ElmKey. Almost immediately, the structure began to violently shake. He snatched his hands away, startled.

"We may have a problem," Kadesha admitted.

Jacob touched the ElmKey again, curious. This time the shaking was more intense, and bits of rock fell from above.

"The tremors will get worse when we remove the ElmKey. I think we might need to get out of here, fast." She handed Jacob the satchel. "You're quicker than me."

"How much time do you think we have before the place collapses?"

"I have no idea, but let's hope it's enough to get out of here."

Chapter XXVIII

With Kadesha already on the move, Jacob grabbed the ElmKey and stuffed it into Boocka's satchel before spinning away and racing back down the golden steps at breakneck speed. He ran so fast it felt like his legs would give way at any minute, while the tower shook and rumbled in what seemed to be an echoing prologue for something even more disastrous.

The stairs crumbled around him and then completely collapsed as he jumped from the last step and rolled across the ground. He lay there for a moment, hoping to catch his breath, but the ground then began to split underneath him, teasing a fall into nothingness where oblivion surely waited. A crippling fear consumed him as he stared into the deep, dark vacancy.

"Come on," Kadesha shouted back, as she jogged towards the door at the right-hand side of the gap with the statue underneath.

Jacob leapt to his feet and propelled himself in the same direction. He was gaining on her now, almost neck and neck as they ran through the door and up another set of stone steps that led to an empty room, except for a single rope dangling from a rather large crack in the rocky ceiling.

"You first," Jacob wheezed.

As Kadesha began to climb towards the crack in the ceiling, Jacob did not dare glance back but heard more rumbles. The steps and ground behind him began to split and crumble, making him terrified he would be cast into the unknown. He had no idea what lay beyond the tower, but it was not his intention to find out.

"Come on, come on," he muttered to himself, as Kadesha continued to crawl upwards.

Finally, there was enough space for two. Jacob gripped the rope at the last possible second, just before the ground broke in two underneath him, leaving him hanging precariously over the darkness. He pulled himself up behind Kadesha, but it was harder than he had imagined and took his maximum physical and mental strength to not give up and let go.

Closing his eyes, he continued to climb, and by the time he opened them again, Kadesha was through the gap and waiting with an outstretched hand to help him up. At the top, he rolled onto his back and stared up at the strange rock formations that hugged the ceiling. One spiked rock suddenly dropped towards him, but he rolled away quickly, and it smashed into the ground, inches away from him.

"That was close," he said nervously.

Scrambling to his feet, he found Kadesha on her knees, breathing erratically and continuously shaking her head. "I can't…go on," she puffed.

"Yes, you can."

Jacob pulled Kadesha onto her feet, gave her a moment to regain her breath, and then led her across the dangerous terrain. Rocks from the ceiling continued to fall, and Jacob had to duck and dive to ensure a solid mass of stone did not crush him. Kadesha was struggling to keep up. Jacob knew she was exhausted; her eyes were almost closed, and he could see sweat glistening on her forehead. It was then he began to doubt their chances of getting out alive. Still, he pushed on, practically dragging Kadesha towards the stairs while the structure continued to collapse around them.

Another rock, larger than the others, dropped from the ceiling towards the middle of them. Jacob let Kadesha's hand go and dived forward. He turned to see her falling back as the rock crashed through the ground, creating a split that ran the length of the room. Each side was pulled away by the pressure, until the split became an insurmountable gap, leaving Jacob on the side of potential safety, and Kadesha on the other.

"No!" Jacob screamed.

A plume of thick grey smoke rose from the gap, and Jacob felt the quakes getting worse.

"I'll find a way across for you!" he cried, as more smoke rose from below.

"Forget about me," she called back. "Get back to the surface. You must return to Uthovaya with the ElmKey and prove you are the rightful King."

"I won't leave you."

Jacob was frantically searching for a way across now, the panic in his soul rising like the smoke from the split ground. He noticed Kadesha was not moving very much at all. She just stood there, looking resigned to her inevitable fate, and making Jacob even more apprehensive.

"Look for a way across," he yelled in frustration.

"You are wasting time. I do not matter in the grand scheme. You must go."

Jacob ignored Kadesha's pleas. Leaving her behind was not an option. They were a team; if Kadesha could not leave, then neither could he.

"Will you listen to me?" he heard Kadesha cry.

Suddenly, a strong wind rose from the split, creating a vacuum that pulled loose rocks towards it – and Jacob as well. He crawled away from danger and then gripped solid rock to stop himself from being dragged into the abyss with the other debris. Kadesha was still calling his name, but he could barely hear her cries over the howling gale. It took several minutes for the wind to die down, and they could communicate once again.

"Jacob, you must leave without me," Kadesha ordered.

"Stop talking like that."

"Then you leave me no choice."

"Wait, what?"

She waved in his direction and then moved wearily towards the split. The moment seemed to pass in slow motion, but when she purposely leapt into the void, everything sped up again. She disappeared in an instant. Jacob watched her vanish into the darkness and then screamed her name in vain.

Standing all alone, he felt like someone had punched him in the gut. Tears stung his eyes as he staggered backwards, but his legs gave way from shock, and he sat helplessly in front of the yawning chasm where Kadesha had made the ultimate sacrifice.

He remained there for what might have been a lifetime but came to his senses when a second wind rose. It was stronger this time, pulling him towards the nothingness with obvious intent. Every movement sapped what little remained of his energy as he dragged himself away from the deathly drop. He was still dazed and confused when he started to ascend the final set of stone steps towards the light of day.

A glimpse of daylight brought the hope of survival, only for the stairs underneath him to disintegrate. His body twisted in mid-air, and then he was falling into the darkness. Before it could swallow him, two strong hands appeared from nowhere, gripping his wrists and pulling him to the surface. As he lay in the hot sand gasping for breath, Jacob opened his eyes and saw who had saved his life.

Gunnar Veto.

He had cast away his blue tunic, presumably because of the heat, and rolled the ruffled sleeves up on his white shirt. Jacob could see exposed wires on his left shoulder connect to a black glove that ran the length of his forearm and possibly further up. It was obviously how he generated the electricity.

"What have we here?" Veto grinned, removing Jacob's staff and launching it across the sand.

Jacob was then pulled to his feet, but he was too busy surveying the scene in front of him to fight back. Orla, Boocka, and Hudson were on their knees in the sand, while six armed soldiers stood behind them with rifles. The Shadow-Flare loomed in the background.

"Where's Lady Kadesha?" was Boocka's sudden cry.

Out of breath and choking back tears, Jacob shook his head. It was all he could do to avoid falling apart on the spot. He was almost paralysed with shock, devastated at the loss of someone who had changed his life for the better.

Boocka did not need Kadesha's fate spelled out to him. He broke down in tears, his anguished howls enough to pierce even the most insensitive of souls. Orla quickly followed in teary-eyed mourning, while Hudson slowly bowed his head in obvious respect.

"Tragic," Gunnar Veto said, his tone dripping in sarcasm.

"Shut up," Boocka snarled.

Veto smirked in response, and then paced in front of Jacob for a few seconds, eyeing him with a steely look that made Jacob uncomfortable. The unease grew even worse as Veto tentatively approached him.

"Prince Jacob," Veto said, taking a bow that was steeped in mockery. "You've given us quite the run-around. If I didn't know any better, I'd say you were trying to avoid me."

Jacob remained silent. The idea of casually chatting with the man who was indirectly responsible for his parent's death, probably killed all the colonists on Charn, and murdered Mr. Janmano made Jacob feel nauseous. He hated the Antantan with an absolute passion.

"Answer him," a soldier barked, slamming the butt of his gun into Jacob's face.

Sharp pain exploded through his skull, and Jacob tasted warm blood. Veto raised his hand, and the soldier backed away, allowing Jacob to straighten himself up and face his nemesis once again.

"How did you find us?" Jacob growled as he struggled back to his feet.

"You should have chosen your friends more wisely."

Boocka turned angrily towards Captain Hudson. "It was you?"

"Don't be stupid," Hudson shot back. "If I wanted to betray you, I would have done it long before now."

The culprit came quickly to Jacob. "It must have been Junt Kidd," he sighed.

Boocka turned back to Hudson, and an angry exchange took place over Junt's involvement. For his own part, Jacob did not blame Hudson. They would never have gotten this far without Junt's input.

"You can search him now," Veto said to one of the soldiers.

Jacob waited until the soldier got close and then tried to wrestle the gun from his hands, but the soldier was too strong and ended Jacob's mini uprising with another blow to the face. He regained his composure and tried again, but the soldier aimed another well-timed hit, and that one knocked Jacob to the sand. Dazed and confused, he was powerless to stop the soldier from removing the satchel and handing it to Veto, who smirked as he rummaged through it and brought the ElmKey into the daylight.

"It's beautiful," Veto said, staring intensely at his new acquisition. "The president will be delighted we have such a powerful artefact in our possession."

"It doesn't belong to the president," Jacob told him.

"You're right, but it doesn't belong to you either. Both ElmKeys were put on Lozaro by a race we know next to nothing about. Our president has long studied the Creators, hoping to learn their secrets. The Lost ElmKey will hopefully tell us more about them."

Veto put the ElmKey back in the satchel and then pointed at Jacob with his natural arm.

"Get him on board," he snorted to the soldiers.

"What about the others, sir?"

Veto did not even hesitate before answering.

"Execute them."

Panic gripped Jacob, immediately. He could not handle the prospect of his friends losing their lives, especially Orla, who he had persuaded to come along in the first place. He had to do something, anything to save them.

"Wait," Jacob said, pushing a soldier's arm away as he tried to grip him. "The others have nothing to do with this. You've got the ElmKey, and you've got the last Crestmore. Don't punish them for following me."

"They are criminals," Veto fired back.

"No, they followed me because I asked them to." He looked straight at Orla with tears burning his eyes. "Please, let them go."

Jacob turned his attention back to Veto. Amazingly, he seemed to be considering the request.

"Um, sir," a soldier interrupted. "I think you should take a look at this."

"What is it?" Veto replied grumpily.

The concerned soldier appeared to be pointing into the distance, where three black objects were speeding towards the gathering. As they got closer, it became apparent they were Pulse-Fighters.

"The Revolutionaries!" Orla screamed in excitement.

"Get the prince," Jacob heard Veto shout.

Everyone scattered as the fighters flew just above them. The force of the wind sent several soldiers and

Jacob flying. By the time he staggered back to his feet, the fighters had swung around again and were firing shots at the soldiers and the motionless Shadow-Flare. After whooshing past a second time, the fighters turned again but came to a quick stop just above the ground. Green-clad Revolutionaries leapt from the aircraft and traded fire with the Antantan soldiers. More Antantans exploded from the Shadow-Flare, providing backup to their distressed comrades.

Emboldened by the sudden turn of events, Jacob sprang into action, sending a trooper onto the sand with a spear manoeuvre. Boocka was next to get involved, using his head to ram a soldier unconscious. Orla was grappling with two others, while Hudson was on the ground wrestling with a particularly burly one.

Sensing his chance, Jacob bolted towards the Dynasty Staff, but sudden pain exploded in his head again, and he found himself back on the sand, fighting to stay conscious. Veto loomed over him, pistol in hand, and sporting an angry expression.

"You're coming with me," he growled.

Jacob was lifted over Veto's shoulder and heard him give the cry to evacuate. As he was carried up the Shadow-Flare's gangplank, Jacob got one last look at a despairing Orla, before the doors closed.

Chapter XXIX

Orla watched the Shadow-Flare rise into the sky with her best friend on board and immediately felt a sense of hopelessness that made all her past fears about losing Jacob become a terrifying reality.

"Do something," she cried to Boocka.

"There's nothing we can do," he replied coldly.

"No!" Orla ran in the direction the Shadow-Flare had flown. She burst across the sand like Jacob's life depended on it, as though sheer will alone could somehow bridge the gap between herself and the monstrous flying symbol of Antantan oppression, but the harsh terrain and sizzling hot weather slowed her down quickly. She collapsed in defeat, doomed to watch the Shadow-Flare become a dot on the horizon.

"Are you alright?" she heard Boocka ask, as he trudged up behind her.

Orla spun around. "What kind of question is that? Of course, I'm not alright. They've got Jacob and the ElmKey."

"I know. It's all gone to hell."

Orla retrieved the Dynasty Staff from the sand and then made her way across with Boocka to Hudson and the soldiers. All were checking the Antantan bodies, presumably to ensure none of them were still alive. As she got closer, she recognised one soldier as Commander Jackson, the man they had met when visiting the Uthovayan base.

"Where's Lady Kadesha?" Jackson asked.

Boocka turned away as Orla delivered the horrible news. "She didn't make it."

Jackson hung his head. "I'm sorry."

"The Antantans have Jacob," she added. "And the ElmKey."

"Damn," Jackson replied, squinting in the glare of the sun. "Just when I thought things couldn't get any worse."

"How do you mean?"

"Operation Creeper is finally ready to launch, but we've hit a few problems. Some of our financial backers have gotten cold feet, and I doubt losing the rightful heir to the throne will help the situation."

Orla was confused. "Why does that even matter? We already have an army ready to go, and Cyclops are providing the weapons, so who cares what the financial backers think?"

"It's a bit more complicated than that. Those backers are the ones who will keep the country afloat after the coup until we get back on our feet. We need the transition to be as smooth as possible for the Uthovayans."

315

"I don't believe this," Boocka raged. "What can we do about it?"

"There's a vote being held later tonight," Jackson explained.

"We have to be there," Orla said, firmly.

Boocka shook his head. "What good will that do? They're not gonna listen to us."

"We'll make them listen," Orla said, aware of the determination in her tone. "If we don't, then Lady Kadesha and most likely Jacob will have died for nothing."

Jackson nodded and then ushered everyone on board the Pulse-Fighter.

"You coming as well?" Boocka asked Hudson.

"Damn right. I'll come back for the Veteran when this is all over."

"Even though Jacob's gone, and you can't claim the rest of your fee from Ryker? Not very mercenary-like."

"Ye sound surprised."

"Can you blame me?" Boocka laughed. "But I have to admit I got you all wrong."

"Ye didn't really. Finding out Jacob's real identity makes me think there's more to this story. I fully expect to discover you've been the princess of Krokira all this time. Ye think I'd miss that?"

Orla interrupted their bonding session by gently pushing Hudson towards the Pulse-Fighter. "We'll have plenty of time to tell you the full story. It's a long way back to Uthovaya."

Chapter XXX

Jacob could feel eyes full of hatred glaring at him. It seemed like every Antantan soldier, officer, and member of the flight crew had gathered to watch Gunnar Veto frogmarch him through the Shadow-Flare's monotonous grey corridors. Some gnashed their teeth and shouted abuse, others spat in his direction. One female officer rushed forward and planted a thunderous right hook on his chin. It stung, but he tried not to show as much. Why give them the satisfaction?

The hateful welcome came as no surprise. Jacob had always known the Antantans despised anyone with Dakew blood. But something told him their reaction came more from the fact he was the last surviving Crestmore, a family who stood for everything the Antantans did not. In that moment, he felt enormous pride in himself and the family name.

Although his prospects looked bleak, Jacob could not help but admire the irony of the situation he had found himself in. Nobody knew him back in Uthovaya; nobody cared to know him. It was that feeling of invisibility and restlessness that convinced him he needed to get away from the capital and make something of himself. He had achieved his goal, albeit not in the way he envisioned at the time.

Now, he was something more. Still, others bemoaned his very existence. Not that he would change it for the world. Orla's decision to visit Oakhedge and Kadesha's introduction into his life were the best things to ever happen to him.

Kadesha.

His mind trudged back to her final moments. The falling rock, the desperate search for a way across the chasm, the blind panic as he came to understand Kadesha's final words before leaping to her death in a remarkable act of self-sacrifice. Had Kadesha not given her life, he would have been plunged into the void with her when the structure completely disintegrated. Now, he was trapped on board the Shadow-Flare, facing certain death that would render Kadesha's bravery meaningless.

No. The Revolutionaries would surely launch Operation Creeper without him. It was imperative he somehow escape the Shadow-Flare and take his position on the throne, though. Hopefully, the Uthovayans would believe he was the rightful king even without the Elm-Key and power of elemental magic. It was risky, probably even reckless considering the likelihood of a civil war, but what choice did he have? Uthovaya deserved to be free once more. It's what Kadesha would have wanted, not to mention his deceased parents.

Still chaperoned by Veto and two soldiers, Jacob turned another corner and found his path blocked by a man he did not recognise. He wore a black and gold waistcoat with a long-sleeved dark shirt, a high collar, and the Antantan insignia on his right breast. He stood upright, staring straight ahead, and emitting authority over the corridor. Despite his powerful persona, Jacob sensed a frosty atmosphere between him and Veto.

"This is Vice-President Gex," Veto said, the disgust practically dripping from his voice.

"Ah, the last Crestmore." Gex grinned.

"You better believe it."

"Charming," he said, raising an eyebrow. "Well, Jacob Crestmore, I have good news for you. The President has decided to turn your death into a national event. You will be taken back to Antantis and marched through the streets of our great nation's capital. Then you will be executed for the viewing public's pleasure."

"Sounds wild," Jacob said, rolling his eyes. "Just one question, if I may?"

"Make it quick."

"Do I get into this event for free, or will I need to pay at the gate like everyone else?"

Gex ignored the sarcastic comment and turned his attention to Veto. "Do you have the Lost ElmKey?"

"Right here."

Veto released the orb from Boocka's satchel and then handed it to his superior. Gex studied the object in his hand and then turned to leave.

"Just a moment," Veto said, stopping Gex in his tracks. "I hope you told the President it was me who recovered it? Can't have you taking the credit now, can we?"

"Credit? Do not make me laugh. The others got away. Even in victory, you somehow manage to fail."

Jacob looked on as Veto advanced on Gex, a look of venomous rage twisting his face into something hideous. Gex seemed unfazed, perhaps because the soldiers had switched from pointing their weapons at Jacob to Veto instead.

"Back off," Gex growled.

"Don't tell me to back off. You know how much I need this success on my record."

"Your record is a list of one failure after another. Adding one minor success won't make a blind bit of difference."

The tense standoff lasted a few more seconds, but Jacob was left in no doubt about Gex and Veto's hatred of one another. After trading a few more insults, Gex laughed in victory and then marched off down the corridor. The soldiers then turned their weapons back on Jacob.

"Trouble in paradise?" Jacob joked.

"Nothing I can't handle."

"Yeah, you really looked like you were on top of things there."

Veto ignored the comment and made his way across to a metal door. "Get over here."

Sensing he had gone as far as possible with the wind-ups, Jacob followed Veto's order and watched him insert a keycard into a control panel. The door pinged open to reveal a grey hallway with three jail cells on each side, and a single metal door at the end. Jacob looked through each cell window as they passed. All were empty, except the last one on the left where a prisoner lay motionless on top of a single bed, covered with a threadbare blanket. It was impossible to tell if the prisoner was still alive because they lay facing the faraway wall.

"In here," Veto barked, inserting his keycard into the control panel by the room at the end.

It was an interrogation room, containing a metal desk with two chairs. Veto ordered Jacob to sit in the chair across the other side and then pushed a bronze lamp into the middle of the desk. Veto then sat in the chair directly opposite, exhaling loudly as he planted himself down.

Despite his dislike of guns as a weapon, Jacob wished one was within his grasp so he could use it on the man who killed his parents. The man who had made so many others suffer.

"Well, where do we start?" Veto asked, leaning forward and clasping his hands together.

"You can start by telling me why I'm in here."

"How do you mean?"

"Well, you already have the Lost ElmKey. What more do you hope to learn? Why not just sling me in one of those cells until we reach Antantis?"

"There's plenty more you can tell us. You spent time with Kadesha, so you must know a lot about the Revolutionaries."

"And?"

"And I'll be expecting information."

"You're wasting your breath," Jacob said flatly. "I won't sell the Revolutionaries out, and you know it. Why not just kill me right here and save us all the embarrassment of a public execution?"

Veto shook his head. "I cannot do that. The President wants to be there when you take your last breath. He was disappointed not to witness it twenty years ago."

"Clearly, watching my parents take their last breath wasn't enough?"

Veto shifted uncomfortably in his chair. "Let's cut to the chase. I did not actually bring you in here to discuss the Revolutionaries. I wanted to ask you something."

Jacob was intrigued by his comment, so he sat forward in his chair. Veto took a deep breath before he continued.

"How did you escape Oakhedge?"

Veto's question confused Jacob. How could the special agent have possibly known his whereabouts when even Lady Kadesha and the Revolutionaries were unaware? Had Veto found out later? Did someone recently tell him? Yes, that must have been how he knew.

Unless…

"Did you know my foster-parents?" Jacob asked tentatively, taking a wild stab in the dark as to the truth of the matter.

"What makes you say that?"

"Call it a hunch."

Veto rose from his seat, double checked the door remained firmly closed, and then aggressively leaned on the desk.

"Who do you think paid those two idiots to take you in? I warned them what would happen should you ever leave Oakhedge, but I should have known they couldn't handle a simple task."

Jacob was shocked at learning the truth. Pirlie and Raszlo had taken him in for money, and not just anyone's money, but Gunnar Veto's – the man who had murdered his parents. No wonder they had treated him so badly. Jacob felt an enormous weight lift from his shoulders as he realised their lack of love was not caused by anything he had done.

"What about my mum's journal?"

"What about it?"

"It's what led us to the Lost ElmKey. Why would you leave it with Pirlie and Raszlo if you didn't want me to know my real mother?"

Veto pulled the journal from the satchel and then began flicking through the pages. He shook his head a few times and then tossed it onto the desk. Jacob reached out to take it, but Veto snatched it back.

"I never once said I didn't want you to know your real mother. I just didn't want you leaving Oakhedge. How was I to know it wasn't a personal diary? I don't speak Dakew."

Only one question remained. Jacob thought long and hard about asking, but in the end, he decided it was best to know the answer.

"Why would you take me away in the first place? Why not send me to the President along with my parents?"

"Does it matter?" Veto sighed.

"You had my parents killed without thinking twice, yet you kept me alive. Of course, it matters."

"That's not entirely true," Veto explained, taking his seat back at the desk. "I hated your parents when I first met them, especially your mother."

"Watch it, Veto."

"You don't understand. Hating the Dakew comes like second nature to us Antantans. We don't even question these beliefs. But your mother…" He stopped and then sat back down in the chair like he was in a trance. "Your mother was different. Fiona showed me it was all a lie. She was such a wonderful woman. I wish there was some way I could make things up to her, but it's too late now."

Confused at his ramblings, Jacob studied Veto carefully. There was a sadness about him, perhaps even regret about how things had turned out. It made Jacob wonder if Veto's relationship with his mother was platonic or something more. Jacob opened his mouth to ask for clarity but decided against it. Some questions were better left unanswered.

"You sing my mother's praises, yet you betrayed her," Jacob said, his eyes filling with tears.

"I begged the President to spare your mother's life when the time came. I explained how much she meant to me, but he wouldn't listen."

"How big of you," Jacob shot back. "She trusted you, and you used that trust against her."

"I know!" Veto yelled, tears rolling down his cheeks as well now. "There isn't a day goes by when I don't think of her."

"And what about my father? Just an afterthought, was he?"

"Seth was collateral damage."

"Spoken like a true psychopath," Jacob whispered, rolling his eyes at the sheer mental gymnastics Veto must have performed to justify his role in the downfall of the Uthovayan royal family.

"I know it's hard for you to believe, but I genuinely am sorry how things worked out. I was only following orders."

"Were you following orders when you murdered my friend, Mr. Janmano? Or everyone else at the Dance for Liberty? What about the colony on Charn?"

Veto stared blankly, looking like a lost soul who had wandered into the day of judgement.

"Why save my life?" Jacob blurted out. "You still haven't told me."

"It was the right thing to do. When I realised, I could not save your mother, I did the next best thing and made sure you survived."

"And I bet you think that makes up for everything."

"Enough!" Veto roared, storming away from the table to face the door. "If there was a way to make up for my actions, I would."

A plan suddenly came to Jacob. Could Veto's moment of weakness be used against him? Perhaps, he could be persuaded to make one last decent decision in Fiona's memory? It was a long shot, but Jacob was convinced it was worth a try.

"Maybe, there is a way you can make things up to my mum." He said, getting up from his chair and walking behind the distraught Antantan special agent.

"What are you talking about?" Veto replied, still not turning to face Jacob.

"Let me go."

Veto spun on the spot. "Let you go?"

"Yes. Give me the Lost ElmKey and get me off this ship."

"Why would I do that?"

"Because it's your one final chance to make things right. The only reason we still have a chance at bringing back elemental magic is because you kept me alive back then. Let me go, and I'll finish the job you started. You can be the man who made it all possible."

Veto seemed to be thinking over Jacob's request but then shook his head. "I'm sorry," he finally said. "But we cannot have elemental magic making a return. That kind of power is too precious to hand over. It came from a race we barely understand."

Despite what Veto said, Jacob got the impression his captor was leaning towards helping him out, so he cranked the pressure up a notch, hoping he could somehow persuade Veto to do the right thing.

"It's not just elemental magic Mum would want brought back. She would have wanted me on the Uthovayan throne. You can make that happen."

"I –"

"Please," Jacob begged. "Don't let the Crestmore name die with me."

Veto sighed loudly and then turned to place his keycard into the control panel. Two soldiers waited on the opposite side of the door, and Jacob knew immediately they were to escort him to his cell.

"I'm sorry," Veto whispered, flatly.

"So am I," Jacob replied, unable to contain the disappointment in his tone.

Alone in his cell, Jacob sat on the uncomfortable bed and stared at the blood-stained walls, preparing for his public execution in front of a baying mob of bigoted Antantans.

Chapter XXXI

"How are you holding up?" Orla asked Boocka.

The Krokiran was slumped in his seat by the window on the Pulse-Fighter and had barely uttered a word since they left the Tavara Desert. It was not like him. Boocka had never been the friendliest individual, but Orla could always count on him finding something to moan about. The fact he had stayed silent for the entire journey worried her greatly.

"What do you mean, how am I holding up?" Boocka replied, suddenly sitting bolt upright. "Nothing wrong with me. I'm fine."

"Don't try to kid me, Boocka. I know you, remember? You're not as tough as you make out."

"Well, maybe you don't know me as well as you think? I'm over it."

Orla knew it was an act of self-preservation. Lady Kadesha had been his employer, best friend, and confidante for years. Her death had taken its toll on him, and it showed in his apathetic reaction.

"Will you be seeking employment as a bodyguard somewhere else?"

It was a loaded question, but Orla hoped it would at least get him talking about his real feelings.

"Are you serious?" he snapped.

"Deadly serious. You said you're over Lady Kadesha's death, right? So, why not get straight back in the saddle?"

"I let Lady Kadesha down," he blurted out. "What makes you think I would do a better job guarding someone else?"

"You didn't let anybody down. There was nothing you could have done."

"Maybe, but I shoulda been there to help her."

"You've given Lady Kadesha years of service, always protected her no matter what. But she said herself you couldn't protect her forever. Don't beat yourself up or be afraid to mourn her."

Boocka nodded. "I hear ya. Maybe, I should be asking how you're holding up?"

A good question, but the answer was not good at all. Images of Jacob being dragged aboard the Shadow-Flare tormented her.

"I'm OK," She lied.

Boocka threw her a sceptical look. "Now who's pretending to be tough?"

"OK, I miss him," she admitted. "I know he's probably dead by now, but I don't want to think of him that way."

"Then don't think of him that way. Keep believing he's still alive."

"I'll try."

Commander Jackson came through from the cockpit. He was sporting a serious expression and looked tense as he addressed the trio in the cabin and told them the aircraft would be landing soon.

Half-an-hour later, Orla turned away from the window as the Pulse-Fighter hovered above a patch of wasteland on the outskirts of the Uthovayan Capital. The ground opened below them, and the Pulse-Fighter descended into the underground base where Ambassador Bellis was waiting for them at the bottom of the airstairs. She wore a fetching white gown and was flanked by two armed soldiers whose stern expressions never changed. Much to Orla's surprise, Bellis made a beeline straight for her instead of Boocka.

"We are so glad to see you back, safe. May I say how sorry I am for your loss. Prince Jacob would have been a real asset to Uthovaya."

"We don't know if he's dead yet," Orla shot back.

"Of course," Bellis said, before turning to Boocka. "And you, my friend. I cannot imagine your pain at losing Lady Kadesha. She was truly a special being."

"Thanks, Ambassador, but we must know what's happening with the vote on Operation Creeper."

Bellis had a worried look that made Orla immediately nervous.

"I am afraid we have encountered an unforeseen obstacle. A serious one that will render the vote meaningless."

"Meaningless?" Orla and Boocka repeated simultaneously.

"I don't quite know how to tell you this," Bellis said, twiddling her fingers, "but Cyclops has voided our contract."

"They can't do that?" Orla cried.

"I am afraid they can. As you are already aware, the arsenal they supplied came with an experimental locking system. Everything has been locked. Weapons, aircraft, tech, the lot.

"Damn that Ryker," Boocka blazed. "Wait, how did you manage to pick us up?"

"We used Pulse-Fighters that were purchased years ago from an independent arms dealer. Thank goodness we did, or they would have fallen out the sky when the locking system took effect."

"So, what happens now?" Orla asked. "Have you cancelled the vote?"

"Not yet. I have not told our backers in the hope we can find a solution. There is no coming back once they know the truth."

Orla turned to Boocka. "We have to unlock that arsenal."

"But how?"

Bellis said, "There should be a control room somewhere in the city where Cyclops administered the lock. It works by sending a shockwave that affects everything in range. I have my men looking for the control room as we speak."

Orla felt more relaxed. At least there was hope, however small. If they could somehow find the control room and unlock the arsenal, they could begin Operation Creeper – if it passed the vote, of course.

She thought long and hard about where the control room would be, but the Capital was a big place. It would be impossible to search everywhere in the time they had.

"Where is Ryker?" she asked. "Maybe we can persuade him to change his mind?"

"Nobody knows where Director Ryker is," Bellis said quickly. "He gave me the lock news by communicator but never revealed his location. I sent some of our troops out to look for him, but they came up empty-handed."

Orla's heart sank. "We owe Jacob and Lady Kadesha more than just giving up."

Hudson, who had remained silent during the entire exchange, suddenly became animated.

"Have ye tried Ryker's office in Culder Street?" he asked.

Bellis shook her head. "He does not have an office here in the city."

"Oh, he does." Hudson grinned, before turning to Boocka and Orla. "Cyclops has an entire building of offices. I should know; it's where we shook on our deal to take you guys to Charn."

Once again, hope sprang in Orla's heart.

"I had no idea," Bellis admitted. "I will send some troops round immediately."

"No," Boocka said, firmly. "This one's on us."

Orla waved her hands to get their attention. "What about the vote on Operation Creeper?"

"It's not for another few hours," Boocka replied. "We'll be back in time."

"Where have I heard that before?" She rolled her eyes, thinking about Jacob's words from before they left Uthovaya. The ones that got her into this whole, sorry mess in the first place.

Bellis said, "You really think Ryker can be persuaded to unlock the arsenal?

"Who knows?" Orla said, shrugging her shoulders. "Just make sure the backers don't find out about the weapons lock. That vote must go ahead – whatever happens."

They travelled to Ryker's office in Commander Jackson's jeep, but found the skyscraper full of offices closed and guarded by a bald and burly Cyclops agent. He looked less than impressed to see visitors coming towards him and urged them to leave immediately. Orla was just about to offer an excuse for their presence, but Hudson beat her to the punch, pistol-whipping the unsuspecting guard and then hiding him in a bush around the side of the building.

"Did you have to knock him out?" Orla fumed.

Hudson merely grinned. "You should know how I operate by now, Miss Paton."

Orla was second inside behind Hudson, through the revolving door, and into the lobby. It was dark, and she detected the unmistakable smell of fresh cleaning solution. As a result, she urged caution when walking across the slippery floor.

"Over here!" Hudson cried.

"Where?" Orla replied, trying to follow the direction of his voice.

Boocka appeared with a torch from behind the main desk. He made his way to the light switches across the other side of the lobby and flicked them several times.

"Power's out."

"Shine that torch over here," Orla ordered.

Blessed with the ability to see ahead, Orla pushed her way past a giant plant, and then took a seat on the edge of a circular water fountain.

"Looks like they've packed up and gone," she said.

"Damn cowards," Boocka snapped, turning away in disgust.

"Ryker's office is on the fourth floor," Hudson said. "We should still check it out. Maybe, we can find something useful?"

The elevator control panel was dead, so with Hudson still in the lead, they tiptoed along the hallway in search of the stairs, only to find a Cyclops agent waiting at the bottom of them. He was facing the opposite direction, but Orla could just about make out a small pistol in his right hand.

"Wait here," Boocka whispered.

Orla watched him sneak up behind the enemy like a ninja but closed her eyes when she heard a thud. By the time she opened them again, the agent was unconscious on the floor, and Boocka was standing over him with a wide grin that made his tusks rise.

There were four offices on each side of the deserted fourth floor; all were closed, except for the last one. It was wide open, and light from a torch could occasionally be seen dancing in the dark. As Orla followed Boocka along the hallway, she noticed lots of documents scattered across the floor, as though someone had been looking for something important.

A familiar voice speaking into a communicator from the office startled them, and Orla turned to Boocka and Hudson. "It's Ryker," she mouthed.

Both nodded, and the three crept as close to the doorway as silently they could, hoping to keep an element of surprise. When they entered the office, they found Ryker at his desk by the window, dressed in a black suit and crumpled white shirt. He looked exhausted, and his previously combed hair was messy.

"What are you doing here?"

"Shut up," Boocka raged. "You've got some explaining to do. What's the deal with locking our arsenal?"

"I don't owe you an explanation."

"Just start talking," Hudson ordered.

Ryker stretched back calmly in his chair. "You were the first client we used the lock with. It was only natural we wanted to test it out."

"Fine time to test it," said Orla, trying hard not to punch the smugness out the businessman sitting in front of her.

"It's nothing personal. I planned to test the lock and then pull out of the deal before Jacob showed up. The only reason I changed my mind was because I saw an opportunity that was too good to miss."

"Opportunity?" Orla said in confusion. "What opportunity?"

Although Orla grew increasingly uncomfortable with Ryker's replies, she needed an answer to what he meant. If Jacob had been the sole reason Cyclops had stayed involved, then his capture by the Antantans explained why they had lost interest.

"That boy is a weapon," Ryker explained. "We could have studied him, learned the secrets of elemental magic for ourselves."

Orla had never heard anything so ridiculous in her entire life.

"Elemental magic isn't something you study."

Ryker stood up from his desk and turned to the wall behind it.

"How do you know?" he asked without turning to face them. "Just because we do not understand something now, does not mean we won't understand it in the future. That's what Cyclops does. It's what the Antantans do as well – invest in science and technology so we can understand the world a little better. Look at the Creators,–They created this world and everything in it. We must embrace the idea of unlimited power like that."

Orla had to admit his speech was convincing, but he had omitted the part where the Antantans had stepped over another country to help fund their technological rise. There was no point in a glorious future if it was only for the privileged few. Ryker droned on and on while Orla considered this, but she snapped back to attention when he began talking about Jacob again.

"After Jacob re-appeared, we intended to ramp up our research into cloning." He spun back around. "Can you imagine an army of Elementalists? They would be an unstoppable force, even more so than the Cybernetic army we built for the Pavellians."

Orla could not believe what she was hearing. They were planning on cloning Jacob with the intention of creating soldiers capable of using magic.

"How can you be so reckless?" Orla growled. "Jacob told me that kind of power must be in the hands of someone responsible. You can't hope to monitor an entire army. If your plan went wrong, we could be talking about the end of the world."

"A bit over the top, don't you think?" Ryker hissed. "We asked ourselves a simple question: could the magic bloodline be duplicated? We think it can. That is as far as we got with the implications. Of course, we would have put safeguards in place, but none of that matters now. The Antantans have Jacob. It's over, and so is my interest in Uthovaya."

SEAN CLARKE

"Well, you better rethink your stance," Hudson
growled, unleashing the pistol from the holster on the
right side of his waist. "Give the order to unlock the
arsenal, or I'll shoot ye on the spot."

"What do you care if they take their country back?"
Ryker spat. "You're a mercenary. Shouldn't you be demanding the other half of your fee instead of joining
their cause?"

"Maybe I think their cause is worthwhile. You've
got five seconds."

"Better do what he says," Boocka added.

"Please," Orla pleaded with the Cyclops leader.
"Don't take away our nation's chance of freedom."

"It's not my problem," Ryker said, showing inexpli-
cable calm in the face of certain death.

"Five," Hudson said.

Ryker still sat with a smug look on his face.

"Four."

"I won't do it," Ryker said, calmly.

"Three."

No response.

"Two."

Still, nothing.

"One." Hudson grinned, as he cocked his weapon.

The room suddenly exploded with light from the
window, and Orla found herself shielding her eyes. She
heard an aircraft outside and the unmistakable sound
of breaking glass. By the time her eyes had adjusted,

Ryker was leaping out the window without a second thought. Rushing to the ledge, she saw him plummet towards the ground in the pouring rain, heading for certain death. Suddenly, he grabbed a hanging rope, and Orla looked up to see a Pulse-Fighter hovering in the sky. He began to climb the rope as it lifted into the air.

"This way!" Boocka cried.

With the Krokiran in the lead and Orla propping up the rear, they rushed out the room and up the stairs to the roof. Ryker was still hanging from the rope, but before Hudson and Boocka could fire a shot, the Pulse-Fighter shot away, taking Ryker to safety, and leaving Orla soaking in the heavy downpour.

"Damn," shouted Boocka as he spat out droplets of rainwater.

Orla could understand his frustration. Ryker had plenty of places to run. He was the head of a worldwide company who specialised in weapons and technology, not to mention he had friends in high places.

"Back downstairs," Orla ordered. "There might be some information on the control room location."

It was slim pickings in Ryker's office. Just a few scattered documents of unimportance and a few leftover personnel files. Both bins were filled with shredded paper.

"What now?" Hudson asked as they trudged down to the lobby and back through the revolving doors onto the busy street.

"Let's get back to the base," Orla suggested. "We need to make sure those backers vote to launch Operation Creeper."

"What's the point?" Boocka asked. "We can't launch unless we find the control room and unlock everything."

Orla got into the vehicle and exhaled. She did not have time to answer because Boocka's communicator went off. He answered and then spoke for a few seconds before hanging up excitedly.

"That was Bellis. She's found the control room."

Chapter XXXII

Running through the corridors of the Revolutionary's Uthovayan base with Boocka and Hudson, Orla felt like her heart could explode out of her chest at any minute. She was hoping to catch Ambassador Bellis before the vote took place, in order to learn the location of the Cyclops control room, but her hopes were dashed when she found Bellis standing at the entrance to the boardroom, surrounded by the financial backers, and in no position to have a quick chat about a problem that was supposed to be a secret.

"We will discuss the control room when the vote is over," Bellis whispered. "You can come inside if you want."

"Thank you, Ambassador," Orla replied, turning to Hudson and Boocka. "Shall we?"

Hudson sighed loudly. "I'll wait here."

"No, you won't," Orla shot back, disgusted he would even suggest missing the vote. "We are all going in. Understood."

Hudson put his hands up in mock defence of his point, before bursting into fits of laughter.

"Fine, if it means that much to ye, I'll come in. Don't complain if I fall asleep, though. Suits and boardrooms bore me."

The boardroom was an average-sized room with no windows and an extraordinarily high-ceiling. Seven raised podiums could be accessed by stairs, and in front of them were wooden seats that looked like they had been hastily assembled minutes before anyone entered the room. Orla could feel the tension in the air as she took her seat beside Boocka and Hudson in the back row. A call from the tannoy announced the vote would be taking place momentarily, and suddenly every chair in the room was taken.

"Do you think they'll vote to launch?" Orla heard one of the colonel's say to another.

"Who knows?" the other replied. "We won't get another shot if they don't."

After what seemed like an agonizing wait, a bespectacled man wearing a dark suit cleared his throat and demanded everyone's attention. He then introduced the six backers one by one: two Humans, two Dakew, and two Remmans. Each took a podium elevated above Orla and the others. Ambassador Bellis came in last, giving Orla a friendly nod before taking position on the last remaining podium.

"Let's begin," Bellis said in a strong and steady tone.

Each backer was given two glowing sticks, one red and one green. A green stick raised in the air meant a vote for launch, and the red stick meant the opposite.

Bellis then explained she would have the deciding vote in the event of a draw. They mulled over their decision for about ten seconds, before all but one lifted their stick into the air.

Three red.

Two green.

The last backer did not budge, perhaps enjoying his temporary power over everyone in the room. Orla held her breath. She knew a red stick would end their Operation Creeper hopes while a green stick would force a draw, all but guaranteeing the launch on Bellis' say so. The tension became unbearable, as the backer prepared to raise one stick in the air. Orla knew something had to be done, something to ensure Bellis got the final vote.

"Wait," Orla shouted to the funder. "There's something I wish to say before you make your decision."

The others looked less than pleased with Orla's request.

"Go on, then." Bellis smiled, ignoring the surrounding displeasure.

Orla took a deep breath and braced herself for the most important speech of her life. Memories of her botched attempt at the ballroom came flooding back, but she stemmed the tide of self-doubt and stood up with unshakeable confidence.

"A few weeks ago, we set out on a quest to bring the Lost ElmKey back to Uthovaya. My friends and I did our best. Unfortunately, it came at a price. I lost something dear." She paused, allowing herself thoughts of happier times with Jacob. "Uthovaya has lost an awful lot, too. How much longer will we sit back and allow the Antantans the freedom to destroy our once proud nation? We've heard the excuses, but this is the chance we've been waiting for. Please, do the right thing. Thank you."

Boocka and Hudson burst into exaggerated applause, but there was no reaction from the deciding backer as she sat back down. After a few moments, the Human raised the green stick above her head.

"We launch!" Bellis cried, pumping the air with her fist.

Orla was ready to burst with pride as she joined her friends in applause. Commander Jackson, who had been guarding the door, also clapped hysterically. Everything they had worked towards had fallen into place, giving them a chance to finish what they started. Orla thought of Mr. Janmano and all those who died in the Capital Ballroom, but most of all, she thought of Jacob and Kadesha, wishing they could be here to witness the historic victory in the boardroom. Losing her best friend – no, someone she had fallen in love with – made the moment bittersweet, but Orla was determined to battle against her sorrow and help drive the Antantans out of Uthovaya. This was Jacob Crestmore's kingdom, not theirs.

"Everyone to the Operation Room," Bellis ordered.

Amidst a collection of computer equipment, base personnel, and large monitors, Orla waited alongside

Hudson and Boocka. When Bellis arrived, she looked flustered, pointing to a large screen on the wall. An image of a squared building appeared.

Bellis said, "This is the control room. The easiest way to get there is through the National Zoo. Find the station where visitors would come in and then follow the train tracks through the tunnels."

"How did you get this information?" Orla asked.

"From a rogue Cyclops agent. He gave us a password that will unlock the arsenal. You must also change the password afterwards. That will buy us some time."

"Sounds easy," Hudson said.

"It won't be," Bellis countered. She flicked the screen to show an image of an elongated flying machine with rotary blades at the top. "This is a Heli-Chopper. Cyclops has deployed it to protect the control room. It has armour-plates for protection, can fire a powerful weapon called a Twin-Cannon, and is armed with at least three missiles."

"I'll keep my mouth shut next time," Hudson said dryly.

Orla turned to the Ambassador. "When do we leave?"

"Immediately. I can only hold off the launch for so long. You must get the arsenal unlocked as quickly as possible."

"We'll do our best,"

Chapter XXXIII

Gunnar Veto felt restless. The Shadow-Flare had almost entered Antantan airspace, carrying the last Crestmore and the key to elemental magic onboard. But what should have been a feeling of euphoria mixed with the satisfaction of a job well done, had instead, become a time of troubled thinking and inner turmoil. Had he made the right decision in not helping Jacob?

He had pondered the question from the moment his soldiers took Jacob away from the interrogation room. Hearing the boy plead for help disturbed him greatly, making him feel guilty to the point he could almost hear Queen Fiona chastising him from beyond the grave.

You monster. How could you be so weak?

The fact Jacob could be his own flesh and blood proved another stumbling block to Veto walking away without giving the boy a second thought.

What kind of man walks away and leaves his own son to die?

Fearing he was going crazy, Veto decided a walk around the airship would do him the world of good, but any attempt to clear his head remained futile, as the guilt over Jacob gnawed away at him like a Weavel Rat gnawing at a carcass. As he headed back to his quarters, he caught sight of an out-of-breath officer hurrying in his direction.

"Problem?" Veto asked, secretly hoping for a crisis that would give him a distraction and clear Fiona's voice from his mind.

"Vice-President Gex demands to see you in his quarters, sir."

"What does he want?"

"He didn't say."

Veto swung back in the direction of the teleport booths. A conversation with Gex was the last thing he needed. It would probably be a complaint of some kind, or perhaps a message from the President congratulating him on a job well done. No, Gex would never give him credit for the successful recovery of Jacob and the ElmKey. He would have taken the credit himself.

Sucking up the disappointment, he travelled by teleport booth and trudged along the corridor to the Vice-President's quarters, feeling almost nauseous as he knocked on the door and awaited a nasally response from his superior.

"Come in."

Veto shuddered and then entered the quarters. Gex stood at his mini bar, sipping champagne from a crystal glass. There was a half-bottle on the bar and another glass with nothing in it. Veto looked on suspiciously as Gex filled it and then handed it to him.

"What's going on?" Veto asked, eyeballing the glass up close to determine if it had been laced with poison.

"A toast," said Gex, chinking his glass against Veto's.

"A toast to what?"

"Our success. Lady Kadesha is dead, the last Crestmore will soon follow, and we have the Lost ElmKey in our possession."

Gex pointed to a small glass cabinet on the floor situated between two chairs. The sight of the powerful artefact Fiona had searched for turned Veto's thoughts back to his guilt over Jacob, but he pushed them from his mind and tried to concentrate on the here and now.

"Is the President expecting us?"

Gex nodded. "I made him aware of the situation, yes. Plans are already underway for the public execution. He was most pleased with our work."

"Our work?" Veto snapped. "Well, that makes no sense considering your previous form. I bet you omitted my part in all this, just like you always do."

He downed his glass in one go, trying not to let Gex see his reaction as the bubbles burnt his tongue. Veto never drank champagne. In fact, he never drank alcohol period.

"Can we forget the squabbling for a moment?" Gex pleaded. "If you must know, I gave you full credit for this one."

"You're lying."

Gex looked somewhere between disappointed and smugger – if that was even possible.

"I'm not lying. The truth is, I did not just call you up here to drink champagne. There is something else."

"Oh?" Veto stammered, his paranoia going into overdrive.

"Recently, I have taken stock of my life. My failures, successes, and everything I have achieved in the role of Vice-President."

"Achieved?" said Veto, laughing into his glass. "That must have taken you all of five seconds."

Gex did not react to the comment. Instead, he dropped a bombshell of epic proportions.

"I'm retiring."

Veto was almost floored by the revelation. If he had been drinking champagne at the time, he would have spat it out.

"Don't look so surprised," Gex continued, as he re-filled Veto's glass. "All good things come to an end."

"Why retire now?"

"I want to go out on a high. What's left to achieve after our latest success?"

"I hope you don't expect me to organise a retirement party."

"Funny," Gex said wearily and without a hint of a smile. "I know we haven't always seen eye-to-eye, but I have always respected you."

Veto burst out laughing. "No, you haven't."

"You're wrong," Gex replied. "In fact, I've always admired your determination to keep going. Even when everything around you is falling apart, you have that inner drive to reach the finish line. If truth be told, you would make a great Vice-President. The President certainly agreed you are the best man for the job. Looks like you finally won back his respect."

Veto stared in disbelief. Although he was suspicious of Gex's story, he was unsure if he could even accept such a position. Not with everything that had happened.

"Are you telling me the President will offer me the role?"

Gex drank from his glass and shook his head. "He almost certainly would, had I not intervened."

"Intervened? What do you mean?"

"Well, the President asked me if I had one final request as Vice-President. I think he expected me to recommend you for the role, but I had another idea. I recommended you be shot for treason, instead, and when I explained the reason why, he agreed and graciously gave me the honour of carrying out your execution."

Gex put the champagne glass down on the bar with one hand and raised a pistol with the other. He had a sadistic smirk on his face, and no doubt felt giddy about the prospect of smoking his nemesis. Veto's mouth fell open. Not only had he lost out on a promotion thanks to Gexs' inability to put a grudge aside, but he was staring down the barrel of a gun as well.

"You are making a big mistake," Veto said, trying to control the panic in his voice.

"Oh, I don't think I am." Gex stepped out from behind the bar, still pointing the gun in Veto's direction. "I don't know how we could have been so blind all this time. You were the one who kept Jacob safe all those years ago. I bet you were doing cartwheels at the thought of getting away with such a blatant act of treachery."

"That boy could be my son," Veto stammered, unable to take his eyes off the pistol pointed at his head. "I had no choice."

"You did have a choice. Staying away from Fiona would have been one of them. You are a freak of nature. Seth Crestmore should have finished you off when he had the chance."

"He didn't have it in him," Veto snarled.

Gex cocked the trigger on the gun. "But we both know that I do. Good riddance to bad rubbish."

Veto closed his eyes and thought back on his life. His loving parents playing with him on the living room rug, his time in the army, Baby Jacob laughing away. They all fizzed before melting into the face of Fiona as the last image he chose to focus on. The love of his life.

Bang!

The gunshot made Veto jump, but he felt no pain.

Strange…why was there no pain?

He opened his eyes to find Gex clutching his chest, a look of shock and horror on his face as blood seeped through his black waistcoat. Veto whirled around and saw the man who had shot him. Officer Briggs, violently shaking, gun still in hand. It was now or never.

Veto thundered towards Gex, charging his electrical arm in the process. Sparks flew everywhere when he delivered thousands of volts of electricity into Gex's body. It was mesmerizing to watch the life drain slowly from his eyes. Almost orgasmic. When it was over, Veto staggered back and watched Gex slump to the floor, his badly burnt body smoking away. Only then, threat neutralized, did Veto turn to his saviour.

"I heard you arguing from the corridor." Briggs shook his head repeatedly, head in his hands as he spoke. "What have we done?"

The young man had turned chalk-white and looked ready to throw up at any minute, so Veto sauntered across and put a reassuring hand on his shoulder.

"You saved my life," he whispered. "For that, I thank you."

Veto took a moment to catch his breath. The President's betrayal disgusted him, but he felt less surprised than he should have been and made the decision on the spot to help Jacob. Just like Fiona would have wanted.

"I need to get Jacob out of here with the ElmKey," he explained as he checked nobody was coming along both sides of the corridor. "The President won't get the satisfaction of killing the last Crestmore. Help me, and I'll make sure your part in all this is never discovered."

Briggs still seemed in shock, but Veto hoped he would see sense. The last thing he wanted was to murder his protégé to keep him quiet.

"Of course, I will," the loyal Briggs promised. "Will we take Jacob to the hangar? There's bound to be a sky-darter down there we can use to sneak him away."

"No," Veto said quickly. "They'll send Quantum-Fighters after it. There has to be another way."

"What about the President's escape pod? He isn't on board, so security will think it's a malfunction."

"Perfect. We would need someone to come and pick the boy up, though. The only question is, who?"

"What about the Revolutionaries?"

"Great idea. Let's get Jacob; I'm sure he can contact them himself."

After hiding Gex's smouldering body in a walk-in wardrobe, Veto took the ElmKey from the glass cabinet and tucked it inside his tunic for safekeeping. Then he led Briggs to the holding cells where Jacob was imprisoned. The on-duty guard bought their story about Gex wanting to speak with the boy, so gaining access was easy. As Veto swiped the cell door machine with his keycard, he was greeted by a surprised-looking Jacob in the corner of his cell.

"Is it time?" he whispered.

"On your feet," Veto ordered.

"I'll just stay here if it's all the same to y-"

"Feet," Veto roared, using all his strength to drag Jacob up.

With Jacob in-between himself and Briggs, Veto led them past the single guard and through the corridors of the Shadow-Flare, trying to look as nonchalant as possible whenever they passed a member of the flight crew. The President's quarters were on the top floor and could only be accessed by teleport booth. Veto went first, followed by Jacob and finally Briggs.

"This way," Veto ordered.

"What's going on?" Jacob asked, obviously realising something was amiss.

Veto inserted his keycard into the panel beside the escape pod door, and it slid to the side, revealing comfortable blue chairs, a medical supply case, and a small armoury containing two pistols and a shotgun.

"Get in," Veto ordered as he emptied the contents of the medical supply case and placed the ElmKey inside.

"Seriously, what's happening here?"

"I said, get in."

"Not until I get an explanation."

"I'm saving you again," Veto replied. "You were correct back in the interrogation room. It won't make up for what I did, but this is the only way to make sure Fiona lives on."

"I...don't know what to say."

Veto took possession of Briggs' communicator and tossed it to Jacob, who caught it with minimum fuss.

"Contact the Revolutionaries. Tell them to come and pick you up. Once you have used the communicator, they will be able to find your location."

"I can't. I don't know their codes."

"Tell me that's a joke."

"Cyclops," Jacob said suddenly.

"What about them?"

"You must be able to get a hold of someone there. Tell them to get a message to Ryker."

"Why would you want to speak with him? Is he helping the Revolutionaries?"

"Does that really matter anymore?"

"I suppose not. Can you trust him?"

"I trust him not to execute me," Jacob laughed. "Which is exactly what will happen if I hang around here."

"Very well. Get on board."

"Won't they come after the pod?"

"They will think it's a malfunction. I will keep things as normal as I can. By the time they realise the truth, you'll be on your way back to Uthovaya."

After making the call, Veto handed the communicator back to Jacob and then launched the pod, watching proudly as it sped away from the Shadow-Flare towards the ocean. He felt the tension in his body evaporate. It was a tension he never even noticed was there. Now, it was gone, like a huge weight had been lifted from his shoulders by Fiona. She would surely be smiling down on him now, pleased he had finally done the right thing.

Veto turned to Briggs. "Go back to your post. I'll clear up here."

"Yes, sir," Briggs replied.

"And Briggs…thanks again."

Briggs saluted his superior and then headed back to work, leaving Veto with nothing but the prospect of a hideous death at the hands of his own President.

Chapter XXXIV

With Hudson at the wheel, the Jeep sped through the Capital's streets, weaving in and out of traffic like a racer who had fallen behind on the final lap. Orla sat with Boocka in the backseat, staring out the window as heavy rain thundered off the glass. Although nervous about their mission to reach the control room, she was also thankful it gave her something to think about other than Jacob and his fate aboard the Shadow-Flare.

Worrying about Jacob was bad enough, but she also had her parents to think about.

Ambassador Bellis had offered to send troops to bring them to the base, but Orla had refused for fear of her father's reaction. All she could do was hope they would stay out of the way, hidden in the sleepy, quiet neighbourhood of Gonga Grove.

The streets were strangely quiet, considering the impending war. Everyone went about their business like it was a normal day. Then again, Orla mused, perhaps it was because of the late hour and the fact no one knew the war was coming. Most of the citizens would be safely tucked up in their beds, unaware of the struggle about to take place. It was a struggle for their nation's future, a struggle for their nation's soul.

As the Jeep swerved onto Thugy Street, Orla peered over Hudson's shoulder and saw the traffic had slowed up ahead. Hudson slammed on the brakes, and the Jeep came to a stop behind an Antantan army truck. Soldiers burst from the cargo area and swung around to head into the traffic.

"What now?" Hudson said, impatiently.

Orla opened the door and stepped out into the wet and windy night. She smelled smoke immediately and heard loud voices, mixed with the occasional burst of gunfire. Urging Boocka and Hudson to wait in the car, she climbed onto the jeep's roof for a better look and saw the street ahead had become a warzone.

As she came back into the Jeep, a friendly-looking Remman gently tapped on the window and urged them to turn back. He then explained a group of unarmed civilians had been stopped by Antantan soldiers for a full-body search. The civilians had refused to co-operate, so the soldiers shot them dead, sparking a full-scale street riot.

Orla leaned forward to Hudson. "We need to go around."

"Fat chance of that." Hudson replied, urging Orla to look in the rear-view mirror at the line of vehicles stuck behind them. "We're going nowhere."

"Well, we can't wait around here all night," she countered.

"Damn right we can't," Boocka replied. "Those Ant-antan soldiers are stopping vehicles up ahead. If we go any further in this direction, we can forget about reaching that control room."

"What do you suggest?" Orla replied. "It's too dangerous to walk through the rioters."

"There's an alley beside that department store," Boocka said, pointing to a potential dark and dingy passport to safety.

"We don't have any other choice," Orla replied.

Hudson turned the engine off. "Let's go."

They exited the vehicle and snuck across the street to the alleyway, using other stationary vehicles as cover from the Antantan soldiers now swarming the area. Suddenly, there was an almighty explosion that lit up the night sky. Orla ran back out of the alleyway and saw more fire erupting in the distance.

"What the hell was that?" Boocka said as he joined her at the alleyway entrance.

"I don't know, but it's not good, whatever it was."

They made their way through the alleyway but found the traffic just as bad on Frenklin Street as it had been on Thugy. There seemed to be more Antantan soldiers as well, randomly pulling civilians from cars to conduct I.D. checks. Orla was frustrated at the lack of movement, not to mention nervous things would go wrong. It was the first time she could recall feeling any pressure. Perhaps, because they were so close to achieving what once seemed like the impossible.

"Over there," Hudson suddenly said.

There was a gap between two buildings on the opposite side of the street.

"We have to get across," Orla told the others.

"Let's fight our way across," Hudson said, excitedly.

"Don't be stupid," Boocka shot back. "We're outnumbered. You want to die out here?"

"Any of you got a better idea?" Hudson replied, looking annoyed by Boocka's response.

Orla said, "Actually, I do."

Without explaining her plan, she sneaked across to a stationary car and dropped to the ground. When Hudson and Boocka stood still, she urged them to join her. All three crawled along the ground, moving underneath cars and trucks to reach the other side of the street. They were only one car away when Orla heard the familiar beep of Boocka's communicator. He spoke for less than a minute, but his concerned expression made Orla nervous.

"That was Bellis. It looks like word got out about Operation Creeper. Some civilians are attacking the Antantan soldiers."

"I guess that explains the explosion," Orla replied.

"How far is the control room?" Hudson asked.

"Not far," Orla explained. "We'll get a better look when we exit the next alleyway."

The words had just left her mouth when the car they were underneath suddenly rolled forward, nearly crushing Hudson under the front wheels as it moved away. Lying exposed on the wet ground, Orla dragged herself back onto her feet and raced into the alleyway before the Antantan soldiers could see her. Boocka and Hudson arrived seconds later.

"Probably the only time I've been unhappy to see traffic start moving," Hudson joked.

Orla led them through the second alleyway, trying to ignore how uncomfortable she felt. Her clothes were absolutely soaked by the time they reached the old zoo, making her movements slow and sluggish.

"Well, we made it," she said as they moved slowly through the arched entrance. "Let's hope we can reach the control room from here like Bellis said."

Orla had fond memories of visiting the zoo with her parents, but it bore no resemblance to that magical place of wonder from her childhood now. The cages were empty, and the visitors centre overgrown with vegetation. It was deserted inside, except for thick vines growing over dusty control panels, and weavel rats and other vermin scuttling across the floor. There were three large holes in the decaying roof of the visitor's centre where the moonlight shone through, and Orla noticed bottles of alcohol beside them. After navigating the visitor's centre, they emerged on the opposite side, right in front of the old zoo train station. There was a damaged red carriage lying on its side by the broken platform. Orla had travelled to the zoo many times on a similar one. She could almost hear the laughter of happy children, all excited to see the animals. It saddened her to see it so run down, so typical of the Capital since the Antantans took over.

Boocka said, "We follow the tracks into the underground tunnels, right?"

Orla nodded. "Bellis said they will lead us to the control room."

The tunnels were dark, wet, and smelly, so Orla spent most of her time trying to hold her breath. Despite the filthy conditions, groups of squatters had claimed the tunnels as their home. Their looks of fear and desperation almost reduced Orla to tears. Those poor souls reminded her of Jacob and everything he went through on the streets just to stay alive. All those times he survived out in the cold or almost fainted from exhaustion made her respect for him grow. She had then watched him stand up and be counted when Uthovaya needed him most. His absence by her side made her heart physically ache.

Swinging around a corner, Orla saw a light from the end of the tunnel and followed it to the exit. Once outside, they scaled the grassy hill and found themselves in the middle of what appeared to be an unofficial rubbish dump, not far away from the control room. It was guarded by two Cyclops agents, but there was no sign of the Heli-Chopper Bellis had told them about.

"Seems light on protection," Hudson whispered as they took cover behind a pile of stinking rubbish.

"Good," Orla said while holding her nose. "We'll get stunk to death if we stay here much longer."

Boocka pulled out his communicator. "Ambassador Bellis, come in."

No response.

"This is Boocka, do you copy?"

The speaker sparked to life. "This is Bellis. Go ahead, Boocka."

"We're right outside the control room. It's only guarded by two bodies."

"No, Heli-Chopper? How strange. The Cyclops agent assured my men it would be there.

Orla shared a worried look with Boocka and Hudson.

"Let's hope that's the only thing he got wrong." She whispered.

Boocka said. "We're going in now."

"Roger that," Bellis replied. "Our bombers and troops are ready to go on your say-so."

"Copy that."

They started their approach, but a Cyclops agent must have spotted movement amongst the rubbish because Orla heard an angry cry followed by gunfire aimed in their direction. Boocka and Hudson fired back quickly, but their efforts were in vain, and one of the agents bolted across to a control panel by the door. Orla saw him pull a small lever and then heard high-pitched wailing.

"He's hit the alarm," Boocka shouted, before aiming a shot that took the other agent out.

"Leave it to me," Hudson replied.

The captain rose from behind a pile of junk to take out both agents. Orla raced forward and tried to pull the alarm lever back up, but it would not budge.

"I need help!" she cried.

Boocka and Hudson helped her push the lever up, and the wailing immediately came to a halt, leaving them standing in silence outside the control room. Orla studied the control panel and managed to unlock the door, but suddenly there was a buzzing noise from a group of abandoned buildings to the right of the control room.

"What the hell is that?" Boocka said.

A Heli-Chopper swung from behind one of the abandoned buildings, and then floated towards them, its twin canon firing seemingly endless bursts that forced Orla and Boocka to roll one way and Hudson the other. Picking herself up, Orla tailed Boocka back to the rubbish dump, where they found cover behind another pile of junk, as the Heli-Chopper continued to shoot in their direction.

"Looks like the Cyclops agent was right after all," Orla said, breathlessly.

"Where's Hudson?" Boocka said.

Orla looked out from behind the pile of junk and saw Hudson pressed against the control room wall, easing himself towards the control panel. He had almost made it when the Heli-Chopper spun around and fired round after round in his direction, forcing him around the back of the building. Boocka then jumped out and took aim, but the bullets bounced off the armour plates, leaving him with no choice but to take cover again.

"How the hell are we supposed to fight that thing?" he cried.

The Heli-Chopper came back towards them, its heavy fire forcing them even further away from the control room. They were almost back at the tunnel entrance now, and Orla could barely see Hudson sneaking out from behind the building. Once again, the Heli-Chopper swung around and put him under fire.

"Get out of there," Orla yelled, desperately.

Boocka struggled for the communicator again. "This is Boocka, do you read me, Ambassador?"

"I read you, Boocka."

"We're under attack from that damn Heli-Chopper."

"You must find a way into the control room."

"We need more time."

"You won't get it," she replied firmly. "Our backers are already questioning the hold-up. If anything goes wrong, they will cancel the launch without a second thought. Get that arsenal unlocked now, or the whole operation is ruined."

"Dammit."

Orla and Boocka crept back up the grassy hill to the junk pile they had used for cover before. The pilotless, Heli-Chopper hovered from side to side in front of the control-room, almost daring them to come forward. Hudson remained partially hidden behind the building to the machine's left.

"We need to find a way past," Orla whispered.

"Dontcha think I know that?" Boocka fired back. Then he turned around with a stunned expression. "What's he doing?"

Orla turned her attention to what Boocka was looking at. Hudson had risen from cover and was giving them a thumbs-up-signal. He repeated the signal two or three times before running behind the building.

"Where's he going now?" Orla said in surprise.

Hudson then re-appeared on the other side. "Whatever happens, get to that control room," he yelled.

The Heli-Chopper fired with its twin-cannon, but Hudson dived to the right and scrambled away towards the abandoned buildings. With the Heli-Chopper in hot pursuit, Orla realised Hudson's plan was to create a diversion.

"Move," Boocka ordered, practically dragging her away from the junk pile.

Orla watched Hudson race away while she ran. He had just reached the first building when the Heli-Chopper unleashed a burst of fire, followed by a missile that brought the building crashing down around him. Orla screamed as he disappeared in a puff of smoke.

She felt strong arms around her as Boocka pulled her into the control-room doorway. There were computer terminals everywhere, each one connected by a mass of wires to a large computer in the middle of the room. Orla fumbled about until she found the unlock key. Once it was done, she changed the password to *BattleforLiberty*.

"We have to help Hudson," she cried, bolting towards the doorway.

Once again, Boocka's strong arms pulled her back. "Are you crazy?" he balled. "That thing's still out there."

"I don't care, we have to help him."

Boocka thought hard for a moment. "I have an idea."

He used his communicator to contact Bellis and asked her to send one of the Pulse-Bombers to their location. She agreed and promised it would take care of the Heli-Chopper. It was an agonizing wait for Orla, but finally, they heard a roar and then the sound of an explosion. Creeping outside, they found pieces of the Heli-Chopper scattered everywhere, and the Pulse-Bomber in the distance, heading away from them.

"C'mon," Orla ordered.

They pulled huge chunks of stone away from the rubble of the collapsed building and found Hudson underneath, bruised, and covered in blood. Boocka checked his pulse while Orla looked on anxiously, tears in her eyes at the state of the merc who had done so much to help them.

"He's alive," Boocka said.

"So, what now? We can't just leave him here."

"I'll carry him," Boocka whispered softly. "We can drop him off at the nearest hospital on our way to Crestmore Castle."

As they trudged through the streets, Orla saw civilians running from their homes, armed with whatever they could find, as word of Operation Creeper spread like wildfire. They had not travelled far when a woman armed with a shotgun rushed towards them from her home.

"This is all we need," Boocka said to Orla.

The pair then explained they were part of the Revolution, before spending a tense few minutes convincing the gun-toting citizen to get back inside the house and not put herself at risk. The woman then called for her husband to come out. He was a doctor and quickly offered to look after Hudson while Orla and Boocka went on their way.

"We don't know how to thank you," Orla said, almost moved to tears by their kindness.

"Just give us our country back," the doctor pleaded, as he and his wife helped Hudson inside the house.

Orla turned to Boocka. "Do you think we can do it?"

"I do," he replied. "Let's get to Crestmore Castle."

Orla nodded as more Pulse-Bombers screeched overhead. Operation Creeper had begun.

Chapter XXXV

Jacob knew something was amiss. His unease had started the moment Cyclops agents released him from the President's escape pod and took him aboard their Pulse-Fighter. He had asked to speak with someone from the Revolutionaries, but his request was met with silence and a variety of funny looks from the torn-faced agents. None of them seemed eager to help with his inquiries about Orla either. At first, Jacob had given them the benefit of the doubt, but as the Pulse-Fighter flew over the Uthovayan Capital, an agent ordered him to hand the ElmKey over, and he realised trouble was afoot.

Making matters more complicated was the fighting on the streets down below. He was pleased the Revolutionaries had launched Operation Creeper but worried about his friends. No doubt, Hudson would be long gone, but Boocka and Orla would most likely be fighting on the frontline. Violence went against everything Orla stood for, but Jacob figured she would put her own beliefs on the back burner to help the Revolutionaries. The thought of her in danger worried him greatly.

"We're almost at our destination," Jacob heard one of the agents whisper to the other.

"How far from there?" asked another.

"Not far. Let's hope the boss is there to meet us like he promised."

As the Pulse-Fighter landed, Jacob realised they were on the roof of Kadesha's safe house. He was bundled out of the aircraft and towards a hatch that presumably led inside the house. It was closed, so the agents frogmarched him across both sides of the roof to find a way down. They eventually found one in the form of a ladder attached to the side of the building.

"Start climbing," an agent ordered.

"Why are we here?"

"Never mind the questions," the agent replied. "Get moving."

Although Jacob was alarmed by the hostility, he suddenly remembered Lady Kadesha's reaction when she discovered Cyclops was involved in Operation Creeper. Kadesha had never trusted Ryker and had made her feelings perfectly clear. Father Gambin was another who had voiced concerns over the director's involvement with the Revolutionaries. Jacob could almost hear his voice again.

He wants something from you. Men like him always do.

Gambin's words echoed in Jacob's mind as he climbed down the ladder, being careful not to go too fast lest he lose his balance and fall. They were high up, but the wind lessened the further down they climbed. It was a relief when his feet finally touched the ground and he could regain his composure. One of the agents pushed him in the back and ordered him to start walking in the direction of the tree cluster at the back of the garden, where the trapdoor to the secret tunnel he had visited with Kadesha and Boocka was located.

Once down below, Jacob saw the buggy from before was still there. An agent sat in the driver's seat while Jacob sat in the back between the two others.

This is definitely not good.

The journey through the tunnels painted a different picture to the last time. Instead of engineers working tirelessly, there was nobody around, and the noise of machinery had silenced completely.

They arrived at the wooden door that led to the Chamber of the Elements, but instead of handing him the ElmKey back and letting Jacob go inside, they ordered him to wait, and it wasn't long before he found out why. Director Ryker appeared from a makeshift hole in the stone. He was armed with a pistol and sported a wild-eyed look that made Jacob uneasy.

"Hello, young Jacob. I'm delighted to see you back on Uthovayan soil."

"Pity your goons aren't so friendly," Jacob said, eyeballing the closest agent. "Where's Orla?"

"I have no idea," Ryker admitted. "The last I saw of her, she was standing in my office, begging me to reconsider my lock on the arsenal being used for Operation Creeper."

He didn't, did he? But then, how?

"Don't look so worried. They have unlocked it by themselves, but who really cares at this point? You see, they get the arsenal, and I get what I really want."

"Which is?"

"You."

Jacob was more than a little confused.

"What could you possibly want with me?"

"In your current state, nothing. But the moment you step into that chamber, power the dimensional gateway, and become an Elementalist, you become the *only* thing I want." Ryker took a few steps forward, making Jacob apprehensive. "I want the power of elemental magic at my disposal, so, you're going to a facility on the other side of the world, where my best scientists can clone you."

It was the most insane plan Jacob had ever heard. Even the recent events in his life paled in comparison to the sheer lunacy of Ryker's scheme, something Jacob would never have thought possible. Yet, there was something about the look in Ryker's eyes that told Jacob he was deadly serious. It was all very well ridiculing the man, but what if Cyclops did have the capacity to duplicate the magic bloodline? They would gain access to a power only reserved for the special few; power that, in the wrong hands, could destroy the planet itself. Jacob knew he had to stop them – but how?

"Give it to him," Ryker ordered the agent with the ElmKey.

The agent stepped forward and held the ElmKey out for Jacob to take, but he refused. It was petty and pointless, but the only option available to him. At the very least, it bought him a little time to think of a more practical solution.

"If you don't take it, then you die," Ryker growled, pointing the pistol at Jacob.

"A word of advice for next time you're in this position." Jacob said. "Don't explain you need someone to make your crazy plan work and then threaten to shoot them if they don't comply."

An explosion from above rocked the tunnels, and then another a few seconds later. Jacob guessed the Revolutionaries had reached the castle, and the fighting was now taking place inside. It meant they were close-by, and possibly able to come to his aid. He immediately wondered if Orla was amongst them, fighting on the front line for Uthovaya's future. He could only hope she would be safe, protected by the more experienced soldiers around her.

"Hurry it up." Ryker screamed.

The disturbances had obviously made Ryker agitated. He was waving the gun around like a madman and threatening to do all kinds of damage.

"This is your last chance." He spat. "Take the Elm-Key and get inside the chamber."

Jacob folded his arms and replied with a firm, "NO."

Ryker burst forward, grabbed Jacob's arm, and wrestled him towards the chamber door. Jacob fought with every bit of strength to stop it from happening but was swept away when two other agents joined in.

"Stop it," he yelled.

But it was too late, and before Jacob knew what was happening, he was inside the chamber with Ryker, who now had the ElmKey in his hands. The two agents who helped push Jacob inside went back out to the tunnel and closed the chamber door behind them.

"Take it," Ryker spat as he held the ElmKey out.

"Not a chance," Jacob said, firmly.

"Then I'll do it myself."

Jacob looked on tentatively, as Ryker pushed the artefact into the slot and then took a few steps back. The colour drained from the ElmKey and seeped out like water into the air, creating a purple whirlpool that blanketed the entire chamber. Small bubbles appeared, floating like feathers. Jacob reached out to touch one, but it did not burst.

"Amazing," Ryker said, trying to touch a bubble of his own.

Jacob had to agree. Although sceptical about magic in the beginning, he had been largely won over by Lady Kadesha's honesty and integrity. Now, all doubts he harboured had been well and truly erased.

Suddenly, the bubbles shot away to the far end of the chamber, as if controlled by some unseen force. They merged to form one giant bubble that morphed into a legless entity that flew in a circular fashion around the chamber. A sudden gust of wind blew Jacob and Ryker against the faraway wall, before a second entity appeared from nowhere, following the same flight path as the previous one.

"What's happening?" Ryker cried.

"I think it's the elemental spirits," Jacob called back,

As he watched the mystical beings circling the chamber, Jacob heard a voice telling him not to be scared, but he wondered if the soothing message came from his own sub-conscious or somewhere else.

Fire engulfed the chamber walls and crackled from every direction. Jacob felt the searing heat from the flames burning his skin. The flames then came together to form a fiery entity that joined the other two spirits above,

"One more," said Ryker, excitedly rubbing his hands together.

Jacob barely had time to respond before the ground suddenly split from under them, teasing a darkness below that Jacob and Ryker fell into. They remained floating in nothingness, as the chamber broke up around them, sending rocks shooting out in every direction. The strange sensation of weightlessness worried Jacob greatly. He could not feel a single part of his body. Ryker looked terrified and screamed until a sudden explosion turned the chamber back to how it was before. Only a single large rock remained, suspended right above Ryker's head.

"Where's the final spirit?" Ryker asked.

The final spirit morphed from the rock and shot down towards Ryker, who was now on his knees. Jacob saw fear in the director's eyes, as the other three spirits joined the first and then circled around Ryker. He staggered to his feet and tried to steady himself, but that was as far as he got before the spirits merged into one and then shot straight through his body like a multi-coloured missile. Jacob looked on in shock as Ryker exploded into nothingness.

The spirits headed in Jacob's direction and entered his body. A sudden surge of power shot through him, making him feel temporarily invincible, as thousands of images entered his brain, too many and too quickly to process. When it was over, he staggered in a daze from the chamber, straight into the Cyclops agents who demanded he remain still. A second unexpected surge of power whooshed through him as he clenched his fists, now engulfed in fire. The panicked agents dropped their weapons and bolted back through the tunnel. It was the last thing Jacob saw before he collapsed.

When he opened his eyes again, Orla was staring at him with tears rolling down her cheeks. Caught up in the moment, he cried out in relief when he touched her arm and realised his imagination wasn't playing tricks on him.

"You're OK." Orla beamed.

"So are you," he managed to whisper back.

"How did you get here?" she asked breathlessly.

"It's a long story," Jacob admitted. "Ryker's dead."

"What happened?"

"I'm not sure. But he isn't part of the magic blood-line. Maybe, the spirits didn't like him trying to steal the power."

"It won't matter now, anyway," Orla said, kissing Jacob's forehead.

"Why not?"

Orla grinned. "Because we've retaken the Capital. The Antantans in government are being rounded up as we speak."

Jacob listened to Orla's explanation, but she might as well have been a thousand miles away when she gave him the news. He closed his eyes and thought of his parents, wondering if they were looking down on him with pride. He had barely contemplated the question when a feeling of elation overtook him. Uthovaya was free from Antantan oppression, and he would be the new King. Yes, his life would change forever, but it would be a glorious new dawn for Uthovaya and its people. He would make sure of it.

Chapter XXXVI

A few days after victory was secured in what had now been dubbed The Battle for Liberty, Jacob stood alone in the Crestmore Castle throne room, staring at the gold-encrusted seats his mother and father had occupied many years before. He had never got the chance to know his long-dead parents, nor would they get to see him carry on their legacy. It was a legacy of togetherness and equality, a country that welcomed everyone, regardless of race, sex, colour, or creed. Jacob was anxious about his chances of living up to their name, but a plan had formed in his mind. A plan for someone else to share the burden with him. Someone who had once been a friend but became something more. Someone he wanted to be his queen.

He reached into his pocket, produced a small black box, and then flipped it open to gaze upon a gold ring with a diamond cluster design. He had found it in a drawer in one of the rooms on the west wing and intended to present it to the person who should have been Uthovaya's saviour.

What if she says no?

Jacob cleared his throat and then fidgeted with his fingers on both hands. He paced the throne room while trying to ignore the fluttering in his stomach and the sweat gathering on his forehead. Wiping his brow with the back of his hand, he took a seat on the throne but immediately got back up again.

"How's it going, Your Majesty?"

Whirling, he stuffed the ring back in its box and found his special someone standing in the doorway, holding the Dynasty Staff in her hands. Orla was dressed in a mesmerising red dress, her blue eyes sparkling in the bright lights of the throne room. He smiled, recalling their meeting under the bridge before Dance for Liberty; it was the first time he had noticed her beauty. Why had he taken so long to notice it? He could not offer himself an explanation.

"I believe this belongs to you," Orla said, handing the staff over with a wide smile.

Jacob took possession of his mother's weapon and then ran a careful eye over it.

"I brought it back from the Tavara desert," she explained. "I…didn't expect to see you again. It's wonderful to be able to give it back."

"Thank you."

"You're welcome." She grinned. "So, how does it feel to be Elementalist?"

Jacob glanced at his hands, remembering the fiery state they were in outside the Chamber of the Elements.

SEAN CLARKE

"I'm scared to even think about it." he admitted. "Maybe, if Kadesha was here, I would be able to use magic without worrying about the damage I could cause."

"She would be able to advise you," Orla added.

There was a slight pause between the pair that made Jacob feel awkward. He was building up the courage to ask for Orla's hand in marriage but could not think of anything else to say in the meantime.

"I have news regarding Captain Hudson," Orla said quickly, sounding relieved she had found a topic to discuss.

"Oh?"

"He suffered a broken arm in the building collapse I told you about, but the doctor we left him with is taking good care of him."

Jacob chuckled. "I doubt Hudson will rest for long."

"You don't know how right you are," she laughed. "He already wants to go back to Pavelle and get the Rad Veteran."

"Where's Boocka?"

"Gone back to Krokira for a few days to clear his head. Said he'd come back once he has time to process everything. Kadesha's death hit him hard."

Jacob nodded. "Looks like it's just you and me for the coronation, then."

He noticed her becoming uneasy, shuffling on the spot, and struggling to look him in the eye.

"You will be here for the coronation, won't you?" he asked, more in hope than anything else.

"I've got something to tell you," she admitted, fiddling with her fingers in the nervous way she always did. "I've been given an opportunity."

"Opportunity?"

"Yes. Remember I told you I needed to get away from Uthovaya?"

Jacob nodded.

"To cut a long story short…." She was speaking rapidly, barely stopping for breath. "Ambassador Bellis put me in touch with some missionaries. They're going to Yolustein to help children affected by the religious war out there, and want me to join them, right away."

Numb with shock, Jacob could barely speak.

"Missionary work?" he croaked. "What about your parents? They won't be happy if you go away again."

"I'm a grown woman. They can't stop me."

"I know, but…"

"Please don't say my country needs me."

"But it does."

"No, it doesn't. We've already spoken about this. Uthovaya needs you, the rightful king. I'm needed elsewhere. Too much has happened for me to stay now. I don't even recognise myself anymore because of what went on during our journey together. I even took a life. That's not me, no matter how I dress it up. I have to get away and find myself again."

Jacob considered his own feelings on the journey; Mr, Janmano and Lady Kadesha were big influences on his life, and he missed them terribly. Although he had found elemental magic and freed Uthovaya from Antantan clutches, the victory seemed hollow somehow, almost pointless. There was still much work to be done if the nation were to thrive again, and the threat of a second invasion from the Antantans played constantly on his mind. He needed to appoint three followers as well, in the time honoured Elementalist tradition.

Orla had to stay.

He went to pull out the ring, but something stopped him. A fear that Orla would need to give up more than she already had to stick around and become his queen. Did he love her? Undoubtedly. Did she love him? He was unsure, but the fact she was leaving did not fill him with confidence. Reluctantly, he kept the ring in his pocket and put a brave face on things, just like he learned to do while living on the streets.

"I...I'll support you in anything you do," he said, barely managing to get the words out. "Just like you supported me."

She bounced on the spot with excitement and then rushed into his arms while Jacob choked back tears, mourning the imminent loss of his special someone. He kissed her tenderly on the lips and felt the familiar surge of electricity that had unexpectedly sparked during their dangerous journey together. There was a moment as they stared into one another's eyes when he thought their lips would lock again, but he battled against the urge and allowed Orla to break away.

"I'm really going to miss you," he admitted.

"Don't," she replied between sobs. "Just promise me you'll live up to the good name of Crestmore."

"I'll do my best," Jacob chuckled softly. "Are you sure you won't stay for the coronation?"

Orla shook her head. "I want to, but if I don't go now, they'll leave without me. I'll be thinking of you. I promise." Before leaving, she turned back around and blew him a kiss. "Good luck, my Prince."

Then she slammed the door shut and disappeared from his life. Jacob stood alone in the throne room with only the ghosts of his ancestors for company.

A Message from Sean

Thanks so much for reading, *Crestmore: The Lost Elm-Key*.

Your thoughts on the novel mean everything to me, so if you enjoyed it, consider supporting my work further by leaving a review on Amazon. Reviews are important for an author because they help us get more exposure.

You can also check out my website:
www.seanclarkeauthor.com

Thanks again.

Lightning Source UK Ltd.
Milton Keynes UK
UKHW010636040221
378234UK00002B/510

9 781527 275782